M000041126

ADVANCE PRAISE FOR *CAROUSEL*

"Dear Reader: This novel contains evil Siamese cats, total disregard for Chekhov's gun theory, much French without translation, a madhouse in Cape Cod, several carousel horses named Napoleon, Bertrand the secret knitter, waffles, a merry-go-round, a marriage in crisis, a crazy mother, and references to Les Nessman. What more could you ask for in April Ford's debut novel?"
—COLLEEN CURRAN, author of *Out for Stars* and the *Lenore* trilogy

"Spellbinding and beautifully written, *Carousel* is a galloping ride into love, relationships, friendship, and the burdens of family history. The characters cast their charms, lingering in your heart and mind long after you've finished the book. April Ford is a masterful storyteller and literary force."
—CORA SIRÉ, author of *Behold Things Beautiful*

"*Carousel* is an acerbic but open-hearted novel about break-ups and new beginnings that is as lovingly crafted as its central metaphor. And there is a depth of characterization here sadly lacking in so much contemporary fiction. An amazing debut novel."
—JAMES GRAINGER, author of *Harmless*

"An arch and darkly comic look into obsession, marriage, and family trauma, *Carousel* takes us deep into the tilting, whirling

world of Margot Soucy, its one-of-a-kind protagonist. Caught between three formidable women—intimidating Estelle, insouciant Katy, and unstable Marguerite—Margot must determine for herself the answer to the question that dogs modern life: Why do we want what we want, and what will we sacrifice to get it? Her journey will stay with you long after your head's stopped spinning."
—ANNA LEVENTHAL, author of *Sweet Affliction*

"April Ford constructs the exquisitely imagined world of her wildly spinning *Carousel* with irresistible characters and intricate plotting. You'll likely find yourself a bit dizzy with giddy and well-deserved appreciation for her considerable gifts in this psychologically acute novel."
—KIMBERLY ELKINS, author of *What Is Visible*

"*Carousel*, April Ford's debut novel, takes us from Montreal's famed amusement park, La Ronde, back and forth through history, following Margot Soucy, a middle-aged former antique firearms buyer and seller, as she experiences a crisis in her longtime marriage to the beautiful and enigmatic Estelle. Featuring Le Galopant, the oldest galloping carousel in the world, family secrets, French, madness, a staycation, art galleries, evil cats, teenage ingenues, and a whole cast of memorable moments and characters, *Carousel* is a wild and rollicking ride!"
—GREG SANTOS, author of *Blackbirds* and *Rabbit Punch!*

"With the precise intimacy of a short story and intriguing depth of a novel, *Carousel* plumbs a marriage in crisis, and in so doing, reveals all the nuances of the relationships that make us who we are—family, friends, and lovers—in all their messiness and wonder. In the end, the novel provides hope that what was once joyful can be restored."
—BRAD WINDHAUSER, author of *The Intersection*

"April Ford's absorbing, beautifully crafted novel weaves a modern tale of mid-life crisis. In deftly constructed scenes and effortless backstory, Ford's painfully flawed, all too human protagonist impulsively confronts doubts about her marriage, with unsettling consequences for those around her, especially her wife. Peopled with appealing, finely wrought characters, *Carousel's* often funny twists and turns of plot end up making perfect sense: You can't escape your origins. Yet, as with the fate of the horses on the grand machine at the heart of this story, Ford shows us that neither can you know for sure where any particular path will lead. The last page will take your breath away."

—ANNITA PEREZ SAWYER, author of *Smoking Cigarettes, Eating Glass*

CAROUSEL

Copyright © 2020 April Ford

Except for the use of short passages for review purposes, no part of this book may be reproduced, in part or in whole, or transmitted in any form or by any means, electronically or mechanically, including photocopying, recording, or any information or storage retrieval system, without prior permission in writing from the publisher or a licence from the Canadian Copyright Collective Agency (Access Copyright).

We gratefully acknowledge the support of the Canada Council for the Arts and the Ontario Arts Council for our publishing program. We also acknowledge the financial support of the Government of Canada.

Carousel is a work of fiction. All the characters and situations portrayed in this book are fictitious and any resemblance to persons living or dead is purely coincidental.

Cover design: Val Fullard

Library and Archives Canada Cataloguing in Publication

Title: Carousel : a novel / April Ford.
Names: Ford, April L., author.
Series: Inanna poetry & fiction series.
Description: Series statement: Inanna poetry & fiction series
Identifiers: Canadiana (print) 20200204467 | Canadiana (ebook) 20200204475 | ISBN 9781771337137 (softcover) | ISBN 9781771337144 (epub) | ISBN 9781771337151 (Kindle) | ISBN 9781771337168 (pdf)
Classification: LCC PS8611.O723 C37 2020 | DDC C813/.6—dc23

Printed and bound in Canada

Inanna Publications and Education Inc.
210 Founders College, York University
4700 Keele Street, Toronto, Ontario, Canada M3J 1P3
Telephone: (416) 736-5356 Fax: (416) 736-5765
Email: inanna.publications@inanna.ca   Website: www.inanna.ca

CAROUSEL

April Ford

INANNA POETRY & FICTION SERIES

INANNA PUBLICATIONS AND EDUCATION INC.
TORONTO, CANADA

For the stargazers

Was it for this I uttered prayers,
And sobbed and cursed and kicked the stairs,
That now, domestic as a plate,
I should retire at half-past eight?

—Edna St. Vincent Millay

PART I

1. LE GALOPANT

THE MOST IMPORTANT DISTINCTION between an antique carousel and a modern-day merry-go-round: The first is made of wood and operates by steam engine. There's a band organ at its centre, the axis around which proud, handcrafted horses transport delighted children. The organ is ideally a Wurlitzer 146, and its music generated from perforated paperboard sheets. There are no other types of mount on the carousel—no howling pigs, braying frogs, or similarly grotesque intruders—and colours other than white, black, brown, and grey mark saddles, bridles, and chariots, not horses. A historic carousel, one that has travelled across the world, and through generations of careful restoration specialists, should showcase horses of uniform colour (dapples, blazes, and socks are okay). The outside horse in a row of three should be tallest when the carousel is stationary, and immobile once the brilliant fleet begins to revolve around the axis. The outside horse briefly loses his majesty, flanked by the two who rise up and down, forward and backward, threatening to leave him behind, yet always resuming their slightly lower status when the organ's last flue pipe whistles.

This unsolicited information, which seemed a little invented or modified, came to me one late July evening in Montréal as I walked alongside the metal railing separating Le Galopant from the unsightly amusement park public, and attempted (rather dispiritedly, for I was not skilled in this way) to photograph the ride for my wife. It was my second try. The first, I had strained over the railing as though reaching for something forbidden, and this had incited a queue of testy, sunburnt families to form behind me. The ticket boy, no older than sixteen and no doubt utterly bored with his job, barked at me to either step forward or find some other occupation, and so I stepped forward and paid two dollars to ride the world's oldest galloping carousel, which I referred to as "merry-go-round," until later corrected.

Even though I was the first person inside the gazebo, a trapping of industrial columns and shingles insulting to Le Galopant's splendour, I was the last to select a horse. I had never considered carousels in any serious way before Estelle, my wife, became enthralled with them after watching a documentary about their restoration. For weeks after, she spoke of nothing but these alleged magnificent creatures who had survived decades, centuries in some cases, of rough handling and mistreatment from processions of sticky-fingered, screaming children who thought of them as nothing more than temporary toys. Perhaps some of the children also thought of the carousel horses as actual horses, like those in their dreams, but inevitably, the loyal steeds were subject to tiny shoes kicking their sides. Tiny hands yanking the leather safety straps cleverly fashioned into reins. Tiny, wobbly bodies bouncing up and down on their smooth backs as they revolved indefinitely around and around.

Estelle loved beautiful things. Despite the setback of being born to parents who, year after year, narrowly made ends meet, she had been gifted with a privileged childhood and treated as the finest specimen of the five Coté girls. She was the middle child—she who was always at risk of being overlooked in the confusion of older and younger siblings, she who was always too small to borrow an older sibling's clothes, yet too slow to grow out of her own for the younger ones. But Estelle's precocious love for aesthetics, her ability by age five to recite the differences between an oil painting and a watercolour (as a teenager, she would fall in love with artistic photography), her insistence on setting the dinner table in summetime with wreaths of field flowers she made herself, inspired little Estelle's parents to put their faith in the future and cultivate her aptitudes so that one day she might become more than the daughter of yellow tobacco serfs from Lanaudière, a community one hour northeast of Montréal whose identity was so bonded to its religious heritage its inhabitants seemed to dwell in a time capsule. Estelle and I were both twenty when we met, but Estelle spoke and moved in the manner of a distinguished person, one who had doors opened for her, coats hung, and cigarettes lit. She *appeared* to come from old money, when in fact it was I who came from a brand of wealth and pedigree (and neither had impressed favourably upon my family's moral character).

I could not speak to her at first. Her perfectly reasonable question, "Where is rue de la Commune?" stunned me with its inhuman musicality, its flute-like tenor. I pointed southeast, and then crossed rue Notre-Dame Ouest as the light changed mercifully to green. Before I stepped onto the opposite side-walk, Estelle was tugging at my coat sleeve, apologizing, but could I be more specific? And where had I gotten my hat? She adored hats, though she believed bandanas and headscarves suited her better. My hat looked like a post-World War One trilby, though she couldn't be certain. Would I mind taking it off to show her? What followed were the next twenty-five years of our lives together.

Children rushed toward Le Galopant in pursuit of the best horse, knocked into me and used the backs of my thighs as springboards to gain stride across the carousel floor, and I wanted to ask, much in the way Estelle would have, why the rush? Every horse appeared identical—white, legs striking out in front and back in a presupposed race, ears alert and pinned at the crest of a bulging neck, uncomplicated eyes and mouth strangely hostile for a children's ride. What would I do once I selected my mount? Would I even have to select him (I assumed the horses were all male), or would he choose me, as I overheard one young girl protest wretchedly when her mother proposed a random horse. The girl would have spat on the poor fellow had she understood such a gesture could efficiently demonstrate her indignation, but instead she moved onward and made eye contact with each gleaming animal until one finally wooed her. In the girl's defence, she chose the only horse whose forelock fell neatly carved between his eyes, so there were subtle differences after all. I wished Estelle could be with me as I circled the platform a second time, in search of the spot that would best conceal my aloneness more than my childlessness. I finally settled on a blue and pink chariot, figuring it would be easier to accomplish my task from a fixed perspective.

I did not, it turned out, take any photographs during my first ride. I spent the two minutes and thirty-nine seconds of the Wurlitzer's "Don't Cry Frenchy, Don't Cry" staring blankly at the undersides of chariot horse's silver hooves. The children, thinking already of their next fun-park adventures, began dismounting as the carousel made its final revolution, and their eager feet squeaking to the ground, tripping over loose shoelaces, exhumed from me, however fleeting, a more sincere desire for my wife. When was the last time she and I had done something together? Something romantic? I asked myself these and other questions as I exited the gazebo, and perhaps my inability to answer any of them was what prompted me to purchase another ticket. This time I would eschew concern for what people thought about a middle-aged woman riding the carousel by herself. I would photograph the sweep of horses as though it were my regular business, and then I would return home with something that pleased Estelle.

I was the only person with coin in hand my second turn; a few sets of parents and wistful-eyed children pressed against the metal railing and watched. While I should have felt some relief in having the experience to myself, I became awkwardly aware of my singleness. Even here, in a venue flooded with sounds, sights, and people, I was alone. I had found once more a way to be alone in an overwhelmingly public space. This had troubled Estelle from the start, my instinct to cordon myself off from everything going on around me, around us, and it was effectively the reason I was at La Ronde sans wife that day. She had been the one to suggest the outing in the first place, but my delayed response, not entirely without purpose, had diluted her enthusiasm over a period of weeks. When I turned to her that morning in bed and proposed bringing her to Le Galopant after she finished work, she turned away from me and said, "I'll be home late. But I'd love it if you went and took pictures. Would you do that for me, Margot?"

After she left for work, I cleared still-sealed boxes from the chest where she kept her novelty cameras. We had moved to the loft in June, and I had failed (again, not entirely without purpose) to unpack and set up the place as I had promised I would. With some bitterness, I deliberated over which type of camera to bring to the park. SLR? Twin-lens reflex? Digital? I didn't care for photographs—another raw point between my wife and me, since she worked as manager for L'Espace Vif, a small but strident gallery that attracted important artists every season with its reputation for showcasing baroque nudes and other verboten concept photography. As I waited for my water to boil, I phoned Estelle to ask what she was hoping for, what quality of image, what kind of mood, wishing to simultaneously impress upon her my keenness to fulfill her request, but the gallery's voicemail service left me to answer those questions myself. I sorted through the cameras and tried to fathom how Estelle could stow a 1937 Minoltaflex or a 1947 Ilford Witness in a chest, but strew flippant of-the-moment art on our walls. Most of the cameras didn't seem to work, but then again I felt wary about handling them. Maybe I was experiencing the same uneasiness Estelle used to experience when I came home with a rare pistol I had acquired for my business partner, Bertrand. "How wonderful! He's lucky to have you," she would say, waving away my prize, even after I exposed its empty chamber. The cameras were all carefully arranged in either original packaging or bubble wrap, except for one: the Polaroid Z2300 Estelle had surprised me with in January, her annual attempt to stimulate my interest in her passion. "*Tiens*, GoGo, it was designed just for you. It's not too modern-looking, but it is digital, so you can see the images before you print them." She explained how I could edit images on the viewfinder—a word I hated immediately—and then demonstrated by capturing my puffy morning face and converting the image to black and white before printing it.

This—pleasing my partner of twenty-five years—should not have posed any challenge for me, yet it did. As I chased a mouthful of hot tea past my front teeth, which were becoming increasingly sensitive from my nighttime grinding, I realized that what pleased Estelle, what had always pleased her, absolutely turned my stomach. It hadn't always, but relationships are interesting and titillating only in the beginning, and those that survive the pre-set obstacles that dissolve others (overcoming jealousies about ex-lovers, negotiating room for two in one's life, learning when to concede and when to advocate, et cetera) eventually become vulnerable to much less. After two-and-a-half decades with a woman whose gasp-worthy winsomeness and intelligence I had avowed to protect and nurture for the rest of our lives, I was bored. So bored, I didn't have the wherewithal even to take steps toward rehabilitating the relationship. But this was not a thought on which I permitted myself to dwell. By the time I set out late in the evening of that Wednesday (I had spent the day organizing ... maybe Estelle would be back at her usual time and agree to accompany me), I had convinced myself that it wasn't a thought at all but a misinterpretation of the ennui I had been feeling since I left my job in March. Add to that the move to our loft, one of the most stressful events for the average person, and it made perfect sense that I had transplanted the seeds of my negative

feelings onto my wife. Through all the recent change, she had been the sole constant. While the other rungs of my life had spiralled away from my reach, Estelle had remained rooted at my side, and it was much easier to criticize her steadfastness than to praise her stability.

After Estelle had spent two weeks searching for the ideal loft for us, I agreed to make an offer. I had to make amends somehow for constantly refusing to be whisked around the city by a realtor who wore fake gemstones on her eyelids. Also, I expected the owners to laugh in our faces (property on the cobblestone street facing the Saint Lawrence Seaway, with pristine interior features like exposed brick walls and original copper piping, *always* provoked bidding wars), thus my participation in Estelle's "Project Loft" was more of a confirmation I was still engaged in our relationship than any conscious desire to expedite another major change.

When I had informed Bertrand I was resigning from Le Canon Noir, a tiny establishment in the surprisingly profitable business of purchasing and selling antique firearms, I had felt in control: I had outfoxed The Midlife Crisis by choosing to do something drastic before succumbing to an impulse, and eventually I would adjust. Otherwise, who in her right mind abandoned a high five-figure career with plentiful and constant perks in favour of uncertainty? I had never risked anything greater than a found dollar on a lottery ticket. Estelle had been complaining for months I was staying at the shop too late, "You care more about a scuff on your British flintlock than my horrible day at the gallery!" so I decided the best solution was to leave my job. It had, in Estelle's defence, become unfairly time-consuming since Le Canon Noir's expansion to the empty lot next door. After twenty years in antiques dealing, I was confident I would have new opportunities; until the right one presented itself, I would enjoy my free time. And then, at the apex of my boredom, I acquiesced to Estelle's plea for the loft on rue de la Commune (how perfect it was, this point on the

map around which our relationship had begun and flourished!).
Major life change number two.

Dusk settled over La Ronde between my first and second rides.
Le Galopant's traditional carnival music seemed anachronistic
set against park-wide booming, thumping dance club hits and
hydraulic-launch roller coasters with names like "Monstre"
and "Goliath" (appalling machines that sped along narrow
fluorescent tracks, flipped upside-down and spun through a
series of loops, with passengers secured in place by T-shaped
bars pressed against the tops of their thighs). How could two
such opposing concepts exist so close to each other? What
similarities did they share to attract equal attention from
park-goers? I could hardly imagine myself as a child wanting
to ride a silly ornamented horse when I could experience the
thrill of shooting through the air like my favourite villain.
There had been no such rides in my childhood, of course. I
never once went to an amusement park, for my mother was
agoraphobic and my father regularly absent. Estelle adored
amusement park rides and always looked at them in young-girl
wonderment, but her tall, slender build was too easily bruised,
so she always settled on the Ferris wheel.

The ticket boy yawned self-indulgently when I presented two
dollars for my second ride. "Don't worry, ma'am," he said, "I
overcharged you before. Thought you were bringing a kid on
board like everyone else."

The sting from his remark inspired in me the impulse to
slap him, to demand whatever possessed him to assume I had
a child. There was nothing remotely "mother" about my attire—grey plaid Oxford bag cuffed trousers, a starched white
button-down with nickel snap cufflinks, two-tone spectator
shoes, and a black merino derby hat. But what if the ticket
boy's mother, or close female relatives, defied conventional
moulds and he was simply programmed to assume every
woman could be a mother? For the possibility, I offered my
humblest expression.

"Since I'm the only person in line, would you prefer to wait? I don't mind waiting. I'm here to photograph the ride for my wife. That's not an issue, I hope?"

The ticket boy's eyebrows tented, and I wondered if his was the same surprise that still quivered across people's faces years after Québec had blessed same-sex marriage. I didn't care what people thought, but Estelle's absence that day, along with the trailing guilt over my morning thoughts, forced me to acknowledge how new our old life was for others. I had known from the moment I walked Estelle to rue de la Commune that she was it. There had been no one before her, not a kiss or so much as a timid exchange of interests. Estelle, however, having entertained the affections of men prior to our union, felt compelled to externalize her rebirth. For a while, she championed politically correct terms and urged me to do the same (I did not). She joined a lesbians-only book club that met every Sunday and never seemed to discuss books. She told everyone who would listen about how none of her male lovers had *completed* her. Eventually she made her place in "the community," and she wept more on the day we became entitled to legal marriage than she did at our wedding the following week.

"If you don't mind, ma'am, since there's no one else waiting, I should run the herd to see what the creaking sound I heard before's all about. You can take pictures while I do it. Just watch the edge of the platform. The basswood's splintered and might catch on your pants." The ticket boy lit a cigarette. He glanced at the *"DÉFENSE DE FUMER"* sign outside the gazebo and then stepped inside his booth. There, he busied himself with the control panel, which reminded me of a toy telephone switchboard I had owned as a young girl, made of bright knobs and dials that generated important sounds when you pressed or turned them. The Wurlitzer vibrated awake when the boy punched a large red button at the top of the panel, and upon his manipulation of a slider and adjacent yellow dial, the steam engine's gears shifted and clicked, and the horses, bold and powerful without the impediment of people, advanced in an unhurried, confident lope to "K-K-K-Katy."

I remained outside the gazebo while the horses made their revolution, suddenly awed by this parade of animals prominently featured in all aspects of world history—transportation, war, colonization and industrialization, sport and leisure. I had never given weight to their greater, universal significance, and the privacy of my experience evoked in me an almost analeptic joy. I, too, could identify beautiful things unrelated to my work! I, too, could make connections between the symbolic and the literal! I could recognize importance and develop new appreciations. Estelle would have pulled me inside the gazebo by now, certain I was bored, and stood us so close to the splintered platform we could feel the breeze of motion skim across our faces. She would have held my hand and rested her head on my shoulder, insisting I receive the moment with an enthusiasm I was normally incapable of seizing. Why wasn't she with me right then? But as I stood by myself, considering each set of three horses as it panned from left to right, I pushed aside all negative thoughts and delighted in each animal's uniqueness that revealed itself. There was the horse with the neat forelock, another with no forelock, a set of three with dapples on their rumps that looked like constellations, and a horse by himself at the end, if a circle could have an end, whose front legs were fully extended in his effort to keep up with his legion. He would be my mount for my second ride. The smallest of the horses, the least gilded of the lot, yet the one who should have attracted the most attention from park-goers for his exquisitely flared nostrils, fine, raised veins along the sides of his muzzle, and gleaming white teeth chomping the air in defiance of being left behind. He had not been a simple creation, I imagined, though that was as much as I could imagine. I knew nothing about the building of carousel horses, let alone how this would have been achieved in 1885, the year Le Galopant was created in Bressoux, Belgium. I recalled some details from Estelle's documentary, how the horses were built in parts—head and neck, legs, barrel and tail—and then fused together with a recipe of glues and screws, but beyond that I couldn't guess the amount of labour and devotion poured into conceiving an entire convoy.

The ticket boy ran the horses until the end of "K-K-K-Katy," then hopped out of his booth. He stubbed his cigarette against the metal railing and, not without a shrug of apology for the distastefulness of this next move, tucked the butt into the side pocket of his jeans. He was the kind of boy who probably had one close childhood friend only, who sat at the back of classrooms not because he was disaffected or repellent, but because his gaunt, sexless face did not draw him attention even if he sat at the front and waved both hands in the air. He was well-read and more intelligent than most of his peers, certainly the other boys, but had not yet figured out how to interact with girls who kindled his interest—and he wasn't sure if they kindled his interest or his impulse to conform to adolescent behaviours he inwardly scorned. I guessed him to enjoy a large degree of freedom in his home life; perhaps his parents both worked full-time in professions that demanded their attention more than their son did, and so they rewarded him with autonomy that was poorly handled at-large by an age group of video game and social media fiends. He would start to gain popularity once he entered his twenties, when his formerly unappreciated features became those that made young men and women swoon as though struck by a Hollywood star—eyes the colour of autumn brush, full mouth, fine-boned hands that should belong to a classic pianist, and a lithe frame that spilled elegantly into three-piece Italian silk suits. Upon my assessment of the boy, I thought it appropriate to ask his name. Nobody new had come to lean over the railing and admire the carousel, and I was worried the boy might retract his generosity.

"Young man, what is your name?"

My question appeared to fluster him, or perhaps it was the absence of preamble. He thrust his hands into the kangaroo pocket of his *Cats* hoodie and looked away as he answered. "Étienne."

"Lovely name, Étienne. I'm Margot."

"Do you want to ride the carousel now, ma'am? The park's closing soon."

"To tell you the truth, Étienne, I get a little dizzy on rides, even something as mild as this. But I'll make a tour of the platform and photograph the horses—I enjoyed watching them on their own. I especially like that last fellow."

"Napoleon!"

Étienne and I turned to inspect the third source in our conversation: A teenage girl holding a spool of pink cotton candy in each hand. She nipped at the spool in one hand and extended her other hand to Étienne, who pushed up the right sleeve of his hoodie and checked his watch.

"They're going to catch you," he said.

The girl grinned and licked the contours of her mouth like a satisfied cat. "You got free food all last summer because of me. Now say 'thank you.'"

"*Merci.*" Étienne accepted the cotton candy then retreated into his booth. The girl smiled at me and offered some of her spool.

"No, thank you. Excuse me, Étienne, may I go in now?"

Étienne encouraged me to enjoy the opportunity, and then ducked from sight as though to escape further conversation. A hand fluttered up to the control panel and programmed the carousel, and the girl called out, "Could you play 'K-K-K-Katy' again? I'll bring you a jumbo dog tomorrow, and a bacon-cheeseburger the next. I'll bring you something every day until I leave if you play my song again!" Étienne's hand paused, fingers flexing and curling in contemplation, and then his other hand appeared and ten trim fingers manipulated the control panel with swift expertise.

"I love teasing him," she said, touching my arm. "So you like Napoleon? He's my favourite, too! I don't know his real name, because they didn't replace the name plaques when they fixed up the carousel. Isn't that the saddest thing you've ever heard? My dad said Nanny and Poppy memorized all the names when Le Galopant was at the World's Fair. He used to make them tell him when he was young. I can't wait until Napoleon's friends are repainted. No one wants to ride the horse all by himself, so I'm very happy you've taken an interest in him."

The more she spoke, the greater the girl's lisp became. At first it evinced only every few words. After a full minute of her wired chatter, it was present in every word, even those that normally wouldn't encourage the tongue to catch on the back of the upper front teeth. Lisp notwithstanding, the girl's speech rhythm and accent were unmistakably American. Having travelled often to the U.S. in pursuit of firearms for Le Canon Noir, I had developed an ear not only for the different accents from state to state but also for the different registers within a particular state. The cosmopolitan versus the rural. The educated versus the underprivileged. Upstate versus downstate. This person licking cotton candy off her lips with the giddy zeal of a child, swaying side to side on bowed legs that were far too long for her body beneath mid-calf leggings, Converse sneakers, and untucked T-shirt, was from New York—somewhere central-state, sparsely populated, and nowhere a person would want to spend the rest of her life.

"I'm Katharine de Wilde," she said, tipping her head sideways as though unfamiliar with her own name. She extended her hand but withdrew it quickly when she saw it was pink with cotton candy residue. "Or just Katy. Or *Kah-Tee*, like Étienne says when I make him. I love French accents!"

I felt a charge of weariness, like I had been trying to photograph Le Galopant all day long and was interrupted every time by buzzing, loquacious people like Katy. In reality, I had been at La Ronde for barely one hour. I hadn't visited any of the park's other attractions, and I had willfully chosen to go so late in the day to be able to blame my poor (or nonexistent) photographs on crowds, time constraints, and poor lighting, to make obvious to Estelle my crossness at her refusal to accept my morning proposal. Katy must have noticed me fidgeting with the shoulder strap of the camera case, for she pointed and said she had wanted a digital Polaroid *forever*, and did I need help taking pictures? Did I have a steady hand? A steady hand was crucial.

"It so happens I have a very steady hand," she said. "Like a professional. That's why my dad lets me shear the ewes. So do you?"

"Do I what, Katy?"

"Have a steady hand?"

Weaker than my desire to engage in further conversation with Katy was my desire to photograph the carousel horses, even Napoleon; however, now there was a way to redeem my situation. The Wurlitzer whistled a song whose origins I could not identify (Étienne had rightly chosen to ignore Katy's coy request). The fleet revolved around the axis for the last time that evening, each polished wood body illuminated against the darkening sky, but the magic I had experienced earlier was gone.

"I'll take your pictures. Who are they for? And what's your name?"

"Margot. And why does it matter, whom they're for?"

"It makes all the difference. Like, if the pictures are for you, you have to be on one of the horses. Napoleon!"

Katy took the Polaroid from me and nudged me inside the gazebo. She followed as I circled the platform in search of Napoleon, and she giggled when I lifted a spectator shoe to the platform but stomped it back to the ground when I realized I had no business attempting to embark a moving ride.

"Just grab on to a horse and pull yourself up, then hold on to the others until you get to Napoleon. Don't worry, Margot. No one has ever fallen on this ride. It's the safest in the park."

I could hear Katy clicking away behind me, immortalizing god knew what in the viewfinder (the back of my head? my luckless effort to be spontaneous? adorable Étienne in his booth?), but I was so intent on making a graceful show that I couldn't break my concentration to warn her about printing images while she worked. A couple for herself was reasonable exchange for her efforts, but she couldn't be dexterous enough to fan a stack dry and operate the camera at the same time. I decided my chances of successfully mounting the platform would improve if I walked alongside it at an accelerated pace, until I gathered enough momentum to leap toward my steed of choice. I did not have a goal at this point, except to land upright and square, ideally with my derby hat still on my head. It was as I travelled the perimeter of Le Galopant that I learned about the distinction between it, a true artifact of the past, and the modern-day merry-go-round—Carousel's spurious, evil twin. Katy clicked less and talked more as she followed me on my little fun-park adventure, and seconds after I launched myself, with the dignity of a felled tree, onto the ride and then atop the most unexciting of all the horses, she sprang, light as a twig, onto the horse in front of mine—one of the constellations—swung her long legs over his rump to face me, and took what Estelle would claim, in the twilight of our marriage, the most telling photograph of a person she had ever seen.

2. THE LORAZEPAM HOURS

"PIERROT GAVE ME THIS AT LUNCH. What do you think?"
"I find the Artist Sans Surname movement infuriating.
The Ass movement."

I had just entered the loft—had scarcely a beat to begin the
slow, painful process of extracting my swollen feet from my
spectator shoes, which had served me loyally for standing and
sitting all day at Le Canon Noir, but proved unsuitable com-
panions for my journey to La Ronde—when my wife accosted
me with a print that appeared to cause her great excitement.
With my left foot halfway out of its shoe and looking like a
cousin of the Hindenburg, I realized I would need both hands
against the wall for balance, and so I offered to Estelle, less
magnanimously than I had planned, the box of blueberry tarts
I had purchased from Monsieur Pinchot bakery. I had figured
if I was going to make a grand entrance with photographs of
Le Galopant to please my wife, to allay the tension between
us that had been incited by the carousel in the first place, I
might as well take a half-hour detour to Montréal's *gourmande*
quarter and splurge on tarts.

"Excellent. I forgot to get a dessert," Estelle said, not both-
ering to untie the blue ribbon for a peek inside the box.

It was true we were Monsieur Pinchot regulars, and consistent in our selections, but why couldn't she at least feign
curiosity about the delectable *du jour*? Instead, she looked
around distractedly and ferried the box to our temporary

Ikea table, returning to stand before me and ask, "Well?"

I pretended to study the print long and hard, for the sake of alliance, but all I saw was what I had seen initially: the silhouette of a woman around whose body, below her nude, unsettlingly youthful torso, was coiled a reptilian-looking swirl of smoke.

"*Un serpent*, GoGo. She's transforming into a serpent, like the one on the guns Bertrand let you keep? The figure's meant to express dislocation and longing. It'd make sense if you saw the whole series."

I took the print from Estelle and considered it seriously. Its suggestion bore no conceivable resemblance to the crafted gold serpent on either of my early seventeenth-century Barnett trade guns, and I was surprised she would make such a connection.

"It looks like someone's final project for Photoshop 101. I'm sorry, it just doesn't speak to me."

I returned the print and beheld my feet. The flesh in spots where they had rubbed hardest against the insides of my shoes was raw and stained with black dye.

Estelle *tsk-tsked*. "See what happens when you let things pile up?"

"You shush. I have plenty of clean socks, but I was too busy hunting for the right camera to concern myself with the basic staples of my day." I began my plank-walk to the bathroom, fully intending to dodge a squabble about how, if I had done laundry the previous day, as I had promised I would, I wouldn't urgently need to soak myself in the claw foot tub. Estelle tugged at the strap of the camera bag slung over my shoulder, and I shrugged her off. "Not now."

"*Pauvre fille.* Some white Rueda and shrimp pad Thai'll make it all better."

I almost said, "Don't forget about my poor, lonely tarts," but I wasn't feeling playful or even sarcastic. Rather, I was feeling an unexpected protectiveness over the chronicles of my afternoon, and I wanted time alone to revisit them before I passed them on to Estelle, who would, as she did so pre-instinctively it wasn't her fault, possess them as her own.

In addition to the photographs the girl with the spools of pink cotton candy had taken, I had acquired an information pamphlet about Le Galopant's origins, most which Katy had yammered on about as we rode around. The ticket boy, Étienne, had let the ride go on for so long I felt queasy when I dismounted my horse. Katy pleaded with him to run the fleet once more, but he had grown somber after concluding that the creaking sound he heard was the symptom of a serious malfunction. He didn't want La Ronde's management blaming him for making things worse.

"I'm not even supposed to let grownups on," he said grumpily, when Katy pouted her sticky pink mouth.

"That's not true at all. You just have to politely tell the … bigger people to ride in the chariots—not that you're big, Margot. You look *amazing* for your age. Right, Étienne?"

A few revolutions into our ride, Katy had dangled the Polaroid in front of me and insisted I take charge. The way she proceeded to tuck her chin-length sandy bangs behind her ears and gawk expressly at everything but me and the Polaroid was neon indication she wanted to be photographed. The candid, "I can't believe you caught me at such a favourable moment!" shot she could show her friends back home. I didn't oblige, of course, but I did slyly capture her profile as I panned the viewfinder over the backs of the horses, and I felt strangely anxious about this photograph. I had printed it during my commute home on the metro, and I was worried I hadn't let it dry completely before tucking it inside the camera bag.

As I drew the water for my bath and waited, I saw that Estelle had assumed my task and set up more of the loft. That morning, only our toothbrushes and her travel cosmetics case had occupied one side of the marble counter, at the centre of which sat the pleasingly deep and wide basin sink, one of the loft's features that had most appealed to me as an insincere

prospective buyer. Now there was one of Estelle's arty, confusing vases on the other side (she regularly received bizarre,
impractical thank-you gifts from artists, which she always
managed to find some practical use for), a pedestal toilet paper
holder beside the toilet, and, most curiously—for this was not
an acquisition we had previously discussed—a translucent, teal
digital scale shaped like a cat's head. When I tapped the surface
with my toes, two electric green eyes blinked open at the top,
and a needle-toothed grin illuminated across the bottom. I
stepped onto the scale and cracked my knuckles, as one does
in anticipation of disagreeable news, and the scale began to
purr. I jumped off and hollered to my wife.

"I thought we had a deal."

Estelle laughed on her way to the bathroom, her face bright
with pleasure when she came to my side. "I couldn't say no.
Roland gave one to each of us and begged us to try it out. He's
shooting a series on bathroom alter-egos."

"Roland's projects are incomprehnsible at best. And what
in hell is a bathroom alter-ego?"

Estelle tipped her head back and shifted her eyes from me
to the scale, and then back to me. "I think we have a winner."
She licked her forefinger, which looked as though it had been
dipped in our dinner preparations, and then fluttered her hands
in the air. "*Vas-y*, get into your bath. I'll be back in a sec."

Between the snake woman and the scale, I wondered what
might be consuming my wife, whose most ordinary tastes were
normally more discriminating and sophisticated. That she had
recently become taken with carousels now struck me as part
of this new, threatening continuum of the whimsical, against
which my unadventurous self was preparing to resist.

I stepped back onto the scale and jumped off once again
when it spoke. "Dear me," it said. "Someone's had one too
many hazelnut wafers."

"Perhaps you need to be returned to your manufacturer,"
I snapped.

Estelle reappeared and sighed loudly, but patiently, like she was about to change an infant's diaper. "Roland asked us to play with different settings to see how they made us feel. We're his beta-testers. He's planning to photograph subjects before they step on and after the scale gives its reading. They'll be nude, of course, but he's more interested in their faces, especially their mouths. He claims our alter-egos are most visible when our mouths are open." She presented a tray with two bowls of shrimp pad Thai, a half-empty bottle of white Rueda, and two crystal glasses. A cinnamon-scented beeswax candle flickered at the tray's center.

"So then it's all a lie? I can have more hazelnut wafers?"

Though I wasn't overweight, I certainly wasn't what anyone would consider thin or nimble. My five-foot-two frame carried my sixty-two kilograms equitably, so while there was nothing about it that inspired people to compliment specific features, there was also nothing about it that invited suggestions I might consider wearing this particular type of pant leg or that style of neckline. I was perfectly invisible in the eyes of fashion hounds and trend gurus, which was fine with me. Estelle, conversely, was runway trim, long and lithe from her morning Yoga sun salutations and evening Pilates routines. Being beautiful was part of her job description as manager of a gallery that served a public seeking to define itself by the art it owned. She was L'Espace Vif's emissary, responsible for wooing new artists and imploring benefactors, but she didn't have an inflated sense of herself. (Though I felt she sometimes went to extremes where her footwear was concerned. She was five-eight in stockings, and I believed my trepidation about being alongside her in four-inch heels not unreasonable.) Her modest confidence, which reflected in her sunniness and refusal to leave any option unexplored, attracted artists and benefactors the way it had attracted me the day she tugged at my coat sleeve on rue Saint-Paul.

Estelle turned her back to me and placed our dinner tray

on the marble counter. "I won't look," she promised, hearing my lack of progression from clothed to naked to submersion in the bath. She was dressed in a floor-length white cotton sheath, not transparent but so fitted I could see she had no underwear on. She rarely wore a bra for she didn't need one, and she disguised her insecurity about her breasts, which I thought were lovely, mouth-sized details, by wearing fabrics that alluded to her absence of top-level undergarments. Had she been a coffee shop barista or a barmaid, customers would have leered at her liberally and made derogatory remarks. But at L'Espace Vif, everyone was proper and contained in order to balance the effects of the lewd artwork. It was, in that sense, an opportune environment in which to get away with being fashionably improper, especially if your nametag boasted an important title.

"I think you'll be happy with the carousel pictures," I said, giving up on my plan to enjoy them first in solitude. I placed the camera bag on the floor at Estelle's feet and proceeded to remove my clothes, folding them neatly on the toilet seat and laying my derby hat carefully on top. I eased into the claw foot tub, relishing the bite of cold water on my twin Hindenburgs. When Estelle turned to me, she offered me a glass of Rueda.

"Here's to finally setting up our loft," she said, chiming her flute against mine. "Maybe we'll be done before the new year." She started to remove my clothes from the toilet seat but reconsidered and sat on the tufted mat beside the tub.

"So?" she said, plunging her hand under water to grab mine. "Should I offer him space for an exhibit?"

"Whenever you ask me this, I know you've already made up your mind. What about the pictures? I had a little help from one of the rubes, this odd teenage girl who—"

"Margot, please, can we talk about Pierrot first? I have to make up my mind by tomorrow. His series is called 'Images of Erotic Distress and Divination.'"

"Sounds like he was molested as a child. Is he Catholic?"

Estelle sipped her wine and stretched out her legs. In both private and public, she enjoyed drawing my attention to their meticulousness; she was perhaps the only middle-aged woman in the history of the world who had not one blemish on her legs. Not a murmur of cellulite or spider veins, no scars from skinning her knees in the sprints of childhood, not even a freckle or a mole. I loved that they were mine. Their single "imperfection" revealed itself during winter and only if Estelle forgot to apply her Dior Brilliant Bronze tanning gel to keep the covered parts of her skin uniform with the uncovered parts.

"I think maybe it's time for us to see a couple's counsellor," she said, withdrawing her hand and worrying her wooden bead necklace.

"Okay, fine. Offer him space. If you like his work that much, I don't see why it matters what I say."

"Margot."

"I've had a bit of a day, okay? Why don't you ask me in the morning? Wake me up with some Earl Grey and I promise I'll be agreeable."

Estelle's voice quivered. "Did you hear me?"

"Yes, I heard you."

"Really? Because I said we need to see a couple's counsellor."

"Actually, you said you think maybe it's time for us to see a couple's counsellor. Have you been waiting all day for this? It's one of Marianne's brilliant suggestions, I bet. Next you'll tell me she's been thinking lately about experimenting and wants to try a threesome with us. No, forget that. She knows I wouldn't touch her with a leaf blower."

With pronounced and sloppy abruptness, Estelle seized the camera bag and dropped it onto her lap. "Never mind. Sorry I said anything. Now isn't the time, right? Right now we should enjoy our meal, you should enjoy your bath, and I should enjoy these pictures you seem to think will make me so happy." She unzipped the bag with the greed of a dieter unwrapping a chocolate bar. I set my glass of Rueda on the floor beside the tub and snatched the bag from her before she could look at the print of Katy.

"There's some editing I want to do before you see the pictures," I stammered. "I started on the metro, but you know me and modern things. I couldn't even figure out how to … I need more time. Would you mind? Would you let me do something nice for you? It might save us two hundred bucks in couples counselling."

"Can I see the one you printed?"

"That was just a test. It's nothing."

Estelle took my flute and emptied it into hers, and finished the wine in one baleful swig. "I've been thinking a lot about it," she said, rising unsteadily and claiming the bottle of Rueda from the marble counter. "I finally talked about it this afternoon with Dr. Weinstock." She swigged from the bottle and pushed my clothes and derby hat off the toilet seat with her foot. Her big toe flashed a thin silver artisan-style ring I didn't recognize. My derby landed on its crown, and if I hadn't been so concerned about splashing water inside the camera bag (thus ruining the print of Katy, which was in that moment more important to me than the proper handling of my hat), I would have scolded Estelle for her recklessness. *You can't just wipe merino wool dry like a plastic tablecloth!* But I appreciated the precariousness of my situation, knew it best to let Estelle get whatever was in her system out of her system. This sometimes happened when she indulged in too much drink.

"Dr. who?"

"Of course you wouldn't know who I'm talking about, because I haven't told you I've been seeing him. And do you know why? Of course not. It's like you went deaf the day we moved into this place, so why would I bother to tell you anything important?"

"Seeing? As in more than once? What are you talking about? Estelle, you're not making any sense. And you're slurring."

Estelle leaned against the counter and took the bottle's neck deep into her mouth, closing her lips around its base. She glared at me, licentious and beautiful, radiating Verdejo grapes, secrets, and thespian ribaldry. I stepped carefully out of the tub, my willingness to meet her challenge in competition with my illogical need to preserve a photograph of some teenage girl who, but a few hours ago, had tormented my last bit of patience. Estelle looked triumphant as she finished the wine, as if to say "Ha! Now you can't have any." What I wanted was elusive and alive under her white cotton sheath. It was something, were I to give weight to my wife's desultory pronouncement, I could lose thanks to Marianne and Dr. Weinstock.

"No," Estelle said, turning away when I took the bottle from her and kissed her on the mouth.

"That hurts," she protested when I bit her neck, yanked up her floor-length sheath so I could reach underneath. "Margot, I'm not in the mood."

But the mood under her sheath told differently. The Rueda was directing her body language, hastening her physical responses and silencing her inhibitions, and at her body's request, I would comply. At the reception of our official wedding night, she had allowed her family, friends, and coworkers to intoxicate her with well wishes and iridescent blue cocktails. When finally we were alone in room 1742, the famous Bed-In suite of Montréal's Queen Elizabeth hotel (which had cost me no less than a month's salary), instead of wanting to make love, she had wanted to forage the mini-bar. We had been partners for sixteen years, but it would be the first time I experienced Estelle's unutterable fantasy, one she could permit herself to act out only after she was too drunk to consent. Her body's quickness to orgasm, from the mere suggestion of touch she claimed unwanted, and her convulsive response to pleasure in spite of her verbal contestations, stirred in me that night my own unutterable fantasy: When Estelle was in that state, I could take what I wanted quickly, ferret away what was only circumstantially mine.

Estelle bucked her hips against the marble counter and reached once again for the Rueda. I grabbed her wrist and stopped her from throwing the bottle across the bathroom, and with my other hand I grabbed between her legs and worked the heel of my palm forward and backward until her breathing deepened and her thighs unclenched. It would be over before she could think of another way to fight me. I pressed into her until she winced from the grind of her tailbone against the marble. I felt satisfied by her wince; she had threatened our marriage! A series of deep stabs with my fingers, more bites on her neck, and then Estelle released and slumped against me. Her hand loosened and the bottle burst against the tiles. The front of her sheath was entirely transparent, her skin flushed the colour of *petite mort.*

"I'm not like her," she wept. "Margot, I'm not like your mother was. I'm sorry. I'm so sorry. I don't know what's wrong with me. That's why I've been seeing Dr. Weinstock. I need help, and I don't want to drag you down." On she went, weeping into my shoulder, kneading her hands along my spine with such purpose it was like she hoped to learn something new about me.

"Not now." I kissed her face, her eyelids and the tip of her nose, and then pulled away and wrapped a towel around myself. "Take a bath, darling," I said, draining the tub to run fresh water. "You'll feel better."

When I turned back, Estelle looked at me like a little girl stricken from having failed her spelling bee. She raised her arms over her head and waited for me to undress her. As I rolled the sheath up her body, I paused often to kiss her. Once she was naked, I slid the elastic band from her ponytail and smoothed her hair.

"Echidna," I said.

"What?"

"Pierrot's print reminds me of Echidna, the Greek she-dragon."

Estelle lit up. *"Mais oui.* Why didn't I think of that?"

"I'm impressed I just did."

"And you operated a digital camera. It's been a big day for my GoGo."

I reached above the sink, where the medicine cabinet yielded acetaminophen and Estelle's prescription bottle of Lorazepam. I shook out two pills of the former, one of the latter, and filled her empty glass with water.

"Take your bath so we can look at the carousel pictures together in bed." This would give me time to study the one of Katy, for it had been nagging at my consciousness more than anything else since my arrival home.

Estelle hadn't made any progress in our bedroom. It was as I had left it that afternoon, her chest of novelty cameras still open, my men's lightweight flannel nightshirt slouched over the lamp. The room gave the impression of a suspended departure rather than a celebrated arrival. I closed the chest and dragged it beside the Queen Anne burl walnut highboy I had gifted to Estelle our fourth year together, which she cunningly re-gifted to me the following year, on our "wood" anniversary, confessing that the dresser was too impractical for her everyday use. As a demonstration of her rue, she had filled each drawer with silly bric-a-brac she knew I enjoyed but was too proud to acquire on my own: Bazooka Joe bubble gum, miniature green army men, a Lego medieval village set, T-rex-patterned handkerchiefs.

Rather than lose time making the bed and fluffing the pillows as I customarily did before we turned in, I sat on the edge and turned on the digital Polaroid. The images Katy had captured were, as she had promised, the work of a steady—and remarkably skilled—hand. Estelle would be pleased. There was a series of the horses from behind, the undersides of their lovely silver hooves flashing the lens; a series of the horses in profile that emphasized the precision of their sculpted muscles and manes; and a cheeky shot of Étienne brooding into the horizon, evidently unaware he was the subject of Katy's whim of the moment. Katy had photographed me, too, and the shot was so abysmal that in the morning, with fresh eyes and a fresh mind, I would have to figure out how to delete it. After a few more horses, I came to the photograph I had taken. I compared it with the printed version, and I was severely disappointed. Whatever magic I had believed existed in the shot had remained at the park. It was just a picture of a teenage girl who was all limbs, her smile too wide and luscious for her face, and an obnoxious sliver of a gap between her top front teeth like the sort admired in select famous actresses and models, but which, in common women, betrayed orthodontic negligence or inferior social class.

"What are you looking at?"

I jumped to find Estelle standing before me, wrapped in a plush lavender towel and smelling of cinnamon body wash. She sat beside me and nipped my earlobe. "I'm sorry," she whispered. She slipped her fingers down the front of my towel as she worked her lips along my neck. With the two versions of Katy looking up at me—a funhouse, mocking me—I couldn't allow things to go any further. Besides, the resurrected desire I had felt for my wife in the bathroom, had felt in twinges throughout the day, was once again dormant.

"I've had quite the day, Elle."

Estelle pressed her teeth against my collarbone as she considered my statement. She wrapped her towel more tightly around herself and crawled to the top of the bed and then under the sheets. "Sure. I get it."

I turned off the Polaroid and hid the print of Katy in a pocket inside the camera bag. "Tell me more about this Dr. Weinstock. And since when—no, why, I mean really, have you been seeing him?"

"Do you want the short version or the long version?"

"I have nowhere to be in the morning."

A yogi's controlled exhalation, silence, and then: "What about our rule?"

"I didn't start this conversation."

A pause. "But if we get into a fight."

"We'll stop right away and wait until tomorrow."

"Promise?"

"Yes."

"Remember, you asked." Estelle pulled the sheets up over her shoulders. "I thought there was something wrong with me, like a depression, because everything was upsetting me, so I went to the guy Marianne recommended. You have to believe me, Margot, everything under the sun was upsetting me, not just you. Sometimes I'd have to take emergency breaks at work to go sob in the washroom. Jean-Jacques's been the biggest jerk lately, and I can't take it, working with him day in day out and listening to his bitching every time we don't get an artist. I'm doing the best I can. I actually left one of our meetings in tears. So," another exhalation, less controlled this time, "I went to Dr. Weinstock, assuming after he heard me talk for five minutes he'd diagnose me with clinical depression and send me to a walk-in for a prescription of Paxil or something. But instead he told me to come back the next week. Sort of. He asked me to come back."

"And you went back."

"Yes. That was in March, right after you quit Le Canon. Right before we found this place."

"Why?"

"Why, what?"

"Just, *why*, Estelle? You've been seeing a therapist for five months? What's so terrible that you need to see a therapist for five months?" Though just that afternoon I had entertained notions of our relationship being in a perilous state, now I felt the searing panic of a person about to be ejected from even the unhappy securities of her life. My wife had been doing something significant and transformative behind my back. How else was I supposed to feel?

"Oh, fuck, I shouldn't have said anything tonight."

"But you did, and I'm guessing it wasn't all the wine talking." I turned to her and good thing I did, for her face slick with tears quelled my anxiety enough for me to consider her explanation.

"Look, lately you've been, I want to say it nicely … brash? Angry? All the time. Your decision to quit Le Canon was *your* decision, remember. I complained a few times about missing you when I got home from work, and you imagined I was asking you to quit your job. That's a lot of pressure on me. And you've been on this bender about your parents—*tu es obsédée.* I get it, but I didn't appreciate you griping about it the one time this year my family was able to come visit. And I've stopped asking you to work functions, because I never know what you'll say to set someone off. Like you did with Marianne? When she asked what you'd like to do next and you said sell firearms to Al Qaeda? I mean, she was genuinely interested."

At this last I laughed, which earned me a scowl, but not one entirely rooted in opposition.

"Come on, Elle, it's too tempting. She's so gullible. Remember that time she wired money to Micronesia based on some email claiming you were stranded there?"

"*Tu vois?* That's just it. You enjoy being cruel. What has any decent person in our lives ever done to you?"

"Is Marianne still your friend?"

"That's not the point. You always do this." Estelle fought back a yawn.

"Let's continue this conversation tomorrow, baby girl."

After a contemplative moment, she turned down the sheets on my side of the bed and beckoned sleepily to me. The Lorazepam hours were upon her. The sun had set behind the crystalline Saint Lawrence Seaway, *calèche* horses nickered as they passed one another along streets hugged narrow by nineteenth-century stone structures alight with nouveau bars

and restaurants, a string quartet stationed at one of the Seaway's docks implored the night crowd with a hopeful, festive
rendering of a Prince song. As I settled beside my wife and
lay my head on her shoulder, I thought about our first time
together as a married couple: it had given us an opportunity
to redefine our relationship. Though we had been together
for twenty-five years, in some ways I had come to think of
the day of our sanctioned marriage, sixteen years after Estelle
stopped me on rue Saint-Paul, as who we were in the world.
People seemed most comfortable understanding relationships
in terms of years legally married, so while Estelle and I were
firm when we stated we had been married for nine years but
together for twenty-five, some people, especially those who
regarded our kind of marriage as a young concept, viewed
us as a relatively new couple—a couple still figuring out that
things could never fit exactly.

"Margot? Tell me about Le Galopant. Is it magnificent?"

"I wouldn't go that far."

"Then I don't want to know."

"Not according to the photographs I took, anyway. I guess
my alter-ego led me to believe I'd done a better job. Maybe
I've had one too many hazelnut wafers after all. I'll go back
tomorrow and try again. Would you like to come?"

"I've got Pierrot all day. Why don't you keep going back
until you take the perfect picture? I'd love that."

Estelle kissed my forehead and tangled her legs with mine,
the slipperiness of our bodies in our un-air-conditioned loft in
the high of summer making it difficult for us to hold onto each
other. Estelle endured, turning toward me on her side to secure
an arm and a leg across me. *We are a unit*, I imagined was the
mantra in her mind. *We are a unit, and you can't leave me just
because I haven't told you everything.* As I let the sounds of
the quartet on the boardwalk lead me into sleep, I committed
to beginning the next day with insoluble resolve to rescue my
marriage. I planned out how I would start the day—making

breakfast for Estelle and serving it to her bedside—and I pushed aside the troubling thought that doing for her now what I had lived to do for her in the early years of our relationship was somehow more antagonistic than restorative.

3. LE BONHEUR

MY MOTHER HAD ALREADY GONE MAD by the time she gave birth to me. Three years earlier, in the doomful February of 1965, she met my father at a roadside diner in Watertown, Massachusetts, off Route 3, where she and her parents had stopped for lunch on their way to Boston to pay wishes and farewells to distant American relatives freshly drafted into the war. Being a coquette Québécoise of seventeen at the time, accustomed to lots of attention and little responsibility, she did not take notice of the gentleman looking at her from across the diner, but instead became fascinated with a poorly kept poster of a nineteenth-century French painting taped onto the wall outside the restroom. At that age, my mother enjoyed art for the initial impressions it could make upon her, but she never sustained interest long enough to spend more than a moment appreciating any one thing before becoming distracted by something more visually exciting. Whenever somebody tried to explain art to her—the origins of a particular painting, the significance of a bronze statue, the craftsmanship behind a Persian tapestry—she waved her hand as though batting away a fly. "Ça ne m'intéresse plus," she would say. "Art is made to look at, not to study and recite like catechisms. If you know too much about it, it becomes boring." And so my mother was almost grown-up before she appreciated a work of art for the first time as something more than an object for her whimsy (much later, I would blame this for her tumble into madness).

Art to my mother, until that point, had been purely a pleasure of the moment—how instantly a painting or sculpture
or tapestry took her breath away, made her eyes glisten with
wonderment, flushed through her a heat that reached the tips
of her limbs and made her feel like she was standing on a cloud,
or floating; however, the poster in the diner, though faded,
curled at the edges, and stained with fingerprints from people
waiting in line to use the restroom, did much more than inspire
in her feelings of physical bliss. *"Maman, Papa!"* she called to
her parents, who were contently nibbling on hero sandwiches
and enjoying the freedom to stretch their legs as far under the
ketchup-red booth table as they wished. *"Maman, Papa,* what
is this? What is it?" My mother pointed to the image of robust
Percheron horses rearing toward one other and away from
their handlers, striking their feathered hooves in all directions
and reaching their rippling, metallic necks toward the heavens.
She had never held a particular interest in horses, but she recognized in that painting a natural order of power, a freedom
inherent to those creatures that man had been trying to capture
and control, in both kindness and cruelty, since the moment
he had understood the possibility. My mother's parents were
unable to tell her anything about the painting other than to
agree with her interpretations and offer her a fountain soda,
and that was when Morgan Wright, the shrewd man across
the diner, who had been eyeing my mother from the instant she
arrived, took the opportunity to weave apologetically between
tables and around waitresses until he stood beside Marguerite
Soucy and told her, without being waved away, all about Rosa
Bonheur's, "The Horse Fair."

Morgan Wright: Born on January 5, 1925 in Grand Rapids, Michigan, to a set of mercantile Welsh immigrants who
worked long, back-breaking hours in the lumber industry and
eventually established one of the city's most successful furniture
businesses. Everybody in the Wright family was part of the
business, even Morgan's mother, and his four older and two

younger sisters. By the time of Morgan's birth, future plans for his education at Yale University had already been laid out. As heir to the family's legacy, he would study business economics and not only ensure Wright & Co.'s longevity (at the time there was actually no "& Co.," but Mr. Wright had known at least enough to name the company to appear larger than it was), but also its expansion through the northeastern United States of America. Perhaps he would even forge a relationship with the Ford Motor Company and the Wright girls would learn to upholster Tin Lizzies. Versatility would be key. The family's entire future was pinned to that five-pound jaundiced baby on the morning of January 5, 1925. He would ensure their survival, emotional as much as literal. As fortune would have it, Morgan outgrew the myriad health complications that had set a dark tone in the Wright household during the first eighteen months of his life—infant botulism, whooping cough, rheumatic fever—and by the age of ten proved himself a bright and curious chap who compensated for his slight size by learning to play ball and creating a family team of throwers and catchers. At the end of long school and work days, and every day in summertime, Morgan shepherded his parents and siblings to the ball park near their home, insisting that an hour of throw and catch would lift spirits and ensure sound sleep for all. By the time Morgan was thirteen, he had developed, much to his parents' relief, a keen interest in furniture-making, especially billiard tables, which had gained popularity among the wealthy and promised to afford the Wright family unanticipated luxury. A billiard table, young Morgan declared one night to his father—who expressed initial skepticism about the venture—is a toy the rich are willing to buy. We'll make a lot more money selling toys to a few rich people than we will selling tables and chairs to all of Michigan. Only a child prodigy could tease out the logic in such an idea, and luckily for the family, Mr. Wright chose to put faith in his son's proclamation. When Morgan left for Yale five years later, by then a sturdy and handsome young man with no lingering effects from his early-life trials, Wright & Co. had combined resources with another local business and rebranded itself Wright & Ellis. Shortly after Morgan completed his studies at Yale, Wright & Ellis became the preferred supplier of custom pigeonhole billiard tables in the northeast, and the business began its foretold expansion across the map.

Now, imagine such a man as Morgan Wright, educated, successful in business, neatly suited in a black double-breasted long coat and wide-brimmed fedora. Then imagine Marguerite Soucy, a hummingbird of a girl from Saint-Télesphore, Québec visiting the United States of America with her parents for the first time, to meet distant family members whom she might never see again if the newsmen's nervous murmurings about Operation Rolling Thunder came true. At seventeen, Marguerite understood nothing about the world beyond the farm where she had lived since birth, and she did not feel particularly compelled to search beyond the cornstalk borders of her family's property. Her parents had reared her too tepidly, too guardedly, not out of inability or poor parenting strategy, but in attempt to protect their daughter—their only child— and themselves, from the persecution directed toward families with fewer than three children. Québec farming families were expected to produce large broods. Failure to do so indicated one of two things, and neither inspired sympathy from the community: Either one half of the couple was infertile, or the other half was impotent (the latter brought far greater shame onto the family and was almost always kept secret), or the couple as a unit did not believe in procreation and was driven by sinful ambitions like money and empty pleasures of the flesh. Of course, the Soucys were not driven by ambitions other than excessive work hours to ensure their survival and a nominal space for their produce in the central market, and any money they had that was not designated to the obligations of quotidian life was spent on Marguerite to compensate for her remote and lonely childhood. And so, when Morgan Wright approached Marguerite Soucy that afternoon at the roadside diner in Watertown, Massachusetts, and explained the origins of the painting with which Marguerite had become desperately enamoured, Marguerite, accustomed to lots of attention and things generally going her way, thought to herself, *I like this man with the funny accent. I would like him to buy me a fountain soda* (which Morgan did), *and then I think I shall make him fall in love with me* (which Morgan did, though the process took longer than Marguerite could have anticipated, and by the time she would "arrive" at her goal, she would be, as she always had been, off onto other things). The Soucys, not being people to judge or condemn, remained silent and smiled politely when Marguerite led her new gentleman friend by hand to the table and introduced him as a very important person.

"Oh, my," Morgan laughed softly, "I don't know that I'm terribly important, but I do know a thing or two about art, and your daughter has asked that I request your permission to bring her to a museum while you visit family members. I promise to drive her once we are done directly to the address you provide me. We shouldn't be longer than the afternoon."

Marguerite's parents, understanding very little English, nodded and smiled and turned to their daughter and asked, *"Est-ce que cet homme te plait, chérie?"*

Marguerite clapped her hands the way she did when a piece of art excited her, and her parents gave their blessing to Morgan Wright in the form of more nods and polite smiles. After Marguerite left, plunging her small fist into Morgan's, which felt to her smoother than bisque, Mr. Soucy turned to his wife and said, *"Allons-y,"* and the couple departed, too. The Soucys had not given an address to Morgan before he left with their daughter, Morgan had not asked for an address before he left with their daughter, and even years later, no one discussed whether those oversights had been innocent or intentional.

Morgan didn't bring Marguerite to a museum. There was no museum of the sort he had described to her parents, not even a roadside trailer showcasing the variety of backwoods kitsch working-class people purchase as holiday stocking stuffers in hopes of being complimented for having smart, original taste. From the car windows, Marguerite saw nothing but fast-food rest stations and truck stops between the diner off Route 3 and the American side of Niagara Falls, where she and Morgan ended up ten hours later, but her interest in the horse painting had been promptly transferred to Morgan's bottle-green Lincoln Continental. The car ride had started off awkwardly, between the unaddressed, looming language barrier and, more unsettlingly, the obvious age difference between Marguerite and this person whom she reasoned to be kidnapping her. Nothing about him suggested he harboured malevolent intentions, though, and since Marguerite entertained only the fantasy she was being kidnapped and not a cold, dark fear she would never see her parents again, she thought she might allow things to progress as they would and see where they brought her.

A half-hour into the ride, she was bored with the repeating highway scenery and no longer enthused by the Lincoln Continental. (Its best feature was its exterior. The interior, while roomy and fashionable with its blood-orange leather seats and carpeted floor, was just another car.) Eventually, Marguerite cleared her throat and attempted to speak in confident, unbroken English. "*Monsieur* Rrrright, how do you ... how do you say what age you are?" She forced her eyes on the road ahead, but they flickered toward Morgan when he released a hand from the steering wheel and laid it reassuringly on her stockinged knee.

"*J'ai quarente ans,* my dear Marguerite." His years at Yale had not been wasted in any sense, and Morgan was pleased to have the opportunity to speak French freely with his young companion, now that they were alone. As he had anticipated, his fluid tongue caused Marguerite to tense. He would have to take pains to ease her into his plan, and so he withdrew his hand without ordeal and opened the glove compartment. He removed a slender pewter case and rested it on his thigh, flipped the lid up with his thumb and extracted a cigarette.

"Would you mind if I smoked?" he asked, tucking the cigarette into a corner of his mouth and offering the pewter case to Marguerite.

Marguerite blinked as though dust had been kicked into her eyes, and then smiled in a manner I would come to recognize as the prologue to her long bouts of madness, but that was also, my father once told me in an effort to soften me toward her, the smile of a woman to whom the world had promised too much and given too little. "Non, *Monsieur*."

She had seen her father smoke, but never in the house, and she hadn't seen him smoke so much as discovered him one evening, in the shed at dinnertime, after her mother asked her to retrieve him from splitting wood so he could enjoy fresh-made *paté à la viande* and apple-maple cider with his family. (And *tarte au sucre* for dessert!) Marguerite was then a young girl of six or seven, and in the quiet way such girls have on evenings when the snow is falling so delicately it purifies every sound into soundlessness, she remained at the shed entrance and watched Benoît Soucy puff on a cigarette and tilt his head up with the smoke as it wound toward the rafters, his unshaven face soft and relaxed. She watched her father puff on his cigarette until it was finished, and only when he turned to toss it outside did he notice his daughter, huddled against the shed doorframe, a dune-coloured braid cast over each small, quivering shoulder.

The physicality of their communication, the expression of awe on Marguerite's face and the initial panic on Benoît's, tethered father and daughter together with something new and more powerful than blood: They now shared a secret. When Benoît went to his little girl and scooped her consolingly into his arms, lifted her easily onto his shoulders and headed for the house, Marguerite felt her body rush with warmth. She pressed her mittened hands around her father's ears to share the warmth with him, and in that moment, high above a world with which she was just barely acquainted, Marguerite was imprinted with the impulse to trust men who reminded her of her father.

Since the gods of happenstance had orchestrated everything for Marguerite to bond with her kindly kidnapper, she allowed her eyes to rove the interior of the Continental anew, beginning with Morgan, whose thin, distinct lips were curled around his cigarette while his fingers simultaneously guided the mink fur-encased steering wheel and tapped in rhythm to Sonny and Cher's "I Got You, Babe." Yet another trigger, as this was one of her mother's favourite songs. Anaïs Soucy enjoyed humming it as she strung damp clothes by the potbelly stove, and sometimes, if Benoît was nearby, she shyly sang the monosyllabic words loudly enough for him to hear. Marguerite had never considered what it meant to be forty. Her parents weren't yet forty (though she wasn't certain of their exact ages), and while surely there were many forty-year-olds who lived in Saint-Télesphore, she couldn't picture them, especially when she looked to Morgan for reference. He looked younger than her parents, which confused her further. Her father's face, even when it was smooth and taut from the sting of aftershave, was marked with deep lines around the eyes and mouth, and faded straight-razor nicks from his impatient boyhood. His hair, especially when it was trimmed and tamed for Sunday mass, was as uncomely as their sheep's wool. Anaïs, small-framed and skittish, had once been a beauty, but her hands had grown swollen and textured like poorly sanded tree bark from scrubbing clothes in the washbasin on cold winter days, and her lips cracked and bled even in the high-summer heat. Morgan Wright, in spite of his early sickly years and subsequent teenage years of manual labour at the billiard factory, was as preserved as the Hudson's Bay Company mannequins Marguerite loved so much to touch at Christmastime, when they were robed in extravagant animal hides. Not that Morgan's face was featureless like the mannequins', but the consistency of his complexion, the precise arches of his thick eyebrows, the way his lips appeared to have been pencilled on, made him, in Marguerite's impressionable mind, as she would tell me years later, "exasperatingly *exotique* and puzzling."

Morgan smoked halfway to the filter, then rolled the window down and tossed his cigarette. In watching him do this, Marguerite caught, in the corner of her eye, several large shapes occupying the back seat of the Lincoln. When she turned for a better view, she saw three boxes wrapped in brown paper, a different name stamped on the top of each one. Before she could ask about the boxes, Morgan once again placed a hand on her knee.

"Those are for my nephews," he said. "*Pour mes neuveux.*"

"*Ah. Des cadeaux?*"

"Well, sure. Gifts."

They rode in companionable silence like that, Morgan's hand on Marguerite's knee for a few miles, until Marguerite pointed daintily with her forefinger at the pewter case still atop Morgan's thigh. Morgan nodded his head slowly, imploringly, until Marguerite understood his invitation and helped herself to a cigarette.

"What kinds of gifts?" she asked, bringing the filter to her lips but not placing it between them, accepting the brass Zippo Morgan offered to her. She held the spade of flame to her cigarette, blackening its tip the way a lit gas stove blackens the bottom of a stew pot. After a few seconds she stuck the filter between her lips and puffed. Nothing happened, and Morgan allowed Marguerite to repeat her actions once more before taking the Zippo from her.

"Like this, darling girl," he said, taking a fresh cigarette from his case and demonstrating. "The first time you puff in, don't inhale the smoke, just let it flow out. If you inhale that first puff, you'll have a sharp taste in your mouth and won't be able to enjoy the rest."

Marguerite brought another cigarette to her lips and Morgan ignited the Zippo. She puffed in quickly and deeply, and burst into coughs so violent the cigarette flew from her mouth and catapulted off the dashboard and onto the carpeted floor. She gasped between coughs, and her pretty little hands flailed as she grabbed for the cigarette. Morgan got to it first and flicked it out the window as he parked the car on the side of the highway. He rubbed between Marguerite's shoulder blades in slow, soothing circles, crooning "there, there" while she covered her stunned, reddened face with her hands and sobbed.

"*Désolé!*" she cried. "*Désolé.*"

Morgan continued to rub between her shoulders, working his palm down to the middle of her back, easing it around her side and nudging her gently toward him. He took a last puff of his own cigarette. "God help me," he whispered.

Marguerite didn't seem to notice she was sitting so close to Morgan now that the sides of their arms were touching. She reached into her pea coat pocket for her handkerchief and blew her nose with the fervour of a child fed up with suffering from a cold. "I'm sorry for being *un gros bébé*," she sniffled.

Morgan's reply, which was to pull her even closer and kiss the top of her head and whisk a fallen eyelash from her cheek, aroused in her a greater urgency to weep, but she caught hold of her breath for ten seconds and resumed composure.

"Can you keep a secret?" Morgan crooned.

"*Oui.*"

"Those gifts for my nephews? They're really care packages, enough to get them started until I can bring more."

"What is it, a 'care package?'"

At this, Morgan pulled away from Marguerite and took her chin between his thumb and forefinger. That was the first time my mother noticed his eyes, deep-set, mesmerizing green eyes that contained secrets like the one he was about to reveal to her. And secrets he would keep from us beyond his death.

"My darling girl, it is so important that you keep this secret. Can you promise me with all your heart you will keep this secret? Forever?"

How exciting for a small-town girl to be suddenly swept into a mysterious world by such an opulent man! Her unbearable sadness of moments earlier was lustily replaced by the thrill of the unknown, of her accessory to this unknown. Her kidnapper clearly meant her no harm, and that he considered her special enough to involve in his plans was by far the most formidable thing ever to happen to Marguerite Soucy of Saint-Télesphore, Québec, whose parents, though she loved them eternally, had been able only to offer the stability of what any person requires in order to lead a decent, simple life. When she saw them next, she would be filled with newness and knowledge to share with them, to improve their lives and open them to the sorts of fantasies she had seen in the artworks that competed for her attention.

After a pause, Morgan let out a shallow breath and spoke. "You know how just hours ago you were on your way to Boston to bid farewell to relatives going to fight in the war? Well, sometimes people want to go to war, and sometimes they don't. My nephews don't, but the government is trying to force them, so we're on our way to save them."

"Save them?"

"To bring them to Canada, where they'll be able to have good lives—the kind they're meant to have."

"*Ah, oui.*"

But of course my mother didn't understand what this truly meant, the consequence of what Morgan was about to do, the butterfly effect his actions on that day would have years into the future. Hers and mine.

Morgan went on to explain how in 1950, three years after he had completed his studies at Yale and proceeded to expand his family's business, he received a letter stating that he would fight in the Korean War. His mother saw the envelope first and buried it beneath carrot and potato shavings from the evening's dinner preparations. After dinner, as Morgan tossed his pork-chop gristle into the waste bin, the envelope peered through the carrot and potato shavings like a jester's cruel, laughing face. Immediately the next morning, Morgan contacted Dean Mason at Yale. He had made inroads with the dean because of his perfect grade point average and service to the campus community, and asked if there was any way he could help. Morgan did not want to fight in the war; he was simply not that sort of man. Dean Mason, too, was not the warring sort, and because he was a month away from retiring and moving to New Jersey, where he would breed polo ponies and spend time with his grandchildren before they metamorphosed into defiant carriers of his DNA, he had nothing to lose by making phone calls and visits around campus that very day.

The following morning, as Morgan knotted his ascot and palmed the sides of his hair flat above his ears before he left for work, Dean Mason phoned and said, "Congratulations, Son, you've been accepted into Yale Divinity School's three-year Master's program. Your background in economics, along with your stellar success in expanding Wright & Ellis into such a profitable luxury business, will surely prove useful to other students in the Divinity school. Perhaps even to the school itself. God knows the building should have electricity and a coffeemaker. I'm counting on you to make these things happen, Son." And just like that, Dean Mason turned young Morgan Wright into exception IV-D of the *Selective Service Regulations*, which the U.S. government had revised in 1948, after ceding to some of its logistic shortcomings during the Second World War.

Now here he was, fifteen years later, about to assist his three nephews in dodging the Vietnam War. His sisters, Francis and Joyce (his other four, so far, had birthed all daughters), lovely and kindly as they were, had each married a rather dull man whose aspiration to become an employee of Wright & Ellis wasn't to assist the business in expanding further, but to secure himself a job he could depend on. The children of both men were the unfortunate consequences of these unions, pleasant and easy on the eyes though they might have been, and Morgan couldn't bear—more so than his sisters couldn't bear—to see them off to merciless, premature deaths.

I can't be sure my mother understood all of this even years later. By then, my father had abandoned us more or less permanently, except for his invitations, which were as reliable as my mother's mental states, for us to join him on his business venture *du jour*. In the Lincoln by the side of the road that day, what young Marguerite did understand was that she wasn't being kidnapped after all, but rather she was assisting Morgan in his plot to get his nephews safely into Canada, to Hamilton, Ontario, to be exact, where they would assume new identities and new lives and survive by Morgan's generosity until they achieved autonomy on their own merits.

"I can purchase a train ticket to get you back home, and you can phone your parents before you board the train to let them know you're coming back." Morgan said this with great solemnity, his eyes down and heavy with shame, or perhaps with the desire to keep Marguerite to himself, which was naturally the possibility my mother-to-be preferred to entertain. The loneliness she imagined Morgan felt was the projection of her own still inarticulate loneliness of an only child growing up in a small Catholic farming community. But because Benoît and Anaïs had been such consistent, loving parents, Marguerite had been endowed with perhaps an overly sympathetic imagination when it came to other people's inner lives and wants.

"*Où vas-tu aller après* ça?" she asked, finding it difficult to picture Morgan returning to his big-city life filled with glamorous billiard tables and expensive dinners with wealthy clients. In spite of his grand automobile and elegant attire, she had come to view him as an uncomplicated man, one who enjoyed specific company and the opportunity to talk about interesting things. Did he have a wife? Children of his own? Did he read the stock reports every morning and sip black coffee while his wife spooned scrambled eggs onto the children's plates, scolding them affectionately when they pestered their father with questions about gifts for upcoming birthdays? Marguerite had never had a boyfriend. By the time she was fifteen, when many of the girls in her grade were tittering about boys in the other school or fainting over Jimmy Gilmer and the Fireballs or The Beach Boys on the radio, Marguerite asked her mother if there was something wrong with her because she didn't have any of those feelings or reactions.

"*Mais non, chérie*," her mother had said, wrapping her small frame around her daughter with the might of a bear. "That's not love, anyway. *Ce sont des niaiseries.* When you are in love, like your *papa* and me, you will do anything for him. *N'importe quoi.* You can't do anything for some man on the radio, can you? Or for those silly boys at the other school who don't even know how to act properly around girls their own age."

Marguerite wasn't sure what she was willing to do for Morgan. Being far from home, though, sitting on a comfortable blood-orange leather seat inside a bottle-green car, beside a man who told her things that sounded right out of the French translations of the Harlequin Romance novels her mother hid in a box under the firewood behind the potbelly stove (*Came a Stranger*, *Take Me with You*, *Bride in Flight*, et cetera), Marguerite decided she must be on her way to being in love. She felt lightheaded, she felt like squealing, she felt there must be something she could do to make Morgan lose his glum expression and take her in his arms and kiss her so violently the car tipped over.

When instead Morgan's voice broke through her reverie, asking if she would like to take a train home from Hamilton, Ontario, Marguerite released the breath she was holding and flung her arms around Morgan's neck, both of them panting with surprise from the force of her action as much as from the action itself. When their mouths met, Marguerite, having never kissed anyone on the mouth before, faded back to her reticent self and waited for Morgan to take charge, just like in the books.

"God help me," he whispered.

4. BYE BYE BIRDIE

I WAS EIGHT WHEN I FIRST EXPERIENCED my mother's madness in full spectrum. It was 1976, and Wright & Ellis had satellite factories in six states. My father, as usual, was away on business. In addition to billiard tables, the company manufactured other novelty items such as home theatre units and Lazy Susans for the female "household entrepreneur"—the latter being a scheme, my mother asserted, to keep women where men thought they should be.

Imagine the reality for a fidgety child being told one minute to settle down and watch a boring grownup movie with her mother (when said child would much rather chase seagulls along the bay or build driftwood forts by the ocean), and then the next minute her mother starts singing and dancing just like the actress on TV. I was thrilled, and I jumped to my feet to join her. Together we swished our imaginary skirts and pouted our lips like Ann-Margret, waved dramatically and blew kisses at each other. I didn't know the words to the song except for the first line of the chorus, and after my failed attempt at miming, I stepped back and watched my mother to learn from her. It was as though she wasn't in our living room but in front of a large crowd of people, and she had to exaggerate every movement, elocute every syllable so even the people at the very back could see and hear her inimitable performance. After the song finished, my mother clapped her hands and bowed before the audience. *Merci. Merci beaucoup!*

"Margot, dear," she said, breathing heavily and wiping sweat from her forehead, "rewind the song, please."

I had become proficient at operating our SONY CV video recorder, which was still considered a household luxury more than a decade after it had been introduced to the world. My father had come home with it after one of his business trips (he always came home with extravagant gifts for my mother, to make up for the unbearable emptiness she proclaimed to feel during his absence). She didn't like this particular gift at first, as it was, I agreed, a hostile contraption of discs and buttons, and bigger than our television. So the next gift my father brought home was a factory-new Wright & Ellis walnut cabinet, long and low to the ground with curved corners, inside which we could hide the video recorder and on top of which there was ample room for the television and arrangements of crystal vases filled with the orchids and gerberas delivered to our doorstep every morning when my father wasn't home with us. One laggard day when my mother lost interest after our first round of an anti-German, pro-American war board game called, *The Battle of the Bulge*, she suggested we watch a movie on the SONY, which meant, "Margot, dear, why don't you see how that thing works? You're just like your father in that way, all about figuring out how things work." By lunchtime, when my mother came to the living room with a tray of de-crusted, triangle-shaped tuna sandwiches and a pitcher of squeezed lemonade, I had figured out how to work the recorder, and so began my mother's love of watching her favourite scenes two, sometimes three times in a row, which could turn an hour and thirty-minute movie into a three-hour affair, especially if it was a musical. *Bye Bye Birdie* was the first time I saw my mother involve herself so fully in a favourite scene (the first scene of the movie), and I had no clue how utterly long that day was going to be, how, in some ways, it would go on forever.

As I rewound the scene, giggling at how silly Ann-Margret's face looked moving backward in slow motion, my mother skipped up the short flight of stairs to our kitchen and dialled the rotary phone.

"Mom? It's ready! Can we sing and dance again? But this time may I be Birdie? The boy she's saying bye-bye to?" I peered up the staircase at her and she waved her hand to shush me.

Her voice was springy and barely contained when finally the switchboard operator transferred her to my father's line.

"Me and Margot miss you so much, darling! When will you be home? Really? Why so long? Well, would you do us a little favour on your way back? A little favour to make us happy?"

While my father spoke, my mother beckoned me into the kitchen and pointed to the cabinet above the refrigerator. The door was made of transparent glass, so I knew what was in the cabinet, but I didn't know what my mother wanted me to do with it. She issued a series of "um-hums" to my father while pointing to the cabinet and then to a kitchen chair. When I sat on the chair, she pressed her lips firmly together and shook her head so fiercely her bun fell loose and caped down her back. She mouthed words to me that I couldn't understand and then threw one arm up and rolled her eyes to the ceiling. I remained on the chair, an instinct so deep in me I wasn't yet aware of its existence causing me to sit straight-backed and poised to run off if necessary.

"I know, darling, but we're so *bored* here. There's nothing to do when the weather's so unpredictable—you can't expect us to walk all the way into town and get caught in the *rain*."

It was true the walk from our house to the town's centre, where the penny candy store, Lema's, the post office, specialty shops, and restaurants were, took us twenty minutes at a good clip. But what did she mean about the weather being unpredictable? It was a balmy, sunny day—it had been a balmy, sunny week, and my mother and I had taken regular advantage of the conditions until that morning, when she suddenly decided we should spend time together, just the two of us. "Those townspeople are so snobby and nosey, always asking where Morgan went to this time, nattering amongst themselves about how he must have a real good job to afford a house so close to the bay."

We had moved to the house by the bay when I was three. Before Wellfleet, Massachusetts, we had lived in Grand Rapids to be near my father's sisters, so all the childbearing women in the Wright family could bond and help one another raise the brood. The Wright sisters had been bonded since birth in a tight-knit family way that was as foreign to my mother as Africa, and all the family fretting and hubbub made her feel oppressed rather than included. Though she was still in contact with her parents by telephone, she hadn't seen them since the whole en-route to Watertown diner ordeal (which meant that to me, my Québécois grandparents were only as real as the hand-signed cards and occasional photographs they sent).

Once Morgan and Marguerite had transported the Wright nephews safely to Hamilton, Ontario, instead of Marguerite taking the train home as Morgan had suggested, the two drove to Saint-Télesphore. When Benoît and Anaïs arrived at the farm a few days later, having finished their visit with the distant Boston relatives, and assuming their daughter had gone off to a new life with the remarkable man from the diner, they were bewildered and even alarmed to discover their little girl waiting impatiently for them on the front porch, the remarkable man beside her warming his hands around a steaming mug. Morgan stayed the night with the Soucys, and the next morning over a tense, ceremonious breakfast of blueberry pancakes and beans baked in maple syrup and lard, took his chequebook from the hip pocket of the Japanese silk kimono he always travelled with and asked the Soucys, in fluent French, if they would allow him to have their daughter's hand in marriage.

"I understand," he said, "that she's not yet eighteen, so my proposal might cause you some concern. But I promise to oversee all of her needs, including further education if she so wishes, or art classes with the finest mentor in Grand Rapids.

Will you consider it? *Ta fille mérite une belle, grande vie.*" He signed his name across the bottom of a cheque, tore expertly along the perforated line, and then laid the cheque on the table before my grandparents, beside the mason jar of freshly sapped maple syrup. Stamped in antique-style lettering across the top of the cheque was *Wright & Ellis*, and written in flawless cursive on the "dollars" line was "fifty thousand." Thus on February 11, 1965, my father-to-be purchased my mother-to-be, and the transaction of my future arrival was completed.

I sat alert on the kitchen chair after my mother hung up the phone. I watched her rearrange her hair into a bun and smiled guardedly when she looked at me.

"The movie's ready," I said, unable to speak normally, my voice stuck somewhere behind my thundering heart. Was I in trouble? Was my father coming home early from his trip to scold me? Their conversation had begun cogently, but had ended, at least on my mother's side, in the coded language of dissatisfied adults.

"Margot," she finally said, brushing breakfast crumbs off the kitchen table, "would you please do as I asked and get the Delamain from the cabinet?" Then she walked away, down the hallway to her and my father's bedroom.

The Delamain: A bottle of 1950 Grande Champagne cognac from Mr. Ellis, of Wright & Ellis, to my parents on their wedding day. The bottle had never been opened because my parents were waiting until their twenty-fifth anniversary, by which time the cognac would be "vintage and *délicieux*," my mother had told me when I asked about the bottle one day while she had it down from the cabinet so she could polish it. I thought polishing a bottle was silly, especially a bottle of maple syrup. "No, *chérie*, this is a very powerful drink, and very expensive. We keep it apart from the other bottles so our guests can't get at it. This is mine and your father's—something just *pour nous*. One day when you have a husband, you'll know what I mean."

Why my mother couldn't get the Delamain herself now that she was off the phone was a mystery I was too flustered to solve. Mostly, I was relieved that I didn't seem to be in trouble, at least not immediately, and I was happy to do whatever I could to delay any more cold looks from my mother like the one she had given me while she was on the phone with my father. I pulled the kitchen chair in front of the refrigerator and climbed onto it, rose to my tiptoes and reached my arms as high as they could reach, but I came nowhere close to the cabinet. I considered how I might scale the refrigerator or balance a chair on top of the first one; I knew I would be in trouble if I didn't get the bottle. My more practical solution was to climb onto the countertop and reach the Delamain that way. The countertop was slippery under my bobby socks, but I could lean against the refrigerator for support. *Eureka!* My shaky, sweaty hand pulled open the cabinet door and grabbed onto the bottle, and I certainly would have completed the feat successfully had my mother not come suddenly running into the kitchen, her face newly made up with statement eye shadow, rouge, and some horrible shade of orange lipstick.

"Margot!"

The bottle slipped from my hand and landed on top of the refrigerator, just out of my grasp. It rolled slowly, and I'm sure my mother could have stopped it, but she just stared as the bottle inched toward the edge and then plummeted to the linoleum floor and burst. Even then she still stared. It was I who scrambled off the countertop and tried to round up all the pieces of broken glass with my bare hands, as though maybe somehow I could repair the bottle and restore all the cognac. The cognac's odour, so sharp and noxious it caused my airways to constrict, was quickly becoming a thick sticky seal on the floor. Dull triangles of glass poked into my hands and shins. I picked them off and dropped them into the pile I had started. I did whatever I could so I wouldn't have to face my mother, whose bare feet were in front of my hands, tapping the floor like either she was listening to an upbeat song or counting down the seconds before she yanked me by the shirt collar and issued some severe, never-ending punishment.

"Margot? Would you like to go for a walk? It's so nice outside. No need to be doing house chores."

I stopped and peered up at her. My mother had undone her bun and was arranging her hair neatly and evenly over her shoulders.

"There's a new exhibit at the gallery in town, and I'd like to see it. When I'm upset, art makes me feel better. You know that. Don't you want to see your *maman* happy?"

"I'm sorry I broke the bottle. I can give you all my allowances and birthday money from *grandmère* and *grandpère* Soucy I saved to buy a new one."

My mother shook her head pityingly and offered her hand to help me up. "*Non, ma chouette*, you've done something so bad that all the allowances and birthday money in the world can't fix. You truly have. But we'll talk about that later, when your father gets home."

"When's he coming home?"

"Oh, who knows? Maybe he'll be so upset with you he'll never come home."

It would turn out, at least in part, she was right.

The walk into town was slow, as my mother was still barefoot and we had to make frequent stops so she could brush sand and stones from her feet. In addition to putting on garish makeup, she had changed into beach clothes: a sheer wraparound skirt over her black two-piece bathing suit, a loose-fitting white cotton blouse, and a bright yellow wide-brimmed sunhat with a spray of fake daisies and a hummingbird pinned to the front. She wore a pair of cat's-eye tortoiseshell sunglasses that covered most of her face, and her forearms were adorned wrist to elbow with thin silver bangles. Once we reached the road that forked either to town or to the bay, I asked if we should turn back for our towels, just in case. I was happy to be outside, in spite of the way cars honked and boys whistled as they passed us on the road, but I didn't want to see an art exhibit.

"The tide's low right now, dear. There'll be nothing but smelly old seaweed. Tomorrow morning we'll go, I promise."

At least my mother was in a better mood. Because she usually purchased an artwork when she visited the gallery, my father had asked her to limit her visits to once per week. We had been already that week, but this was an exception, she told me, since I had ruined her day.

The gallery was tucked around a corner at the south end of Commercial Street, on a little slope that fed into a marshy area flourishing with hermit crabs. I loved going down the slope and taking off my shoes so I could walk among the tiny creatures who darted in and out of their holes in the muck. Sometimes I brought a magnifying glass with me so I could study them as they scuttled sideways from one hole to the next, freezing as soon as my shadow loomed over them. I did my best not to step on the hermit crabs or their homes, and I always felt bereaved when I spotted a crab whose miniscule body had been cracked to death by a careless wanderer. Since I didn't have my magnifying glass with me that day, and since my mother seemed especially mercurial, I didn't resist when she steered me into the gallery upon our arrival.

The gallery was empty except for the old woman who always wore a starchy eggshell-blue pantsuit. It was a small, square space, with a high ceiling and one wall of windows overlooking the marsh. The other walls were populated with photographs of eerie, impersonal subjects like abandoned industrial buildings and burnt-out store signs, and there was a display table at the centre of the gallery with postcard versions of the photographs and picture frame samples. Usually, local artists supplied their works to the gallery, and their works remained on exhibit for a month unless they sold out sooner. My mother liked to visit an exhibit more than once before she selected something to purchase, and since she hadn't brought her chequebook with her that day, the woman in the starchy pantsuit stayed back while my mother made her tour of the space.

"Remember that time we brought you to your father's factory?" she asked, stopping before a floor to ceiling photograph of a boarded-up factory. The exterior of the factory was out of focus, but there was a hole in the board through which you could see, in sharp relief, a toilet with the seat missing, a light bulb dangling above the toilet, and an overturned child's sneaker with a piece of soiled toilet paper stuck to its sole. I thought the photograph was offensive, an invasion of someone's privacy, so I pulled away and said I wanted to see the hermit crabs. My mother turned toward the starchy pantsuit and shrugged with a laugh of nonchalance and inside jokes among adults.

"She's been in knots all day. Yes, Margot, why don't you go outside and air yourself? Please tell me, Mrs. Blaustein, who took this photograph? I don't see a name."

Outside, tourist season was hatching. The first arrivals were long-toothed attorneys and nasally psychiatrists who preferred to vacation in June, when the squealing, insufferable children of other tourists were still in school. They strolled in and out of local shops with no real interest in learning about the struggling artisans who owned and ran the shops. My parents had chosen to have me home-schooled, since the bus didn't stop near our house, my father was away so often, and my mother didn't know how to drive. We local kids never bothered the attorneys and psychiatrists. For us, the town of Wellfleet was boring. We lived there year-round, and the parents of all the local kids knew better than to let their progeny run amok, repelling the migratory affluence so vital to the town's survival in the off-season.

The presence of the first tourists made me yearn for the beach. I needed something big and soothing at that moment. My little hermit friends in the marsh weren't good enough. June water was too chilly for the tastes of the first vacationers, who, if they went to the beach at all, sat far from the tide, under large floral-patterned umbrellas, and read newspapers or played backgammon. This meant the beach was still the playground of the local children, though I had no friends, so when I went, either alone or with my family, I amused myself alone until the tops of my shoulders turned red.

I peered through the gallery window before I headed up the slope to Commercial Street. My mother appeared deep in conversation with a lady wearing a sundress that shimmered like the inside of an oyster shell. If I ran all the way to the beach (far beyond the north end of Commercial Street, but attainable in my desperate imagination), surely I would have time to get my feet wet before my mother finished up at the gallery. And maybe by then she would be in a *laissez-faire* mood, have forgotten all about the cognac, and agree that we should spend the rest of the day by the water—after all, she was dressed for it. But as I geared myself to dash to my coveted destination, my mother exited the store and called me over. She smiled and held up a brown paper bag inside which, she said, were postcard versions of photographs she thought my father might enjoy.

"When we get home, we'll look at them together and you can help me choose one for Morgan's birthday." Then, when I stared with an expression she mistook as petulance instead of colossal disappointment, she pinched my cheek and said, "Oh, fine, I'll show them to you now if you're going to be a big baby about it. But we'll still have to come back, because I don't have my chequebook."

We sat on the green wood bench outside the gallery. My mother showed me each postcard and narrated its critical features, but all I saw was a bunch of *things*, and I couldn't understand why they merited special attention. All of the photographs were in black and white except for the last one, which I found peculiar because it looked like something from a time way before ours. It was a musket. I had never seen a musket before.

"Before rifles, there were muskets," my mother said. "They

were used in war during the sixteenth through eighteenth centuries. See how long and narrow the barrel was? Imagine trying to hold it steady while you aimed at enemies. The French called it a *mousquet*, and the Italians called it a *moschetta*—like a fly, because it was so small and fast. Do you think your father would like one?"

"They still make them?" For the first time, I was interested in something that had snagged my mother's fancy.

"No, dear, the photograph. This is a sample, remember?"

"How do you know all that stuff about it?"

"Mrs. Blaustein told me. Plus there's a description. See?" My mother showed me the back of the postcard. Though I was too fidgety to read the whole thing, I believed everything she had just told me was recited, for I had never known her to speak with such authority and precision.

On our way home we stopped at the market, where there was an aisle of inexpensive last-minute beach supplies. My mother grabbed a pair of pink plastic sandals.

"Mom, we don't have any money!"

"Hush." She strutted up to the register and smiled widely at the bony-faced boy behind it.

"Excuse me, young man, but the most unfortunate thing happened to me just seconds ago. I took off my sandals before going into the art gallery—I didn't want to trek dirt all over the place, you see—and when I came back out, they were gone. Now I'm afraid I spent all my pocket change on these lovely postcards for my husband, who's such a big fan of the photographer, you see, so I was wondering if I might take these cheap little sandals on loan until my husband gets back from work later today. I promise I'll come back with the dollar, plus a little something extra for your kindness."

The boy blinked and blushed under my mother's flirting gaze, but when he lifted his head and looked toward the back of the market, where Joe Lema was rushing to prepare meats for the deli counter, my mother released an ill-tempered peal of laughter and tore the price tag off the sandals.

"Now, really, young man, you needn't worry about little ole me. My husband's *very* known around here—he's Morgan Wright. Of Wright and Ellis billiards."

By the time the boy had gotten over himself and opened his mouth to respond, my mother and I were out the door and walking brusquely for home. She held my hand firmly and pulled me along with her, and we walked like we were in a race until we reached the steep hill up to our house. At the front door, my mother stepped out of the sandals and threw them over her shoulder. They landed in the bushes under our kitchen window.

"Good riddance to those. They're like wearing barbed wire. No one would pay a dollar to wear barbed wire on their feet."

She continued ranting about barbed wire, highway robbery prices for useless items, the snobs and gossips at the beach, and went inside. In her haste to remove the sandals, she had dropped the bag of postcards. I picked it up and hid it under my T-shirt until I could get to my bedroom. The only postcard I cared about was the one with the musket, so I would find it and then leave the rest on the kitchen table for my mom to look at while I cleaned the cognac from the floor.

Immediately after she went inside, my mother flopped onto the six-foot long upholstered vanilla sofa in the living room and sank into a fretful sleep. The day slipped by. She didn't wake to prepare supper, and I wasn't especially hungry. It was best to let her be. Every so often I heard her moan or utter something in French, but mostly I was fixated on the postcard with the musket. What sort of person carried a musket? How did the musket work? What did a person look like after being shot by a musket? I held the postcard up close to my face and tried to make out the details of the gun; I stood in front of the mirror on my dresser and tried to imagine myself holding one, my posture pillar-perfect like I had seen soldiers of war do in the movies. When I grew bored with imagining, I tiptoed into the hallway and grabbed the broom from the cleaning closet, unscrewed the straw bristles from the handle, leaned the handle upright against my right shoulder and marched soundlessly up and down the hallway until I grew bored with that.

The telephone rang and startled me back into my bedroom. After four rings I realized my mother was not going to answer, so I went to the kitchen and picked up the receiver. There was a brownish-orange blob like crystalized candy on the linoleum floor where the Delamain had crashed, and the mound of glass I had begun to ready for the dustpan was still waiting for me.

"Hello, Wright residence. May I ask whom is calling?"

"*Who* is calling, Margot. It's 'may I ask *who* is calling.' "

"Sorry."

"How was your day?"

"Okay."

"Well, glad to hear it. Is Marguerite around?"

"She's sleeping."

"No, I'm not. Hang up, Margot." My mother had picked up the phone in her and my father's bedroom. She sounded distressed, like she was crying or going to cry. I started to say goodbye to my father, but now that my mother was on the line there was no room for me.

I was about to wet a rag and clean up the cognac when I remembered my father's collection of encyclopedias in his smoking den. I wasn't allowed to touch them when he was away, but if I made haste I would have enough time to grab the "M" volume and learn more about muskets. My mother never went into the den (she claimed to have been scarred by her experience in the Lincoln Continental, yet she would indulge in menthol cigarettes on special occasions), so she wouldn't notice the missing volume for a night. Her voice sounded pitched and intense as she spoke to my father, and I lingered in the hallway for a minute before creeping down the short flight of stairs to the living room, and then down another short flight of stairs to the games room, a finished basement complete with a billiard table and full-service bar my parents used to entertain business associates and established people who vacationed in Wellfleet. The smoking den was behind the bar, a secret room with swinging doors like the sort in Old West films.

No one had been inside for a while. The shades were drawn on the basement-level slat windows, and the air was laden and opalescent with cigarette and cigar smoke of parties past. Flora, the crisp, scowling Columbian maid who came to clean the house every Wednesday, wasn't permitted in the games room or the den. My mother was worried Flora would nip at the alcohol, having heard Columbians weren't to be trusted in this way, so cleanliness in the basement was subject to my mother's whims. The most I had ever seen her do was slide open the slat windows and light a stick of bergamot incense in the belly of the pearl Buddha that sat on a rounded corner of the bar.

My father sometimes spent hours alone in the den to unwind from the stresses of his travels. One time, when I was maybe five or six, I peeked inside. He looked regal in his Japanese silk kimono, his sealskin slippered feet resting intelligently on the ottoman. The kimono was held closed at the waist by a black sash, but it lay open at the bottom, revealing slender olive-skinned calves frosted with fine brown hairs.

"What is it, Margot?" my father had asked, looking up from volume "H" of the encyclopedia. He brought a tumbler of translucent molasses-like liquid to his mouth, the ice cubes clicking against the glass in a familiar, dizzying way.

"What are you reading?"

The *Encyclopædia Britannica* set, bound in deep red leather, its pages gilded with gold, was displayed in a tall crystal case beside where he sat.

"I'm trying to figure out if it was a heron your mother and I saw on the water yesterday. A heron's a bird."

"Oh." I stepped into the den but hugged up against the swinging doors. "Is that a book about birds?"

"It's a book about everything that begins with the letter "h,"
darling. Come, come. Let's learn about herons together."

I hurried to my father and he removed his feet from the ottoman. I wanted to sit on his lap, like girls in the movies sat on
their fathers' laps, but that invitation was never extended to
me in all the years I knew him. Sometimes my mother would
ensnare me in ferocious, spontaneous hugs and haul me onto
her lap, but she, too, never patted her thighs tenderly and
invited me to share a moment with her.

I felt mischievous and important being in the den by myself.
Before I went to the sacred books, I strutted around the room
and pretended to be my parents' party guests. "Why yes, this
is a lovely place! Mr. Wright must *surely* have lots and lots of
money to have a place like this." "One time, when I was here
in the summer, Marguerite ordered us all into the backyard,
where she gave us a fashion show. Can you believe it? Morgan always brings home all sorts of expensive clothes for her
because she's so beautiful. I'm so jealous!" "Well, one time
when *I* was here—"

"Margot Anaïs Soucy! *Qu'est-ce-que tu fais là?*" My mother slammed open the saloon doors and stared at me with a
wild, unacquainted expression, like even though she knew my
name, she didn't know who I was. In my haste to escape the
forbidden den, my bobby socks caught on the shag carpet as
I ran past my mother, and when I grabbed onto the bar top to
keep from falling, I knocked the pearl Buddha off. His round
little belly exploded with ashes and one of his chubby arms
popped away and rolled across the floor like a child rolling
down a grassy knoll. My mother lunged at me and grabbed a
fistful of my T-shirt.

"I never wanted to have you, you little brat. *Tu es imbécile,
Margot. Nulle. Imbécile. Éffrayante.* I didn't ask to be stuck
in this life, keeping you busy, waiting for my husband to come
home from his business affairs—he's a bloody deserter like
his nephews. It's in the Wright blood so it's in yours, too. You

watch, you'll do the same thing. To me, to the man you choose to marry, to your own children." As she seethed, she shook me and slapped my cheeks until they burned. When she let go, I fell onto my bottom and immediately crawled for cover behind the bar. But this wasn't necessary; my mother turned her anger onto herself. With horror, I watched as she bit her forearm and hit herself in the head with her other hand. She stomped her bare feet on the Buddha until he cut through her skin and became streaked with her blood. I watched, huddled up against the bar, as my mother bit down on a new part of her forearm and spun around and around, white-eyed like an animal swarmed by hornets.

"*Déserteur, déserteur*," she screamed over and over.

If we had lived closer to our neighbours, surely someone would have heard the commotion and stopped over to inquire. But our house was on an acre of land all by itself, and between us and our nearest neighbour stood a strip of forest just thick enough to insulate our sounds. Underneath the terror I felt at seeing my mother become so unhinged, I felt an insufferable, informed sadness: there was something wrong with her. Not in the sense there had been something "off" since morning, from the opening of *Bye Bye Birdie* to our impromptu walk to the gallery to her escape into a sleep that seemed to soothe her no more than her spastic movement through the day. No, even as a child of eight, I understood there lived in her a catastrophic flaw, something as much a part of her as her lungs and pancreas, which had, until then, been suppressed by perhaps accidental forces. Now that it had emerged, like a swimmer finally succeeding in breaking the surface after being held under water by a bully, it was swiping and clawing at everything in its way from fully becoming itself.

Eventually my mother calmed down and sat on the ottoman, dropped her face into her hands, and wept until her devastation trumped mine and I felt obligated to go to her.

"*Oh, chérie*," she said weakly, wiping tears from my cheeks, "it's time for you to meet *grandmère* and *grandpère* Soucy. You will learn to speak proper French, eat *la tire* when it's maple syrup season. Doesn't that sound good?"

It sounded foreign and permanent, but before I could protest, my mother drew me against her knee and began swirling my hair round her forefinger, jerkily at first, but then her movements slowed and her touch began to feel nice. Too exhausted to pull away, or even to flinch, through my plenum of nausea, confusion, and insecurity, I accepted, albeit feebly, those last affections from her.

The next morning, Flora woke me and told me to pack only the essentials in the paisley pattern valise my mother had left for me in the kitchen. I decided the valise was too unsightly and chose instead a brown leather duffle bag that belonged to my father and which he had told me in secret I could keep. Inside, I fit enough underwear and socks to last me a week, the postcard of the musket, and then, when Flora was busy scrubbing cognac off the linoleum while she waited for me, I snuck into the den and grabbed volume "M" of the *Encyclopædia Britannica*, which I concealed by wrapping in an old blanket I told Flora I would need if I wanted to nap on the bus.

5. THE GIRLFRIEND EXPERIENCE

*M*A CHÈRE FILLE:
I took a stroll through the arboretum the other day and so many things reminded me of you. But I'm sure you can guess which reminded me of you most: the hermit crabs! I don't know if I'm imagining things or if this supposed global warming is actually affecting our planet, but I could swear the crabs were bigger than I remember them being behind the gallery. And they ran into little hills, like anthills, rather than into the ground like they used to. I did my best not to step on any of your favourite creatures from God. I said hello to them for you.

Alors, quoi d'autre à te dire? *Morgan isn't doing well, I'm afraid. I wanted to wait until the next letter to tell you, because I so dislike giving or receiving upsetting news, but it seems your father's decadence has caught up to him. Heart troubles, the doctor says. All those steaks and rich chocolate desserts aren't good for a man even as limber and elegant as Morgan Wright. I'm doing fine, though I have the opposite problem—I've let my waist balloon a little, but my doctor says it's not an issue since I take daily walks and do oodles of garden work. I enjoy a little nip at lemon meringue or pumpkin pie every so often, but I'm always satisfied after a few bites. Not like your father. Remember how he could devour an entire pie all by himself? Remember that pie he brought home on your fourth birthday? Boston Cream. You'd never seen anything like it. Oh how your eyes got so big and black when your father pretended he was going to keep the rest of the pie for himself after he cut you a sliver.*

I know I've asked you a few times already, but I want to make sure you're actually reading my request and not skimming over it because you're too busy with this or that: Please come see me. Some people here are beginning to think I'm loopy, because I talk about you all the time, but you never make an appearance. I pretended it was you phoning me the other day when really it was Morgan, to tell me about his heart and why he wouldn't be able to visit for a while. I think some of the residents in here don't even believe Morgan's my husband—how could such a devastatingly handsome man be with someone like her, they must be saying to themselves. Would you come see me, chérie? I know it's far and you're busy with your life and family, but perhaps you and your husband could make a little trip? A little weekend for two? Also, when you come, I would ask that you bring me a souvenir, maybe a tarte au sucre and that can of maple syrup with the little children playing in the snow? I promise I won't eat it all at once! Actually, I would share it with Mabel, the lady in the room next to mine. She doesn't seem to have any family at all, the poor thing. It's just heartbreaking.

The other day I watched this movie about a girl who was a real-life escort—what a fancy name they've come up with for whores. I don't know why they would show such a movie here, but what else is there to do, sometimes? En tout cas, the girl was from New York, I believe, and the movie was more of a documentary, following her around as she did things for men—éffrayant! I had to turn the television off after the first act (there was no one else watching the movie), because I simply couldn't bear it anymore. Really, what a distasteful line of work, and shame on whoever made that movie. I do wish they'd let us choose what we watch here. Sometimes we get to vote, but I never bother since my choices are almost always over everyone else's heads. Except for Mabel, she enjoys musicals, too, but the only one she ever wants to watch is the remake of Chicago. *She says Catherine Zeta-Jones is a distant cousin. My left foot she's a distant cousin. Even if she were and showed up here tomorrow, I wouldn't give her the time of day. I can't stand these ridiculous modern-era actresses—that's the whole problem, they're actresses, not singers.*

Well, it's dinnertime now, so I should dust my face with some rouge and such. I'm going to sing for everyone afterward! Most of the residents fall asleep during talent hour, but Mabel, the dear, always wakes up in time to clap. I wonder if your father will remember that next week's our anniversary. I bet you he'll be too caught up in his heart problems, but I'll pick a nice bouquet of field flowers for him anyway. I always think about the Delamain on our anniversary. I was so upset with you that day.

Gros bisous,
Maman

I WOKE UP ALONE the next morning, but I knew Estelle hadn't left for work, because the black and white georgette tunic dress she reserved for high-stakes workdays was draped over the Eloise wingback chair in our room. I felt a little hurt that she hadn't brought me breakfast in bed as I had planned to do for her, but then I reasoned she had a big day ahead at L'Espace Vif and was no doubt flitting about our loft, practising her offer to Pierrot. She was probably so nervous she hadn't consumed anything but espresso, so I likely still had time to prepare a sustaining, if not gourmet, meal for her. If by chance she had broken her routine and left wearing a different outfit, then I would make a lunch for her and deliver it, like a secret admirer, to the gallery doorstep.

The iPad docked on the windowsill above the kitchen sink was tuned to CBC Radio One's *The Current*. Anna Maria Tremonti was commenting passionately about the science of carbohydrate addiction, and her buoyant rant compelled me to prepare a breakfast that would surely leave me comatose on my mohair settee twenty minutes later (I would give Estelle only a half-portion, and garnish the rest of her plate with an arrangement of fresh fruit). But just as I ignited the gas stove to heat my yet-to-be-tried cast iron Belgian waffle-maker, a gift from Bertrand when I resigned from Le Canon Noir, my wife came into the kitchen, guns blazing.

"We need to talk," she said, placing a Xerox box on top of the bar-style counter kitty-corner to the stove (this was one of many boxes I should have unpacked and sorted through already, and as reprimand, Estelle had sentenced them all to the basement storage locker of our building until I fulfilled my obligation). She dragged a barstool against the dark bamboo floor and sat down, then stood and pushed the stool back under the counter. She removed the lid from the Xerox box and peered inside with an expression of utter revulsion, and then poured herself a glass of orange juice from the pitcher she must have squeezed earlier.

"And a good morning to you, too, darling," I said, as I whisked a container of egg whites into the waffle mix.

"*Now*, Margot. We need to talk *now*."

I poured the mix into the waffle-maker and clamped the lid shut. Waffle preparation, even with a top-quality appliance, is an involved process if the waffles are to be the perfect degree of crisp on the outside and tender but cooked fully through. I couldn't manage a conversation at the same time. Besides, I was hungry, and I wanted to enjoy finally using my gift.

Estelle picked up the box and dropped it loudly on the countertop. "*Coucou! Es-tu là?*"

I stared at the second hand on the egg timer. Whatever she had found in this particular box could wait. It was probably something inconsequential like a credit card statement listing a purchase I hadn't consulted her about, something a little frivolous like a DVD set of *Hoarders*. Her huffiness was the symptom of a Lorazepam hangover (she was such a delicate flower), not my perfectly harmless off-the-book expenditures. And hadn't I forgiven her for Roland's scale?

"You can't ignore me like this." Estelle sent a flock of envelopes wreathing through the air. A few envelopes landed near me, and it took only a peripheral glance for me to recognize the dramatic cursive addressed to "Margot A. Soucy care of Le Canon Noir" and understand that my wife was not huffy but irate.

"*Dieu*, Margot! You couldn't be bothered to rent a safe? Or leave them at work? Did you want me to find them?" She reached into the box and snatched up more envelopes. "And it appears you never answered back. Of course you didn't. I mean, I know the expression 'everyone's got something to hide,' but that's for little things like granny underwear and emergency tweezers. *This?* This is not a little thing."

Estelle marched over to me and turned off the burner. Before I could fathom what she would do next, she shoved her hands into oven mitts, picked up the waffle-maker and turned it upside down over the sink. As I watched my morning aspiration glob down the drain, and as I avoided eye contact with my wife, who was entirely warranted in her behaviour at that moment, I felt the same guttural stupefaction and failure a dog must feel on a moonless night after his owner has hanged himself in the woods. Estelle pointed to the countertop and I went, head bowed.

There was more than a decade's worth of envelopes in the box—the one box I should have tended to immediately after our move, whose contents I should have transferred to a bank safe like Estelle suggested. Shame on me for my negligence. I had been hoarding the letters since the day my father institutionalized my mother at the start of the new millennium. I had stopped replying to the letters a few years after, and I had stopped opening them altogether a few years after that, save one from my father in which he pleaded with me to visit my mother during his extended business trip, which wasn't a business trip at all but a flight from public view, because the government had learned of his having smuggled three nephews into Canada during the Vietnam War. (Apparently, after Gerald Ford's death, one of those nephews had assumed he could begin his life anew and tried to return to the U.S. as a lawful citizen.) But Morgan Houdini Wright of Wright & Ellis Billiards was a wealthy, connected man and his flight from public view short, so I never visited Marguerite Soucy in her white-collar seaside asylum. I wouldn't have visited her even if my father had been tried and sentenced to life in prison.

"You told me she died, Margot. *You told me she died.* Of some horrible illness, what was it?"

"Cholera. She contracted it when they vacationed in Senegal."

"No, you said malaria. Obviously they never went to Senegal."

"Why are you asking, then? And actually, they did—"

"Then you said your father died shortly after from a broken heart. *A broken heart?* How could you make that up? How could I *believe* it? I'm so shocked at my stupidity right now I can't even pretend to know how I feel about yours."

Estelle cried, smacked her open palms against the countertop, pulled her bangs behind her ears so violently that her hair got caught in her rings and ripped from her scalp. It wasn't until she knocked over the pitcher of orange juice and shrieked that I realized she was dressed for work, hoop earrings, nametag, and all. How long had she been awake? What had prompted her to go down to the storage locker?

"I was looking for something, since you've done such a shitty job unpacking."

"What were you looking for?"

"None of your business."

"But maybe if you tell me what you were look—"

"Oh, fuck off! I hate you right now. You made me feel like

the villain for seeing a therapist. So what does *this* make you?"

Estelle was right about everything. I had been caught in a lie, and she had reason to be incensed (though I knew she was, as she had said, at least equally upset with herself). She had every reason to question other things I had told her about my family history—though all of it was true. Once she calmed down I would make her see there had been worse crimes committed than a woman choosing to emancipate herself from her family of mad hatters, and that the choice had been mine alone to make. Estelle had never met my parents, or *grandmère* and *grandpère* Soucy; her only connection to my family was through the anecdotes I had entrusted her with, the few photographs I had shown her. So when she accused me of having lied to her about unrelated things, too, like my previous day's outing to the amusement park, a very recent history we shared in equal parts, it was my turn to become enraged.

"You're being hysterical." My fingers flexed and twitched. If only I could busy them with my waffle-maker. "Of course I have photographs of Le Galopant."

"You said some rube took them. Maybe while this *rube* was doing your work you were piaffing around the goddamn city bragging about your stupid hats. How am I supposed to know?"

The upset orange juice pooled toward the Xerox box. Estelle and I both panted and swallowed hard as we watched the edges of the cardboard soak up the juice and darken. Finally, and not without a hitch in her voice, Estelle said, "Meet me at Dr. Weinstock's office at three this afternoon."

"Not that again."

"Nineteen Redpath Street, top floor, door on the left. Meet me there, Margot, or you can find a new place to live." She pivoted away and took her briefcase and keys from the Ikea table and left the loft without closing the door. The executive snap of her heels on concrete bounded off the corridor's high ceiling, and her cellphone voicemail to Dr. Weinstock ricocheted back into the loft as she descended the stairwell. "Hello, this is Estelle. I'm calling to let you know Margot will be joining us this afternoon after all."

OLIVIER, AS HE INSISTED I call him the moment he swung open the door, was a hilariously short man. At first I wondered if the floor of his suite was severely slanted, which is frequently the case with Montréal's older two- and three-storey century buildings. But after I performed the polite gesture of wiping my shoes on the welcome mat ("Please, no need to remove them. That's what hardwood floors are for") and stepped inside to formally greet the therapist, it became clear his diminutiveness was not an optical illusion. There were, however, several *trompe l'oeil* prints along the walls of the two-person capacity hallway, including one I knew well, William Michael Harnett's 1890, "The Faithful Colt." I had learned of the painting about five years into my firearms career, late by the standards of people who assumed I knew everything about every aspect of guns in world history. Initially, I had felt no connection to the representation of the yeoman's loyal ivory-handed sidekick, as I considered myself a dealer exclusively of European firearms. A Canon Noir patron who had showed me a postcard of the painting returned the next day with a full-size print and requested that I locate and purchase for him one of the actual Colts. Appended to the patron's request was a sizeable contribution—an investment, really—toward Le Canon Noir's expansion, which had been Bertrand's dream for as long as I had known him. It was during that journey across the U.S., which led me to a widower in Chadron, Nebraska, who was interested in selling her late-husband's collection of Colts (it was the only thing of worth he had left her), that I learned about American-made Civil War firearms, all gorgeously, expertly cast from the moulds of the French and British firearms I had previously thought superior. So while any gun enthusiast could make himself look fancy and informed by posting "art" on his walls, Olivier Weinstock, whom I couldn't envision in a million years twirling a revolver in his cherubic hand, earned my willingness to respect him for being in possession of such a marking piece of firearms history. Perhaps our meeting would go better than I had forecasted.

Through the open doorway behind Olivier, Estelle sat reading a magazine, completely unresponsive to my arrival. There were more prints on the walls of the waiting room, and classical music played at low volume from a digital stereo rather too large for the cubbyhole space. I cleared my throat for Estelle's attention, and then Olivier cupped a hand under my elbow and ushered me to the end of the hallway and into a surprisingly capacious room with a selection of sofas against three walls, and tall sash windows on the fourth, looking north to Mount Royal. I chose the middle sofa, for it appeared the most used thus surely the most comfortable, but Olivier invited me to instead take a seat across from him at his Marxist-red tanker desk. The desk was wide and deep. Everything on its surface, except for a box of tissues and a glass of sparkling water, which were on my side, was arrayed within reach of the therapist's short little arms.

"Estelle had her session already," he said, speaking easily, as though we were picking up on a conversation that had been interrupted by a phone call. "Now she's doing some meditative exercises while you have yours."

"Since when is reading *Chatelaine* meditative?"

Olivier squeezed his chin thoughtfully. I wondered if he believed this grossly cliché action lent him authority. "One can meditate in a variety of ways. Do you meditate?" he asked.

A pause, which turned into a drawn-out silence, which turned into a stare-down of me against Dr. Weinstock, my wife's breakfast ultimatum. "I thought we were going to have a couples session. You know, together?"

"We'll reach that point eventually, but first you and I must get to know each other. Build trust."

Olivier went on to explain how these things worked, therapist-client relationships, and was swift to correct me when I referred to myself as a patient. No, no, he said, offering me a trifold pamphlet I might wish to read while I soaked in the tub later that night, I would be a patient if he were treating me in his capacities as a medical doctor, but he wasn't treating me at all, nor was he treating Estelle. He was helping us understand ourselves.

"What in hell does that mean? Please, enlighten me: How have you been 'helping' my wife 'understand' herself for five months? Does she get her money back at six months if she doesn't feel helped?"

At this, Olivier leaned back in his chair and adopted an imperious air that filled me with distrust. "I'm sure you can appreciate the principles of doctor-patient confidentiality," he said.

"Absolutely. And if I were your patient, I would comply. But you just told me I'm not a patient. In fact, we're nothing to each other until there's a monetary exchange for services rendered."

Through the windows behind Olivier, I watched deeply tanned businessmen at the helms of convertible Audis and BMWs. The men were accompanied by sleek young women who, I felt certain, were neither their daughters nor their nieces. Rollerbladers, joggers, power-walkers, and dog-walkers pushed northward through the first of August heat, and I wondered if everyone was heading to the top of Mount Royal for a rewarding afternoon view of the pastel cityscape. Outdoors, the humidity was oppressive, and even people moving at leisurely paces were cast in sweat. Inside Nineteen Redpath Street, the acclimatized, de-humidified air, while a nice reprieve, lacked heft and character. Everything about Olivier's office, now that I began to assess it, lacked heft and character. The Harnett print, for example, could have come from a copy shop at the cost of five dollars. Maybe the classical music playing in the waiting room was really Muzak. And Estelle was reading *Chatelaine*.

If this man were a serious practitioner, whether five feet or six feet tall, he would surely supply his waiting room library with serious matter. Could it be my wife had been fooled into spending her money on one of those new-age quacks, the type who, at mid-life, experienced a crisis that drove him to abandon mainstream culture and enroll in some ludicrous short-residency program to become a specialist of the soul? When once I had proposed a similar theory to Estelle, only with regard to the one-year graphic design programs that were popping up like dandelions all over Montréal, conning high tuition from the wallets of ordinary, talentless people with the promise of turning them into successful artists, her reply nonplussed me. "Don't be such an elitist, Margot. There's so much competition that talent gets overlooked all the time. Are you saying only certain kinds of people deserve to be noticed?"

Had Estelle not knocked on the office door, I was about to demand proof of Olivier's credentials, which, when I turned and looked behind me, I saw displayed in their full glory beside the door: Bachelor of Science in Psychology, McGill University. Doctorate in Clinical Psychology (Perception), University of Wisconsin-Madison. Certificate of this, award for that, a framed *National Geographic* article about Malaysian religious divorce rituals.

"Forgive me for intruding, but I, well, I heard you yelling, Margot. Is everything okay? This was probably a bad idea. I've been sitting in the waiting room feeling like a complete jerk. I shouldn't be out there answering a questionnaire about what sort of coffee is right for my personality. I need therapy for my problems, and I'm sorry I dragged you in like this. I haven't even talked to Olivier about the letters. I mean I came here to talk to him about the letters, but I ended up ranting about Jean-Jacques. He said something to piss off Pierrot and now we've lost him." As she spoke, Estelle inched farther into the office until she was behind my chair and resting her hands proprietorially on my shoulders.

"But, darling," I said, flashing my pithiest don't-you-dare-intervene look at Olivier, "this morning—and last night—you said this is very important to you. To us. We should at least have one session together, don't you think? With Olivier? Right now?"

"As I mentioned, I don't do—"

"Phooey, Dr. Weinstock. What harm could come of it?"

"This isn't a massage parlour, Mrs. Soucy."

"Soucy-Coté. And I should certainly hope not. Just meet with us together for thirty minutes, Dr. Weinstock, and if those thirty minutes don't help, if they somehow make things worse, I promise to enlist in regular sessions with you until you feel I'm ready to begin couples sessions with my wife. Is it a deal?" I tipped my head back to peer up at my wife, who seemed pleased, and as eager as I to get to the top of the mountain now that she had pondered the view.

Olivier sniffed indignantly, but with Estelle rooted by my side, he finally said, "Alright. But it's not a 'deal,' it's a process. Now in the time we have left for today, I'd like to assign you both some homework."

BEFORE OUR WALK up the mountain, we stopped at the coffee shop two buildings north of Olivier's and treated ourselves to almond biscotti and iced lattés. We sat at the wrought iron table for two on the sidewalk in front and dipped our biscotti in our coffees, sighed appreciatively every time someone opened the shop door and let escape a burst of chilled air that tightened our skin with goose bumps.

"So what do you think?" Estelle asked, stirring her drink with her biscotti.

I reached over and wiped a drib of whipped cream from her top lip. "He's admirably decorated. Did you see his bookcase? The little man authored a *dictionary*."

"Our homework, GoGo. What do you think of the assignment?"

I thought it was preposterous. New-agey, and a screaming symptom of what was wrong with "modern cosmopolitan couples," as Olivier had labelled us. As he had walked us through our homework, I continued my assessment of him and was not surprised in the least when I found no showcase of family photographs and saw no wedding band on his finger. A married person would never advise a married couple in the way Olivier had advised us. Estelle had been the one to ask all the questions, ruminate aloud the possibilities and eventualities, sketch a blueprint with defined levels and a mutually agreed upon safe room in the event either of us felt lost. She had used Olivier's fountain pen and yellow legal pad to generate a "Pros and Cons" list, working promptly and skillfully like an old-time courtroom stenographer.

"I think it's a step in the right direction, and I think we should start right now. Here, on this lovely terrace on this lovely afternoon."

"You don't have to be sarcastic about it, Margot."

I wiped a droplet of latté from Estelle's chin as she bit into her biscotti. "I'm serious. Let's give it a run. Maybe it's what we need."

"We'll have to establish rules, divide things up. We'll need to make time for that."

"Actually, we could sort it all out immediately: What's yours is now yours only, what's mine is now mine only. I pay the mortgage, you pay the bills, we do our own groceries. Fridays are date nights, Saturdays are sleepover nights, and perhaps one weeknight we could host a gathering with friends—go out with them, I mean."

Estelle dissolved the rest of her biscotti in her mouth like a communion wafer. She peered around us with increasingly perky interest, and I watched some mysterious invisible weight ascend from her as if at the hand of her private deity. She dispensed her next words with reservation, in case I really was being glib with her. "It's Thursday."

"And a momentous one it has been!"

"Where will you stay?"

Rolling with the punches as I had been forced to do since my failed breakfast waffles, I guzzled the last of my latté, which was but sunrays away from curdling, and said, "I believe that's for this old faithful colt to worry about. Now," I rose and doffed my derby hat, "shall we stroll to the top of the mountain?"

"Stroll," of course, was the word we used in lieu of hike, or trek, as neither was an enjoyable activity in thirty-degrees Celsius heat. Once we reached the top of the mountain, breathless and excited like schoolchildren going to the playground for the first time after a confining winter, Estelle clasped my hand tightly and we ran as fast as we could to the lookout ledge. Surprisingly few people were there on such a pleasant day: a man with a notebook and state-of-the-art digital binoculars; a young mother and her riotous toddler, who kept trying to clamber the low-set cement barrier of the ledge; bombastic seagulls on high alert for chips and unfinished hotdogs. At the ledge, squeezing my hand almost viciously, Estelle said, "It's like I came to the city and found the part that suited me then, and now there's the rest of it. Do you ever feel like that? Like, where would you be now if Bertrand had never given you his business card? Or what if we had never moved out of that apartment on top of the bar?" She was contemplative and happy. She was acknowledging my effort to make her happy, and in return giving me permission to share in the freedom Olivier Weinstock had granted us.

And so the first thing I took for myself was time. Time to appreciate the skyscrapers, the CIBC tower with its celebrity nighttime searchlight that swept across the city all year long. I looked far west to where the apartment complexes tapered down in height and eventually vanished into neighbourhoods the city had deprioritized from its fiscal responsibilities for decades. I looked far east to where the buildings rejected corporate uniformity and burst to life with festive pink, purple, and lime green exteriors. And I looked south, across the Seaway, where I spotted, tiny as a soda bottle cap, rippling and mirage-like in the humid sky, the amusement park's Ferris wheel.

6. THE FAITHFUL COLT

"SO HERE WE ARE."

"We are here."

"Can I kiss you goodnight?"

"Would your therapist approve?"

"He's our therapist now, GoGo."

"We'll see about that." I pressed my wife gently against the railing leading up to Le Cabinet Particulier and kissed her with first-date restraint. The hotel's affordable luxury and proximity to L'Espace Vif, in the event Estelle thought to drop by the next morning before work, had comforted me into my decision as we considered options on my Blackberry during a light dinner at Comme Chez Nous. I hadn't gone back to the loft to collect toiletries and such, but I could do without for one night.

"I'm sure they provide bathrobes and little soaps," I said, thumbing a tear from Estelle's cheek.

"We can always start tomorrow. Or Monday—a fresh start on a fresh week."

Estelle foraged through her purse, her lack of purpose and her desperation so heartbreaking I almost agreed to go home with her, until I remembered the letters, still splayed around the kitchen like putrid seaweed expelled from the ocean at low tide. I didn't want to go back to that, not after our intimate trip up the mountain, our dinner in a quiet corner of an establishment whose wait staff understood the inviolability of someone sharing a meal with a beautiful woman. Already,

I was feeling better, even inclined to think Dr. Weinstock had some good tricks up his short sleeves.

"I'll clean up my ... mess when I come over for date night tomorrow," I said, starting up the steps.

Estelle watched me until I was inside the hotel, waved, and smiled girlishly when I shooed her on her way. I assumed, as I watched her head southward, homeward, she would turn around to wave again, maybe pantomime how much she missed me already, but she didn't.

A night to myself in a hotel in my home city was a refreshing idea. The things I could do! Retire to the king bed as early as I wished. Roll around the eight-hundred thread count sheets like a devilish Labrador Retriever. Switch the television channels as often as I pleased—hell, I could fall asleep to *Hoarders*. Come morning, I would page the front desk and order eggs Benedict with a side of herbed chèvre, a bottomless mug of some artisanal tea I had never heard of, and a fresh copy of *The Globe and Mail*. The last newspapers I had seen in our place, after Estelle switched all of our subscriptions to digital, were the leftovers we had used to pack for the loft. If Estelle didn't come to greet me in the morning, perhaps I would wander over to Le Canon Noir, say hello to Bertrand and apologize for having not returned his call from the start of summer. I had meant to, but in coping with my new jobless life, and as I prepared for our move, it had seemed my energy was always depleted by the day's end. Also, Bertrand's voice message was an invitation for me to do contract work (his new associate had gotten unexpectedly pregnant and would have to leave in August), and while I wasn't opposed to helping out or to the income, I couldn't let Bertrand know I still hadn't launched into my next fabulous career.

The boy at the front desk wore period bellhop attire that complemented the hotel's Edwardian décor. He smiled starchily, a ferret bearing chemically-whitened teeth. I told him my name and presented my credit card.

"Young man," I said, as he waited for the system to print my check-in form.

"*Madame?*"

"Would you happen to have a waffle-maker?"

"*Pardon?*"

"For breakfast, do you serve waffles?"

"*Répétez?*"

I readied myself for a fumbling, colossal failure. One of my mother's greatest disservices to me had been to not teach me French during my peak language-acquisition years, and then to ship me off to *grandmère* and *grandpère* Soucy, who spoke only the English I eventually succeeded in teaching them, and who behaved like ghosts around me, looking and stepping through their illicit granddaughter. Estelle's French was native and eloquent, and for that reason she had acted as my on-demand interpreter for the last twenty-five years. Most of our friends were all bilingual, and most of my interactions at Le Canon Noir had been with Americans and Europeans who spoke the universal palaver of commerce. I knew enough to get by on my own (I had attended a French immersion high school when I lived in Saint-Télesphore), but I had never developed an accent or the musical quickness of the language. Unless I was engaging in basic conversation, I was forced to construct statements in my mind before speaking them. And in this instance, if I intended to fully commit to Weinstock's prescribed "girlfriend experience," then I couldn't excuse myself from the desk to phone Estelle for help.

I pulled at the collar of my button-down. "*Un waffle makeure?*"

The bellhop blinked.

"*Thomas Jefferson a apporté le va-felle fabricateur au America? Cornelius Swarthout l'a patenté le vaffle éron?*"

A quiver of comprehension across the boy's face, or perhaps a twitch of fatigue.

"Pancakes?" I tried.

"*Gaufres?*" he said.

For all I knew, he could have made up that word. Maybe he was poking fun at me, the strangely hatted Montréaler who was spending the night in a hotel but a few blocks from the address associated with her credit card. Stooping to the lowest level of my dignity, I brought the heels of my palms together and flapped my hands open and closed like a Pac-Man, and then improvised lifting a fork to my mouth. I even pretend-chewed my pretend waffle. The bellhop shrugged and presented the check-in form to me, scribing with his Mont Blanc pen a perfect "*x*" on the signature line.

Le Cabinet Particulier could accommodate a maximum of eighty guests between its four floors. My room was on the top level, facing the manually operated elevator (minus the lift girl) in the east wing, and delightfully cheerful with its green and gold Astoria wallpaper and thin, curvy-limbed furniture. The modern aspects of the room, like the telephone and television, were tastefully concealed in mahogany hutches and drawers. I actually exclaimed out loud when I entered the bathroom and saw the satin nickel shower arm mounted above the tub, and the bidet with working faucetry beside the console sink stand. (There was also a regular toilet.) Quite a steal for ninety dollars! Of course the price doubled on weekends, and my room was in the "economy" wing, but it didn't matter since I would be checking out at ten o'clock the following morning.

The first thing I did was browse the channels until I found a reality show to drum in the background while I turned down the bed sheets and undressed for my bath. *Preachers' Daughters*, a docusoap that exposed the troubles between teenage girls and their preacher fathers who didn't want their princesses to grow up. The show's content was of little interest to me; it was the *schadenfreude* I craved as company. Estelle didn't understand my affinity for such shows. She thought I should watch her favourites instead, *Master Chef, Property Virgins, The Amazing Race*: they provided participants with tangible opportunities for success, she argued, rather than chuck them into the gladiator ring of rubberneck consumerism.

As pleased as I was with the satin nickel shower arm, I elected to soak in a bubble bath. This would be part of my process of learning how to enjoy myself, as Olivier had said I should. Even though I hadn't told him anything especially revealing about myself, he knew plenty about me from his sessions with Estelle. To his credit, he corrected himself a couple of times while explaining our homework assignment, saying "you both" rather than "you" when emphasizing how Estelle and I had to be openly communicative with each other if we were to benefit from the experience. Estelle. How I missed her. The more I thought about her, the sillier I felt soaking in a bubble bath all by myself. Except in necessary instances, like my mangled feet of the day before, I took showers. The idea of luxuriating in my own filth couldn't be made appealing even with all the mango-scented bubbles in the universe. Nevertheless, I forced myself to sit in the tub until the water became clammy and the pads of my fingers pruned, and then I wrapped the complimentary white terrycloth robe around myself and returned to the bedroom expecting that a solid half-hour had passed. My spirits plummeted even further when I learned otherwise. What else could I possibly do? I wasn't tired enough to fall asleep, I couldn't rein in my focus enough to watch the nightly news, and I had no interest in breaking into the mini-bar. The room was immaculate, and there was nothing for me to rearrange the way I would want if I actually lived there. I felt besmirched when I discovered that the one seemingly moveable piece of furniture, a dollhouse-style coffee table, was in fact welded to the floor. Was Le Cabinet Particulier's management that worried about theft? Really, if I wanted to pilfer anything, which I did not, I would choose unused toiletries or maybe one of the deluxe bath towels. A guest would have to be especially crafty to smuggle a coffee table out of the building.

Finally, I broke into the mini-bar. In lieu of alcohol, I selected a can of pomegranate Pellegrino and a package of Milk Duds. I would knock myself into a pricey sugar coma. A few sips and nibbles into my plan, unable to silence the puerile part of me hollering "Rebel! Rebel!" against the new rules of my marriage, I phoned Estelle. There had to be another way, another therapist, something. I would become a better wife—a better person—but this was not a dictatorship. We were not to be commanded by some short man who sat behind an oversized tanker desk and supplied his waiting room with magazines that published questionnaires like "Which *Hunger Games* character are you?"

But when Estelle's voicemail picked up, I said, as nervously as someone who had stepped in dog poo on her way to a job interview, "Hi, my darling girl! I'm probably not supposed to call you, but I just want to make sure you got home okay. And I'm sorry about last night, and this morning. I'm ready to talk whenever you are. You should see my room. You'd love the linens. And the bellhop is charming and I just really miss you. Okay, this one last little thing? It's stupid, but how do you say 'waffle-maker' in French?" If I had really wanted to know, I could have used the hotel's free WiFi, but what I wanted was to hear Estelle's voice. I wanted to know she was thinking about me.

I finished my snack and browsed channels, waiting for the call of nature's soft nurse, but she took no pity on me. My sugar-coma plan had backfired and I was more restless than a disturbed anthill. I considered reading a book, there were two on the coffee table, but then came up with a much better idea: I would write a poem for Estelle. Like many people, I fostered the secret notion that I could be a good writer if I chose; unlike most people, my notion was rooted in reality. I was well-read, I had a superior vocabulary, I knew a lot about the old and modern worlds. And I knew exactly how I would begin the poem, because I had conceived the idea the year before, hoping to have it ready for Estelle on our anniversary. Regarding myself as quite clever—bet you never would have come up with *this*, Olivier Weinstock—I set to work on the hotel's monogrammed stationery. A swift, productive hour later, I had my poem:

"After"
by Margot Anaïs Soucy-Coté

My love smells like autumn when she cries,
of cinnamon, sage, and burnt almond.
Her face rounds with pleasure, my
hands knead the words
from a mouth cast open by surprise.

Love's tears are red silk against cedar.
Her joy I preserve with a touch
to the flush of her neck, lips, and breast
as it spreads in a rush, oh
soft amber!

My love tastes like autumn when she weeps,
her scarlet face on my breast.
Her hands are young finches
fallen from trees,
so fragile and still in their sleep.

Love's downy amber so mild, so chaste,
this unopened wound of the flesh.
Hands that once pleased now
part and reveal, her sin
was to leave me in haste.

I read the poem silently. I read the poem out loud. I read it as though to Estelle on our next anniversary, on bended knee, holding her imaginary, finch-like hand; however, no matter how earnestly I tried to deliver the words with the overtone of affection I believed they should carry, I couldn't help but feel I had composed something morose, a eulogy rather than an ode. While death and love could be argued as one and the same, I didn't want there to be any allusions, any mention at all of dead or dying things. What if they were augural? What if my unconscious self, as I had heard famous authors speak of, was foretelling a fate? Perhaps my connectedness to the world was deeper than I realized. Perhaps ... I tore up the poem and went to the bathroom to flush it down the toilet. This was how it had started with my mother—racing, irrational thoughts, which estranged my father from us more and more until one day he wasn't there at all. I wouldn't allow myself to reproduce that history with Estelle. A love poem wasn't going to save us. We were on the precipice of either the rest of our lives together or the rest of our lives apart, and we needed to make a definitive move in one direction or the other. The liminal space in which we were floating now was causing too much anguish for either of us to endure much longer. All it had taken was one night by myself at Le Cabinet Particulier to fully realize our situation. While Estelle and I had spent many nights, weeks, sometimes even one full month apart when I travelled to find firearms or she to attend conferences, this night was entirely different under the light that Dr. Weinstock had so slyly shone upon us in his office of optical illusions.

When finally I began to drift off, my Blackberry drummed against the night table. I rolled over with the thick slowness of grief, but it was only a text. It read: *Gaufrier.*

MY WAKE-UP CALL rang promptly at seven the next morning, and the hollow-voiced inquiry, *Would I like to order breakfast to my room?* was enough to make my stomach lurch. I might as well have consumed every ounce of alcohol in the mini-bar for the cottonmouth and terrible body-wide malaise I was feeling. I reached for my Blackberry and checked for missed calls, scrolled through my text history, scrutinized my email in case an important message had been sentenced to the spam folder. Normally at this hour, I would be planning for the day ahead, devising ways to avoid unpacking the loft, generating reasons Estelle wouldn't be able to contest. But today, if I were at the loft, I would be contending with more than a decade's worth of letters, reading many of them for the first time, and preparing for the inevitable conversation with my wife. The atmosphere would be fraught, maybe we wouldn't speak much because Estelle would want to preserve her energy for the work hours ahead, but at least I would be there instead of here, able to put on a fresh pair of clothes, curl up on my navy mohair settee, and burrow into familiar comforts.

I almost didn't answer the hotel phone when it rang again. I wasn't in the mood to fumble for words.

"*Madame Soucy-Coté? Vous avez un appel.*" And then, "I've only got a few. Meet me in the lobby."

As I didn't have time to consider why Estelle hadn't dialled my Blackberry, and why she was asking me to meet her in the lobby, imagine my astonishment, after I scrambled out of bed and into the previous day's clothes (which were wrinkled, as I had left them on the bathroom floor), when I arrived to the lobby and was greeted by a very done-up pair of women.

"Marianne, nice to see you," I said, exchanging air-kisses with her and stepping back quickly to escape the confluence of odours emanating from her—cigarette smoke, hard liquor, perspiration, strawberry perfume. And bacon?

Estelle kissed me on the cheek the way she would a second cousin, and I was surprised she smelled the same except for her vanilla-scented perfume.

Both women were wrapped in shiny, slinky, short and fitted affairs, no doubt expensive, but trashy-looking rather than designer-chic. Marianne's fast-food red hair was piled messily on top of her head, some loose strands stuck to the sides of her neck. Estelle's hair was parted in the middle and braided like a Dutch milkmaid's.

"Did you?" I flipped one of her braids over in my hand. "You dyed your hair."

"Just highlights. A home job. *Tu sais*, to hide the grey." Estelle looked knowingly at Marianne, and the women exchanged self-assured laughter with an essence of bitterness.

"I didn't realize it bothered you so much."

"Not me. Jean-Jacques. He said last meeting that we need to—how did he say it, Mare?"

"'Young-up.' Isn't that the stupidest thing you've ever heard?"

"*Oui.* 'Young-up.' So I've younged-up." Estelle wiped her brow as though just in from a gruelling day of work in the fields, and then glugged from a water bottle. "Anyway, we just had breakfast at Le Sandwichier, and now I have to run home and change."

Marianne cupped a hand around her mouth and whispered to me like she was revealing the secret of the universe. "We haven't slept at all."

"Oh my," I said, exhaling against her bacon breath. "And where did you ladies go last night?"

Estelle snorted and elbowed Marianne. Marianne widened her eyes and elbowed Estelle in return.

"Everywhere," she said to me. Then, to Estelle, "Fuck it. Let's go in like this. Aren't we closed today, so Jerk-Jacques can hang a bunch of floating lamps?"

"Oh those stupid floating lamps. I told him they'll desaturate the north wall, but, *no-o*, I don't know what I'm talking about, my eye is too sensitive to light, *la la la…*"

"I say we don't go in until tonight."

"And tear down all the fucking lamps!"

"What's tonight?" I asked Estelle, raising my hand to Marianne when she started to answer.

How could Marianne know more about my wife's schedule than I did? I had been absent for all of one night, for god's sake. Surely Estelle hadn't told her why I had spent the night at Le Cabinet.

Estelle finished her water and glanced warningly at her friend. "Well," she began, stalling to search her purse for her lip balm. "There's this charity event I'm supposed to attend, we're hoping to woo this visiting artist from Denmark, even more so now to amend the Pierrot gaffe, and I wasn't sure I'd go, that's why I didn't say anything, but since Jean-Jacques wants more than anything to blame me for Pierrot, I really should go."

"Then I shall be your escort. Where is it?"

"I didn't get an extra ticket, Margot. Because I didn't think I was going. I meant to give mine away, but I forgot."

With the subtlety of a wrecking ball, Marianne coughed, cleared her throat, and then punched two pieces of gum from a foil blister pack. "I guess I could give her my ticket?"

I had tolerated as much of the pair's adolescent, cagey behaviour as I could. "No, I don't want your ticket, Marianne. But thank you for your consideration. What I want, if you don't mind, is a moment alone with my wife."

Marianne stepped back to consider the brass sconce chandelier overhead. "I'm always worried something like that's going to fall on me. I mean, what's keeping it there? You can't see the cable or anything. Remember that woman a few years ago? On Peel Street? A chunk of building just crushed her right to death. On her *birthday*. God that shit makes me squirrely."

Estelle applied another layer of lip balm.

"Guess I should feed my cats," Marianne sighed, as though had she not been forced out of the conversation, she might have let her cats starve.

"You got new ones?" I asked, attempting to recover my harsh tone. It was possible she didn't know anything, and I wanted to show Estelle I could talk to her friend nicely and without goading her.

"Nope, same two. Antoine was so eager to start his new life he left his *petits puces* behind. I'm just waiting for them to start having problems like all purebreds do. I'll tell the vet I simply can't afford the bills so please just euthanize them both, since if one goes then the other will just get depressed, and I'd rather save myself a second trip."

Wolfgang and Puzzle were the evilest cats I had ever met. At the point when it was obvious their marital woes were there to stay, Antoine, Marianne's now ex-husband (and Montréal's metrosexual poster boy who came roaring out of the closet when Marianne tricked him by saying she was a lesbian) had decided a pair of Siamese cats was a practical solution, something they could nurture as a couple. That was, until the cats turned Marianne and Antoine into house slaves, yowling pitifully every morning when they tried to leave for work, and the ensuing guilt destroyed the remains of the marriage.

"They were tolerable when Antoine was around, I mean they liked him more than me. Now it's like living with two mini-chimeras who try new ways every day to kill me. Antoine paid two thousand dollars for them, but I can't *give* them away on Craigslist." Whether out of frustration over her ex, her cats, or her inability to party all day and all night, Marianne pressed her forefingers against the sides of her nose and issued a single, cinematically perfect sob. "I hate my life right now."

"Oh, Mare-Mare," Estelle crooned, sliding an arm around the divorcée's waist, "I'll walk you home and read you a story until you fall asleep, okay?"

Estelle and Marianne's relationship had been built on the foundations common to beautiful, ambitious women: adulation and envy. One was at her best when the other was down and out, and the women seemed to swap statuses often to preserve the vigour in their friendship. They had met in graduate school, in Savannah, Georgia. Estelle had been granted a one-year visa to complete a Master's in Advertising, and I followed her into the U.S., as was my birthright from my father. I had begun working at Le Canon Noir only months earlier, and Bertrand, instead of terminating my contract after I told him about my new plan and apologized but I would follow Estelle at any expense, made some phone calls and informed me that I would be travelling the Deep South regularly to get my own education from firearms brokers (it was the best he could do to keep me near Estelle). He arranged for us to live in a darling, matchbox-small apartment facing the Savannah River, in an area otherwise populated by wealthy vacationers. Marianne, also from Montréal, was pursuing a graduate degree in Arts Administration, and Estelle met her at the International Students office after they both received letters erroneously claiming their funding had been denied—no small matter when tuition would cost them the first five years of their luxurious careers. They bonded that afternoon over sweet tea and praline cheesecake, and the very next day Marianne moved in with Estelle and me and remained until we all returned to Montréal one year later.

Marianne was the first to land a job in advertising, which miffed Estelle since that was her area of expertise, and so there was a brief chasm in the friendship, Estelle claiming she need- ed time out to decide what sort of career she wanted. Then Marianne phoned one day and said, "Belle! I got you a job," and so the women worked together at a fledgling gallery in the east end of the city, in little more than a cubicle that was open only Thursday through Saturday and paid the equivalent of a part-time cashier position at a convenience store, until Marianne found a better job prospect and brought Estelle along with her. Marianne was fabulous at pitching herself and Estelle as a package deal. Estelle was the allure (not that Marianne wasn't pretty), and so they became a power team, showing up to job interviews together, Marianne doing all the bartering while Estelle presented their portfolios (hers before Marianne's, of course).

But it was Estelle alone who interviewed for the position of manager at L'Espace Vif, and she didn't tell her friend about the new job until all the paperwork was complete and the nametag pinned to her blouse. She also didn't tell Marianne about the assistant manager position opening at the gallery for which she was auditioning her best friend so they could work together once again (Jean-Jacques, and reasonably so, was sceptical about the melodramas such a situation might incur). While I had stayed carefully uninvolved with The Career Sagas of the Ambiguously Ambitious Duo, this time Estelle begged me to keep her plan secret from Marianne, to lie to her about why Estelle had missed so many days of work. Thankfully, serendipity intervened and the situation never escalated to the point where I had to lie. Two weeks after Estelle returned from her "emergency family trip," as she had spun it to Marianne, she ordered her friend to pack up her office supplies and relocate to the thriving west end of the city, and everything returned to business as usual.

And here they were now, gleeful and hungover, a throwback to their grad school days, and of the mind that they had all the time in the world. But what really bothered me was the most important thing about today: It was Friday. I gazed evenly at Marianne until she exclaimed a sudden need to zip to the post office for stamps. After she left, I invited Estelle to my room.

"I really should be going," she said, applying a dollop of moisturizer to her hands.

"I take it *Mare-Mare* doesn't know?"

"Know what?"

"Come on."

Estelle eyed the bellhop at the check-in counter, a different boy from the day before, who was speaking crisp, idiomatic English to someone on the phone. "I know," she said. "I know, but I really should go to the charity event. What about after? Or we could spend the whole day together tomorrow."

"What will I do until then?"

"It's not that expensive here, right?"

How could she say such a thing! Annex our couples homework—our relationship—on the basis of affordability? "Do you not want me to come home?"

"*No*, I didn't mean it like that. It's just, fuck. When I got back yesterday I started to tidy up ... and I read more of the letters. I know I shouldn't have, they're yours, I broke one of our rules, *et cetera et cetera*, but they were right there. All over the goddamn place. I need to take it all in." Estelle wiped the excess moisturizer on her dress and then rubbed her eyes until her make-up smudged. "I need time to think."

Time to think. This was surely Marianne's doing. Excluding her past five months with Dr. Weinstock, Estelle never took time to think when she was overwhelmed. She rushed headlong into decisions big and small, bristled whenever I suggested she plan or gather insight first. She had just spent the whole night out clubbing. A professional woman of forty-five! Marianne, conversely, took her sweet time with everything, like her divorce from Antoine. She had announced to Estelle just three years into the marriage that it was over, but between her therapist, Saturday nights out with the girls, and thrice-weekly acupuncture sessions, she had needed the next 2,555 days to end it with the bogus "I'm a lesbian" excuse.

A family of German backpackers bustled into the hotel and greeted the bellhop with broad smiles and sweeping arms. *Hallo! Was für ein fabelhaftes Hotel! Wir lieben diese Stadt!* The parents, a twenty-something couple with muscular calves and matching cyclist outfits, each toted a twin toddler at the hip, and each boy was inspecting a plastic-wrapped maple leaf lollipop.

"I suppose I should make up my mind soon," I said, seeing another family of backpackers coming up the steps.

"I'll pay, if you want."

"Estelle, if you don't want me to come home for a while, just say it."

One of the toddlers dropped his lollipop on the floor. The other toddler, in what seemed a calculated act of solidarity, looked from his own lollipop to his lip-quivering twin's and then hurled his onto the floor. He stretched his dimpled arms toward his brother, and perhaps if the boys had been able to make contact, which struck me as an intelligent if not genius alternative for three-year-olds to figure out all on their own, there would have come no meltdown, no flustered parents, no influx of new guests who devoured the bellhop with their wolfish enthusiasm, and no snap decision on my part to punish Estelle for something that was still mostly my fault.

"Leave. Go home. Do whatever you have to do." I turned for the elevator, more eager to escape my wife than the sudden circus in the lobby.

"Margot."

I would have been able to exit swiftly and pointedly had Le Cabinet Particulier's elevator been a modern one. But between my body-wide malaise and my apprehension about squashing my fingers in the manual lift's heavy collapsible gate, as I had done in my rush to get to the lobby, I couldn't even bring myself to take the stairwell beside the lift. So I just stood there, my back to Estelle, until she murmured goodbye and left.

7. VAMPIRE

"*MON ESPRIT!* YOU HAVE COME BACK to me!"
I stepped inside the shop and before I could say a timid hello, Bertrand hung up his phone and ran to me with the bumbling grace of a tall Humpty-Dumpty. I had listened to his voicemail again on my way to the shop and become humbled by my utter selfishness in not returning his call. He trapped my face in his talcum hands and kissed me from forehead to chin in the excessive way of a Gérard Départieu character after too many cocktails. "Margot! Your timing is perfect!" He stuck his head outside the shop and looked up and down rue Notre Dame Ouest, and then flipped the "*Ouvert*" sign to "*Fermé*" and lowered the emerald green chenille blind on the door.

"No, please," I said. After my morning with Estelle, I had no desire to hang around my other no-longer home. I had come to apologize and inform Bertrand I was still resolute in my decision to leave the business.

"Oh," he said, walking behind me with his hands on my shoulders, directing me to the back of the shop. "Does this mean you want to sell your shares? I don't know if I can afford to buy you out right now."

"I'd like to be a silent partner—keep my shares, but keep away. If that's okay?" I accepted Bertrand's offering of red bourbon vanilla tea and sat with him on the vintage orange sleeper sofa. I had spent many late nights on this sofa, researching firearms history and comparing pricelists, puzzling out routes across the U.S. that would lead me to specialty museums and eccentric hermits. Bertrand hadn't minded my personalizing the space over the years, and I jerked my hand and spilled hot tea on myself when I saw my postcard collection still tacked to the pushpin board across from us. "The Faithful Colt," a psychedelic red and black revolver from Warhol's 1982 "Guns" series, the musket I had lifted from my mother in 1976—everything was as I had left it. On the green Formica table against that wall was a clump of sticky notes and newspaper clippings Bertrand could have easily organized by removing my postcards from the board.

He placed a safe, paternal hand on my knee. "You could have kept the letters here, too."

After I said nothing—succeeded, even, to suppress my slightest of physical responses to his statement (the fluttering of an eyelid, the dilation of a nostril, the twitching of a finger)—Bertrand changed the subject to one that could keep me talking for hours without talking about myself. "*Alors,* Margot Soucy-Coté, what career will you conquer next?"

I HAD MET BERTRAND long before I possessed any purchasing skills (much less the inclination to make a career out of it), when my sensibilities were still textbook and restricted to what I had endured in college to obtain a degree and escape an aimless job in retail or food service. Estelle and I were twenty-five, living in my studio apartment situated above a gentlemen's club in the east end, living among big-bearded, chain-smoking bikers, blue- and purple-haired squeegees, and prostitutes who accepted beer and heroin for their expertise. It was all we could afford with my inventory job at Le Real Deal and Estelle's evening hostess shifts. On rare occasions, her former "Drawing I" professor invited her to pose nude for his students, and we'd use her honorarium to treat ourselves to a foreign film and drinks. Back then, Estelle loved iridescent cocktails with clever names, though she was usually disappointed by their flavours and would finish the night with a glass of reliable Chardonnay. About a year after we'd been living on top of the club, we decided to go in and see what all the fuss was about (there was always a long queue of men on Friday and Saturday nights). The doorman gave Estelle a slow, shameless once-over and admitted her for free, suggesting she speak with the manager about a job. Not a minute after we'd seated ourselves in the darkest corner of the bar, a heavily rouged, edgy stripper wearing a dollar-store version of the Playboy Bunny outfit offered us a dance. Estelle said, "Okay!" at the precise moment I said, "No thanks," so we compromised and paid the girl ten dollars to sit with us and talk for the duration of Def Leppard's, "Love Bites." Though she spoke fluent French, the girl's accent wasn't regional, and after the song ended she thanked us for being nice to her.

We were living like beggars who aspired to live like bohemians, but we were in the youth of our love and optimistic about our future. Nevertheless, as each of my days proved to be exactly like the previous, I began to lose sight of what "future" meant for us, until my girlfriend suddenly announced she was going back to school. I watched her apply to graduate programs and grow increasingly determined to study in the U.S. ("Their education is *so* much better"), and I grew increasingly worried she would lose interest in me after she experienced more of the world. She was a small-town Catholic farm girl. Her move from Lanaudière to Montréal had been such a momentous change for her that five years later she was still bragging excitedly to her family about city life. Gabrielle and Véronique, Estelle's younger sisters, still lived at home with the Cotés and helped milk the cows and shear the sheep. Caroline and Nathalie, the older sisters, had found honourable, hardworking husbands and set up families within walking distance of their childhood home. To all of them, Estelle had become as exciting as a Hollywood celebrity; they even accepted her relationship with me as a function of her new way of life.

The first time Bertrand came into Le Real Deal, he purchased a vintage Bearcat police scanner. "To keep me company," he said merrily, as he wrote a damp cheque for fifty dollars. The pawnshop dealt mostly in gold jewellery, drum sets, and heavy metal paraphernalia, so when I found the scanner that morning among the day's new stock to sort and price, I placed it by the cash register for later, to see if I could convince the shop owner to dock it from my next pay.

The next time Bertrand came, he presented a list of items he wanted, "Just for fun," and then he asked about the book I was reading. I told him I had studied History in college but had only recently become interested in the details; the broad range of generic, censored materials I had been forced to read and regurgitate in school had snuffed rather than stimulated my curiosities. Bertrand flipped through my book, *British Military Longarms, 1715-1815*, and asked if he could borrow it. I was about to protest (I'd borrowed the book from the library, and it was a week overdue) when he tucked the book inside the breast of his emerald green corduroy jacket in exchange for a business card he placed on the counter. He left the pawnshop unhurriedly, but I couldn't chase after him because I was the only employee on the floor.

If not for Estelle, I would have thrown the business card away. I wanted nothing more to do with this man who kept taking my things. By dinnertime, I was fuming and ready to quit my job just to avoid further interaction with him. Estelle, however, thought the whole affair was a thrilling and preordained development. Later, in bed, she nuzzled me and chittered on about how it absolutely had to be a sign of good fortune. "Think about it, GoGo: Why else do these unexpected things happen?"

"Maybe he's planning to kidnap me." I snapped. "Maybe I'll go to his *shoppe* and he'll trap me in the basement and make a stew out of me, and that'll be the end of that. Of us. Of everything. You'll go off to grad school and forget I ever existed."

But the next morning when I knocked on the shaded windowpane of Le Canon Noir's door, the corpulent man who had poached my police scanner and my book about English firearms greeted me with a bearish hug and a loud, wet kiss on my forehead. "*Jeune esprit!* You will love it here."

"WHO KNEW, EH?" Bertrand sighed, squeezing my knee.

My chest expanded with a breath I feared I wouldn't be able to exhale without weeping. I didn't want him to see me in this state, especially since I had just told him Estelle was doing fabulously, our new loft was showroom-ready, and I was on my way to La Ronde to have lunch with a new acquaintance.

Bertrand stood from the sofa, wheezing a little, and held out his great big hands to me. I took them and pulled myself up, and then excused myself to the washroom.

"I insist you take this last trip to America," he said, leaning outside the washroom door. "It will be good for Le Canon." When I exited, he led me by hand to the front of the shop and pointed sombrely to the darkened room adjacent to the main space—what had been our recent expansion.

My chest swelled anew. "What happened?"

Bertrand shrugged. "With all the police shootings around here lately, I think it's hurt business."

"No, what's really going on?"

My business partner, mentor, and friend of twenty years smiled dolefully and pressed a palm over his heart. "*Il faut toute une vie pour trouver le bon partenaire, mon esprit. Un vieux comme moi, tout seul,* it sucks the life out of you." He stepped closer to me and took a deep inhalation. The slight wheeze I had heard when he rose from the sofa was now pronounced, and I knew by the perspiration and pallor his effort caused that he was suffering from more than aging and loneliness.

I HADN'T PLANNED to return to La Ronde that day, but I had planted the seed of necessity with my lie to Bertrand. I felt bothered by the ease with which I had told him how wonderfully my life was going, so perhaps if I went to the park, found Katy, and invited her to lunch with me in the Old West-themed food court, I could reverse some of the cosmic damage I might have caused. No. I mustn't allow myself to think this way. This was my mother seeping into me. She believed in things like karma. She, not I, let her deluded ideas about the universe and synchronicity inform her decisions. I was pragmatic and measured, and I wouldn't allow the present stressors in my life to compel me into foolish behaviour.

The line into the park was so long I almost turned back. Swimsuit-clad teenagers stood in defensive formations of five and six to ward off anyone who might consider cutting in front, and young, excessively sunscreened children hopped from flip-flop to flip-flop, vying for attention from their aloof older kin. One little girl squeezed her legs together and pressed down on her pelvis. "I can't hold it anymore!" When I jumped back to avoid being rammed by a pair of boys sparring with candied apples and yelling at each other in what they imagined could pass for Japanese, a man in line behind me placed a hand firmly between my shoulder blades.

"Sorry," he said, when I turned to scold him. "The wife wouldn't be too happy if I came home with a broken baby." The infant harnessed to the man's chest seemed safely padded with fat, and unconcerned with everything going on around her as long as her carrier bobbed up and down.

"My condolences," I said, referring not only to the man's air of constipation and the burden harnessed to his chest, but also to the cumbersome fanny pack around his waist, which, though stuffed to the point of a splitting zipper, couldn't possibly contain everything a parent needed for a day at the fun park with baby.

"No, it's my own fault. My nephew's in a hot dog competition this afternoon and I promised I'd come. I forgot all about it until he phoned me an hour ago, so here we are. I really hope it's over fast. My wife doesn't even know we're here, but I guess she'll know after the fact. Shoot, I didn't think of that."

"A hot dog competition?"

The man started to answer, but his baby, misleadingly un-offending with her sprig of blonde hair gathered at the top of her pate by a ladybug clip, issued a high-pitched scream to re-establish her priority. Embracing the ignominy he had brought onto himself, the man swerved his torso side to side and sang atonally until the baby calmed. "Your mommy's all right, your daddy's all right, they just seem a little weird. Surrender. *Suh-rrrren-derrrr*. But don't give yourself away. Hey, *heeeey*!"

"Stealing baby off to an amusement park *and* introducing her to classic rock? Good thing I don't know your wife."

Once the baby was nibbling happily on a pacifier the man wore on a string around his neck, the man groaned and rubbed his eyes. He was average height, average weight (possibly a little more blurred around the edges than he had been pre-fatherhood), and his face, which could have belonged to a twenty-something-year-old as easily as it could have belonged to a forty-something-year-old, was clean and uncomplicated in the way women looking to start families find attractive. I could imagine his wife describing him to her parents when she first met him: *He's got brown eyes, a straight nose, and an even smile. Everything's where it should be. He'll make a good father.*

"So tell me about the hot dog competition," I said.

The man brightened with giddy conviction. I had just given him permission to relive his baby-free youth. "Okay, so my nephew's sixteen and this is his first real summer job. He lets people on to the Tchou-Tchou, the kiddie train with the mechanical cow that glides onto the tracks halfway through? The guy who runs the ride, the boss, he's really into food competitions, like they have in the U.S. How many pies can you eat in five minutes, that sort of thing. Or maybe it's not a U.S. thing but more of a travelling carnival sort of thing—too backwater for a Six Flags operation like this. Anyway, the boss managed to recruit enough people for a hot dog contest, and my nephew's been practising for two weeks. Apparently he's gained five pounds. So here I am, here *we* are, just a quick in and out, and then back home like nothing ever happened. Right, *ma belle petite Rebelle?*"

"Rebelle?"

"This little lady right here."

"Your daughter's name is Rebelle?"

I waited for the man to explain how it was a nickname, endearing wordplay on the dominant attitude he and his wife wished to imprint upon the infant so that she grew up impermeable to the storm of women's beauty adverts in the event she turned out to be an uncomely adult. Instead he asked, "What about you?"

"Me?"

"Have you snuck off on your husband to be here?"

"I'm sorry?"

The man pointed to my ring finger. "I just assumed..."

"*Prochain!* Next!" The ticket agent called me to the booth to pay my entrance fee, but I was too stunned by the new awareness of my wedding band to step forward.

"I'm here to see a friend," I managed, moving aside and offering my turn to the man. "Please. I need to recount my money."

"Got it," he said. "I totally get it. Enjoy the rides!" Before moving ahead, he winked at me in a way that made him look like a pubescent idiot, which infuriated me. He really did not "totally get it." He had no idea how far he was from getting it.

Once I was inside the park, I didn't know what to do with myself. As it was only my second time there, I was unfamiliar with the layout other than to head eastward to Le Galopant. A clown on stilts, whose face was painted like a fleur-de-lis and who squirted water at the children tossing pennies inside the waist of his hooped trousers, tossed a park map my way.

I was astounded by the quantity of young, feral children milling about. Their parents were likely at work on a Friday, but shouldn't young children be at camp, or accompanied by foreign-speaking guardians with fair complexions? There were plenty of teenagers, too, prowling the premises for shaded corners away from security cameras, where they could furtively pass cigarettes and other hazards among themselves. There was a modest population of baffled adults with infants, like the man and his ridiculously named daughter, there was the cacophony of bells ringing as prizes were won, the grind of roller coasters climbing steeply inclined tracks. And, finally, there was me.

"I knew you'd come back. I told Étienne and now he owes me a free ride."

I turned around to be greeted by K-K-K-Katy and her spools of pink cotton candy, although these ones were covered in plastic wrap, and her mouth shone from lip gloss and not stickiness. She squeezed her arms around me and then jumped back to admire me like we were best friends who hadn't seen each other in years.

"Did your family like the pictures? Are you here to take more? I was just going to bring these to my friend at the popcorn wagon. Want to come? She sells all kinds of flavours, but I think the only good ones are butter and caramel. Do you like popcorn? I bet she'd give you a deal, but don't tell her I said that. I'll do all the talking. I'm good at that."

Katy was wearing a white T-shirt with the cover image of The Smiths' *Meat Is Murder* album ironed across the front. The T-shirt was much too large for her and hung off both of her shoulders, which were freckled and cherry tomato-red from the sun.

"You're a fan?" I said, falling in step with her as she led us to her popcorn-vending friend.

"A fan of what?"

"The Smiths. Your T-shirt?"

Katy made airplane wings with her arms and began moving them in wide circles, nearly knocking me in the face with her cotton candy. "I'm so sorry!" she cried, switching the cotton candy to her other hand. "I just really need to stretch myself out. I've been feeling cramped all morning because I had to sleep on the daybed, because the air conditioner in my room broke. Who are The Smiths?" She stopped to do a few toe-touches and jumping jacks, perfectly bizarre things to do in public.

I grabbed the cotton candy from her when she reached the summit of a fifth jumping jack. "Are you vegetarian?"

Katy smiled and draped an arm around my shoulders as we continued on to her friend. "I've been seriously thinking about it. How did you know?"

"It's a gift."

The popcorn wagon was closed up when we arrived, a "BB in 1 hour" sign taped to the exterior. Katy unclipped a small ring of keys from her belt and disappeared behind the wagon. When she emerged from within, she was wearing a red and white striped sailor-style hat and a shit-eating grin. "What'll it be, ma'am? We got big corn, small corn, medium corn, and popped corn. Perhaps you'd like something light on this fine summer day, like a dusting of dill? Or perhaps you'd like your mouth to sizzle with some sour cream and cayenne? Whatever you want, whatever it is, we got it right here. Except cheddar, I think we're all out until next week. Sunday's re-stock day…"

"A cup of water will be fine, thank you. Are you allowed to be in there? Don't you work with the cotton candy?" I held up the spools, which had lost some of their fluffiness and were crusting around the edges. I swatted them at a wasp. Katy took the spools from me and hung them upside-down on the back wall of the wagon, beside tiered packaged Cheetos-flavoured popcorn.

After she served me some water, Katy closed up the wagon and came around front. She had a bottle of strawberry-kiwi Snapple. "So! What roller coaster do you want to go on first?"

"No roller coaster."

"Oh come on. Please? The carousel's out of order, so you can't even take pictures."

Again, Katy was steering us in the direction of her whim, and her perfunctory statement about Le Galopant caused me to feel unexpectedly, almost unbearably, disappointed. I remembered how the handsome ticket boy, Étienne, had been concerned about a malfunction, but surely, given the historical importance of the carousel, someone at the park would attend to the problem? And if not, there had to be a specialist on standby. Le Galopant, as I had learned from the literature I brought home with me two evenings ago, was first known as Le Galopant De J. Bairolle. From 1885 until 1964, it had resided in Bressoux, Belgium, and then from 1964 through 1965 it was showcased in the Belgium Village of New York World's Fair. Next, the carousel went to Montréal, where it alternated between storage and fun parks until it was shut down for restoration. A decade later—now—here it was, once again available for a public largely ignorant, as I had been, of its history.

"You're mostly right," Katy said, sitting on the curb beside the wagon to retie her shoelaces. "This is the first year people can go on it, but you could come see it before now. I saw it last summer and the one before."

"You're here every summer?"

"Since I was sixteen. I stay with this family and help their kids learn to speak good English."

"Proper English."

"What?"

"You stay with a family and teach their children how to speak proper English."

"That's what I said." Katy guzzled the rest of her Snapple and threw the bottle into a garbage bin, then looked at me sheepishly and retrieved her bottle from the bin. "You seem like the sort that gets pissed at people who don't recycle."

The popcorn wagon was in a tucked-away courtyard of the park, along with other concessions wagons and some memorabilia kiosks. Katy brought us to a hot dog wagon and ordered a large fries.

"It's a bad idea to eat before going on a roller coaster, but you should have a little something in your stomach just to be safe." She grabbed a fistful of fries and offered me the bag. "Eat up."

In truth, I was starving; otherwise, I would have politely declined the fries and gone off in search of a grilled vegetable panino or a Greek salad. I even let Katy douse the fries in salt and white vinegar. We sat on a cement bench at the centre of the courtyard and ate in a silence I welcomed. I watched Katy examine each fry before eating it. I watched her chew each fry separately. I watched her tongue sweep clean the insides of her mouth before she contemplated the next fry. And I wondered if she had any idea I was watching her as closely as she was watching her fries. She was utterly captivating, even though most everything about her revolted me in some way or another. She couldn't keep to one topic when she spoke, her attire was slovenly, her eating habits indicated her total disregard of the food pyramid, and she paid no mind to the grains of salt clinging to the fine hairs under her bottom lip. Estelle patted her lips after every bite and sip, and this used to antagonize me. In the beginning years of our relationship, I imagined it was a sign that she would one day start patting her mouth after every kiss and lick. Eventually she would start to gargle and rinse after we made love, and then one day I would nuzzle her neck and she would ask me to wait while she went to apply moisture repellent all over her body. This never happened, of course, and Estelle laughed until she cried when I confessed this fear to her years after I had concluded that it was unfounded.

"...This'll be my last summer here so I really hope they fix the carousel. My grandparents met in the Belgian Village, did you know that? They rode Napoleon together. Back when the ride was sturdy. And anyway, they were just little kids. After that they were inseparable. My dad brought my mom to Montréal while Le Galopant was touring different parks in the eighties, and he practically made me volunteer here when I got hired by the Fortins, just so I could tell him how the ride was doing and send him pictures with my letters. I still haven't bought a disposable camera this year. I'm hoping to convert him to email attachments."

Katy stretched out her arms and legs until her body was a long plank against the cement bench. As her hips slid toward the ground, her T-shirt slipped up her midriff and exposed the tip of a tattoo. I looked away discreetly, but Katy was as sharp as a bloodhound when it came to sniffing out new points of conversation. And so for five minutes she told me all about the tattoo, since she thought it would be inappropriate to show me the whole thing, when all she had needed to say was "It's a bouquet of exotic flowers," and I would have felt sufficiently informed. We would work on that.

I ate my last fry and suggested we head over to Le Galopant. I needed to see with my own eyes what from Katy was surely hyperbole.

"Oh Margot, I don't want to go there right now. It's so depressing. After. After we go on a roller coaster. I know the perfect one for you! I've been paying close attention to you since you came in, so I know what one will suit you best. I'm gifted, too."

God knows why I didn't resist when Katy grabbed my hand and set us both at a fast clip in the direction of La Ronde's loud and menacing thrill ride annex. Perhaps I was relieved to be gusted away from the gloom in my head and in my heart. Perhaps I could gain something from this experience, bring back to Estelle compelling evidence that I was capable of being different. If I was benevolent enough to embark on an obscene roller coaster to make some hyper teenage girl happy, could this not suggest I was primed to embark on a new life path with my wife? A fearless and honest path with invigorating ups and unpredictable downs that we would experience as a unit. It was time, I told myself, to start doing things I didn't ordinarily do. Time for me to kick off my spectator shoes (which, thank heavens, I hadn't worn that day) and try on a pair of mules. Time for me to accept that change would force itself upon me even after I invited it in for conciliatory tea. If I was to repair the damage I had caused to my marriage, win back Estelle's trust, and make her understand that everything I had done, even my lies, had been for her benefit—but that I was willing to change my ways—then I had to allow myself to be jerked away from my comforts. As we passed under the arched purple entranceway of a roller coaster so tall I couldn't see the top of the tracks from where we stood, it occurred to me that K-K-K-Katy was my ticket. Through her impulsiveness, I would learn how to relax my mid-life grip, and from my moderation, she would learn fundamental rules of civility.

"CAN I ASK YOU SOMETHING?"

"You may."

"Why do you talk like that?"

"Like what?"

Katy chewed her bottom lip and dug the toe of her sneaker into the ground. "Like, well, it's like you're always reading from an instruction manual or something."

"There's nothing wrong with instruction manuals."

"When I was in Boston this spring seeing my cousins, I rode the T. You remind me of the conductor. *Next stop, Longwood. This train is heading to Government Centre.*"

"That's a recording, Katy."

The line moved forward as the next round of people boarded the Vampire. We had been waiting our turn for over an hour. I counted the number of heads in front of us, looked back at the ones bobbing impatiently behind us, and realized it was too late to turn back unless I was prepared to pry through a mass of sweaty bodies and duck under the metal divider railings.

"When we get to the platform," I said, "I'm going to bypass the ride and wait for you on the other side."

"I'm sorry, Margot. I didn't mean it as an insult. Please don't make me go on alone. I always go alone. I hate it."

"I'm not *making* you do anything. Do as you wish when your turn comes."

Katy spun toward me and grabbed my forearms. "Ryan never wants to do fun things with me. He says he will but he comes home after work and all he wants to do is watch football or meet his friends at Town Tavern & Lore. He always says I can come with him, but his friends never talk to me and I'm sure the lady who works behind the bar has a thing for him. She's got red hair."

"Then you tell her to back off. And who's Ryan?"

"My fiancé."

"How old are you?"

"Eighteen, almost. That's why he's my fiancé. But we're getting married right after my birthday. Right after I leave here. He promised." She smiled broadly and flashed her engagement ring. The thread-thin silver band that dipped into the approximate shape of a heart stirred in me a compassion that both startled and embarrassed me.

The Vampire came twisting toward the platform, its passengers red-faced and electric-socket-haired. A quartet of girls in the last train was still screaming and waving their arms in the air like fools after the ride thundered to a stop.

"We're up?" Katy said, so evidently braced for disappointment I couldn't say no, even though I felt certain I would lose my fries at some early point in the ride.

"Just this once," I said, moving forward with the crowd, which had become solemn as it approached the Queen Bee of roller coasters. "You should know I'm just as boring as Ryan."

Katy, I gathered, would want to sit either at the extreme

front or the extreme rear, but there was no way this would happen on my watch. After a swarm of pimply boys and girls proclaimed ownership of the prime spots and greedily straddled their respective ski-lift-style chairs, we stepped onto the platform and I tugged Katy by her shirt hem to the middle train.

"Aw-aw," she mock-whined, claiming the chair to my right so I wouldn't have to sit beside strangers.

"For someone soon to be married, you might want to develop a more sophisticated vocabulary."

Katy was silent until the ride operators lowered our chest restraints and locked us in place. "So when the Vampire gets going, are you going to read from your instruction manual on how to scream?"

Cheeky brat! I turned to scold her, but the padded vinyl restraint was so close to my head that I boxed my ear, which meant that once the ride began shooting and dipping and twirling around the candy-yellow track, I was sure to suffer worse damage.

"It only hurts a bit," Katy laughed, her sunburnt face practically catching fire from her excitement.

"A bit as in two Tylenols and a nap will solve the problem? Or as in a trip to the ER and some stitches?"

"You take naps...?" Then we were off.

As with the other trains I had watched, ours instantly turned into a megaphone for repressed screams. Even during the Vampire's slow ascent to the cliff of the first steep drop, people decompressed faster than helium balloons and let out some terrible sounds. A foursome of grown men in the train in front of ours roared like lions and rattled their restraints. Thankfully, Katy didn't seem prone to excess and instead curled her hands around the part of the restraint closest to her ears. "Like this, Margot," she said. "Just keep your neck relaxed and you'll be fine."

Down the first drop we snaked, building speed as we next flipped upside down and soared around the first of many loops. Katy lost her composure as we neared the second loop, and I was certain I was about to lose my lunch. People yelled, people laughed, some people wept, and when once again we were ripped from the comforts of being upright on the track, I clutched my stomach, thus making my poor ears vulnerable to repeated pummelling.

"I'm going to be sick," I shouted.

"What?"

"I'm going to be sick."

"You're what?"

"I need to get off this ride immediately!"

And as quickly as the nightmare had started, it jerked to a halt and the Vampire pulled up to the platform.

Quite possibly the only reason I didn't vomit was my highly tuned sense of dignity. Had the ride continued for a moment longer, I would have lost my hold, but as soon as my brain recognized that it was no longer being assaulted by vertigo, I was able to preserve myself through deep breathing and a slow dismount from my ski-lift chair. Katy was abuzz from the experience and darted off without a word. I wondered if she was going to be sick. A ride operator came to ask if I required assistance.

"Thank you, kind sir, but I'm fine. A little rattled, but fine." I waited for him to comment on the girl who had been with me and was now nowhere to be seen, and I indulged, briefly, in imagining how I would respond if he mistook her for my daughter. I wanted him to mistake Katy for my daughter, and I wanted to neither correct him nor confirm, but to appear like a person who was connected to other people. Without referring to myself as Estelle's wife, as Bertrand's business partner, what did I have left? The operator waited dutifully while I dismounted and experienced the first of many muscle spasms to come that day, but his attention was stitched to the white and faded blue short-shorts of teenage girls bending over the pile of messenger bags and purses they had left behind for the ride. To me, they were all the same—unshapely downy legs spilled into "grown-up" garments—but to a man whose continuous duty was to buckle people in and then unbuckle them five minutes later, this must have been the highlight of his job.

Friday afternoon attendance had peaked. Long queues of people were staked in front of every concessions wagon, game booth, and ride big and small that I could see. I didn't recognize my location within the park. Where was Katy? Had she snuck back in line for another round of whiplash? I felt disoriented, still, from the Vampire, so I leaned against the archway of the ride's entrance for a few minutes in case Katy was coming back for me. After she failed, oddly, to return, I cupped a hand over my eyes and looked for the imposing fleur-de-lis clown with the maps. When that failed, I began walking in the general direction of the park's main entrance, and from there I would make my way to Le Galopant. I refused to believe Katy's claims that it was being permanently dismantled and stored. On my way, I passed the park's other carousel, a much less exciting *objet d'art*, though it certainly drew a crowd. The horses were in rows of three, like with Le Galopant, but they were luridly coloured. Before I had seen Le Galopant, I would have agreed that horses of different colours were nicer to look at. Now, I thought the uniformity of Le Galopant's fleet, their white bodies and the occasional dappled rumps, the way all of the horses looked onward with enlivened curiosity rather than the frenzy of captured beasts, made them more complex subjects. So many spirited creatures seemingly of one mind. Guardians of a secret.

Le Galopant was in a secluded area at the east end of the park, where it was, I surmised, safest from debris kicked into the air by the velocity of bigger, faster rides. Here it was also less vulnerable to mistreatment from the public (when onboard, passengers were politely asked to keep from touching the horses more than necessary). Fewer people went to the east end of La Ronde because it boasted no glittery or gustatory attractions and faced a parking lot. Before I saw the carousel, I heard what Katy had warned me about, and I stopped to listen: No squealing children, no parents bartering for deals on tickets, and no Wurlitzer 146 paperboard sheet music. I almost retracted my steps back to the main entrance; I didn't feel I could contend with any more disappointments, no matter how little they had to do with me. I heard two men yell at each other in jargoned French, an engine start and gravel crunch, and I probably would have run away from the scenario forming in my mind had Katy not materialized before me, hands on her hips, a lollipop wedged between her back molars.

"It's like a crime scene, Margot. Are you sure you're ready for it?"

I was breathless, like I had already started to run. "I'm feeling a little off, actually, so I think I should be heading back. I just came to find you, to say goodbye."

"Oh no you don't," Katy said, hopping to my side and sweeping her arm theatrically toward what truly could not be described as anything less than a crime scene. Yellow tape with the word "Danger" on it was taped around the perimeter of the carousel, and the scotch-coloured teardrop bulbs on top of the canopy were dark. A rusty shovel lay forgotten on the ground outside the gazebo, an offensive, singular vulgarity. The control booth door was open, and I felt hopeful until I realized no one was inside.

"Where's the barker"? I asked.

"The what?"

"Your Billy Bigelow?"

"Margot, you really have to talk in a way that makes sense if you're going to keep sounding like a robot."

Oh, but inside I didn't feel like a robot at all. My chest was constricting the way it had that morning at Le Canon Noir, and I felt my skin floating away from my body the way I had felt it float away when Estelle pranced into Le Cabinet with Marianne. As I squinted to get a better look at the horses of

Le Galopant, their disc eyes wide and mummified rather than enlivened and curious, I felt like something vital had been stolen from me. I began to sob.

"You're that lady with no kids from the other day," Étienne said, joining us.

Katy issued a stern look. "This is very hard for her."

Étienne jammed his hands into the kangaroo pocket of his *Les Misérables* hoodie. "This all just fucking sucks, *n'est-ce pas?*"

"Hello, Étienne." I walked ahead a few steps. Once the two were bantering away, I would sneak inside the gazebo.

"At least I still get paid until they figure out what's wrong," Étienne grumbled to Katy. I heard him light a cigarette. The smoke from his exaggerated exhalation wafted past my face.

"But what if they don't fix it? I heard it's really broken."

"Who told you that? Michel? He's an *ostie de menteur*. So what's wrong with your friend?"

Katy lowered her voice, though they might as well have been talking right into my ear. "Maybe she's having menopause."

"You don't have menopause like a cold or *la grippe, Kah-Tee* It's a thing women go through for years. My mother's been going through it for ages. It makes women get moustaches and chin hair so they have to shave like men."

"Women wax, Étienne. You're so mean. I meant since she's older and crying, plus she's wearing a long-sleeve shirt and pants—and a *hat*—and it's a zillion degrees. Maybe she's having a hot flash."

"Clothes don't make women have hot flashes, *Kah-Tee*. Hot flashes happen because their bodies are making desperate last attempts at being young."

"Then I don't know what's wrong with her, Étienne, but you could show a little kindness and not talk about her like she's a case study in your high school biology class..."

"Sex Ed., you mean. Unless you dissect humans as well as frogs these days in biology?"

Katy and Étienne turned and gawped at me like I had just

proposed we find a garden and pee all over the flowers.

"They dissected frogs in the old days," Étienne said, trying to burn his cigarette to the filter with one long drag. "Now we have simulations from 3-D printers. Right, *Kah-Tee?*"

"I had to dissect a frog, Étienne, and I just graduated."

"But you're *une américaine*. Everything is still backwards where you come from."

"No more free cotton candy for you, Frenchy."

"I've never once asked you to bring me any. It looks like evaporated diarrhea."

"You're so lame. Diarrhea isn't pink, or blue, or..."

"For god's sake, both of you! You're behaving like children."

This was of course the wrong thing for me to say, given that in their view I was one hot flash away from being a senior citizen, but the more they bickered, the more troubled I felt about Le Galopant's future, even if the carousel was repaired this time around. If people who adored it were busy fighting about the facts of menopause and polymer frogs, what did this say about its potential to survive, let alone thrive, in a culture that deferred to immediacy and was impervious to resonance? The number crunchers would invest only in the minimum requirements to keep the antique carousel running, and as soon as it began to cost more than the revenue it generated, Le Galopant would be labelled as a deficit. This much I understood from my Canon Noir days. I was astounded the first time Bertrand brought me with him so I could learn how to conduct a transaction. I watched him write a cheque for nine hundred dollars to a restaurant owner who eagerly handed over an iron-framed 1860 Henry Rifle that had been precariously displayed atop two nail heads above the men's restroom for as long as he could remember. As Bertrand had asked me to before our trip to Pelham, New Hampshire, I had priced the gun at three thousand dollars. When I asked him how on earth he had succeeded in essentially stealing it from the restaurant owner, he said, "*Mon esprit*, that man doesn't see this piece as antique, heritage, or a tangible history. What he sees is that sometimes it falls on patron's heads when they exit the restroom. He sees that wiping the gun with a damp dishrag doesn't restore the lustre and glory it had when his *arrière grand-père* mounted it on the wall after his side won the Civil War. He sees maintenance and responsibility he doesn't care for. It all comes down to reading people the moment you meet them, *jeune esprit*. Like I read you. I could tell you were doing some soul-searching, *oui?* When you're trying to make a transaction, you have to be diplomatic but friendly, and you have to be shrewd. Someone might have the most magnificent firearm you've ever seen, and he might be willing to sell it for bird feed until he senses your hunger. Right then, you've lost the deal. He'll hold onto that gun until he's had it appraised by other brokers, and even if he comes back to you, you'll never get from him what you could have that first time. Then there are the crazy hermits who think everything in their attics is diamonds. So you drive for ten hours to some town without a name, and what do you come to? A model of a revolutionary Charleville musket that doesn't even have a hole in the muzzle. It's a children's toy. But sometimes you meet that wise spinster who hid her husband's firearms collection after he passed away, so that his family couldn't get their greedy hands on it. And she calls you up and she's willing to sell a ten-thousand-dollar gun to you for half, as long as you're willing to stay the night and listen to stories about happier times in her life. *Les jours d'antan.* What's five thousand dollars less to her? She's going to die before she can spend it all. But quality time with another person? She'll take that to her grave. It's like people selling their houses: some want to bolt this town yesterday, and others need to feel acknowledged for the effort they poured in to creating a *home* before they'll let go."

I didn't suppose Six Flags was the crazy hermit or the wise spinster under the lens of Bertrand's analogy.

Étienne stomped his cigarette filter into the ground and

bowed, since we had all stopped talking. "*Mesdames*, I am late for my training." He pulled white earbuds from his kangaroo pocket, fit them into his ears and programmed a playlist on his smartphone. "Will you come visit me at the Grand Carousel, ma'am?" he asked.

If not for the boy's handsome pianist's features, his overtone of sarcasm, his unapologetic air of privilege, I might have received his question as an insult or an accusation. Who was he to question my loyalties? But he could see perfectly well that in the span of two days I had been converted into a one-carousel woman. No doubt he was fascinated by this, seeing an adult sob over a malfunction in a silly children's ride, and perhaps this aroused in him a compassion whose essence he was too immature to understand, but that nonetheless kept him from stopping me when I ducked under the yellow tape and disappeared into the gazebo. Before I returned to my utterly boring room at Le Cabinet for another night of reality television and Edwardian décor that no longer delighted me (my inspection before I went to see Bertrand had revealed that most of the furniture was inauthentic and made in Taiwan), I wanted to be near something subtle and so exquisitely real that it invoked some of the optimism I had felt the previous day on the mountain with Estelle.

Katy and Étienne exchanged more words, though I stopped paying attention as I walked around the platform and ran my hand along each horse. I had circled twice when Katy entered the gazebo. A new unease had settled into me.

"Where are the constellations?" I asked.

"You mean the stars? I'm pretty sure it's too early to see them. It's daytime, silly." Katy hopped onto the platform and it reverberated under our feet. The underside of the canopy shuddered and something creaked.

"Watch it," I said, walking quickly alongside the platform to catch up to Katy and pull her off, if need be, before she caused any damage.

"Jeez. Sorry. But yeah, I guess we should be careful."

"No, Katy, you should be careful. As you can see, I'm on the ground, where I won't cause further harm. Imagine you're in an intensive care unit at a hospital. Would you go around jumping like you were on a trampoline?"

"Would you go touching all the patients?"

"Of course not."

Katy smiled sassily and pointed to the "Don't Pet the Horses" sign hanging from the railing. I refrained from touching my lovely friends as I continued my third round to find the row of three with the dappled rumps. I had seen them but two days earlier; they were, I was certain, right in front of the unfortunately unexciting fellow I had ridden, only I couldn't find him, either. Had the horses been repainted already? Or had some been replaced? I was about to begin my fourth turn around the platform when Katy lured me out of my head.

"I wish Napoleon was a stargazer," she said, straddling a middle horse and standing up in the stirrups to kiss between his ears. "Stargazers are the ones with their heads looking up at the stars. Napoleon's a galloper, just like all the horses on here, even the ones in front of the chariots—usually those guys are standers. Imagine being stuck in the same pose all your life, seeing the exact same thing day after day after day? I'd want to be a stargazer if that was the case. Poor Napoleon, I wish you could see the stars."

Napoleon! He was the first horse I had noticed, and I recalled his being situated three rows behind the constellations. I stepped carefully onto the platform and went to Katy's side, and from there I counted three rows ahead with my finger. One, two, chariot.

"This is not Napoleon," I said. I looked up at Katy, and she shrugged.

"Napoleon is every horse."

"What in hell does that mean?"

Katy rolled her eyes. "Margot, they're all the same. Except for the colour of their saddles and bridles, they're all Napoleons."

"But I saw Napoleon two days ago, and he looked different. And I saw a row of horses with dapples, and now they're gone. Can you explain that?"

Katy gave "Napoleon" another kiss between his ears—which were, I could swear, pointed more forward than those on the first and third horses in his row. She wrapped both hands tightly around the pole, causing it to warp slightly, and swung her right leg over the saddle as she prepared to leap to the platform in a show of foolishness. Fortunately, she met my scowl in time and slipped off her mount quiet as a cat instead.

"The horses always look different when they're the same," she said, sliding the blue elastic band off her ponytail and combing her fingers through her hair. "Some of them used to be brown, did you know that? My dad told me. One day at the start of a new season, a brown horse galloped right off the platform in protest and never came back, and when the replacement horse arrived white, all the horses were painted white since the brown paint mysteriously disappeared. But none of the horses have ever had dapples or different coloured saddles and bridles."

An afternoon with Katy had revealed to me the key to understanding her: Most of what she said (perhaps everything, but I would need more time to confirm this) was rooted in fantasy. Her sense of consequence was exceptionally low. She wasn't a stupid girl, no. In fact, quite regularly, intelligence shimmered across her surface. But she had been, I could tell, raised by a non-dominant hand and voice, and the lack of equanimity in the way she approached everything from conversations with menopausal women to the way she was completely unaware of the space she took up, spoke to me of a motherless girl. That was why I invited her out to have dinner with me that evening.

Katy was as pleased as a freshly shampooed cocker spaniel, and she apologized every other breath for not being dressed appropriately for a fancy dinner, for not having enough cash on her.

"I'll pay you back tomorrow. I promise. Are you sure I'm dressed okay?"

"I said I would treat you, Katy."

"But what about my T-shirt? I can't go to a fancy dinner in a T-shirt. You hate my T-shirt, I can tell."

"Just don't order anything with meat."

My appetite had returned and then some, and I had adjusted to the body-wide ache of having been thrashed around by the Vampire. I wanted nothing more than to sit in a quiet corner of an Italian restaurant and sip house red between bites of a four-cheese pizza. I hoped Katy would run out of things to chatter on about before we reached the restaurant. She was thrilled to be having alcohol legally with a friend who could also legally drink in public.

"I don't do it that much because it really worries my dad. I won't even tell him about tonight."

"You've mentioned him a few times. You're close, I gather?"

As we walked westward on rue Sainte-Catherine, whose sidewalks were congested with storefront shoppers and panhandlers, I felt like a visitor to the city, the way I had often felt upon my return home from a long-distance firearms scavenger hunt. I found comfort in the freedom of being a visitor: instead of thinking of myself as in therapy with my wife and gainfully unemployed, I could think of myself as an unencumbered summer vacationer, familiar enough with the city to give an insider's tour to a friend who had never been, which was practically the case with Katy. En route to the restaurant, she admitted that she came into the city only when the Fortin family went to a Sunday matinée or some festival show. Otherwise, when she wasn't teaching the Fortin children proper English or volunteering at La Ronde, she remained inside the gates of the family's community and swam in the pool or read books from the library.

Once we were seated on the outdoor terrace at Pizzadéli (Katy begged to sit outdoors so she could people-watch), I ordered our drinks, house red for me and a Blue Lagoon cocktail for Katy. Katy fell quiet while she people-watched, and I enjoyed the quiet while I Katy-watched. She had the habit of pressing her tongue against the roof of her mouth, and I wondered if this was psychosomatic or some technique she had been taught to help diminish her lisp. Her fingers were always moving— tapping some surface, wrestling one another, snapping. Her eyes registered emotion before the muscles of her face did, and her mind registered what she said only after she said it. The moment our pizza arrived (I had insisted we split the "cheese medley"), Katy resumed her chatter.

"You never told me if your family liked the pictures."

"Could you not talk with your mouth full?"

Katy covered her full mouth with her napkin. "This is the third time you've avoided my question. Are you barren?"

I chewed my mouthful until it was so tough I couldn't swallow it. Katy slid her Blue Lagoon across the table to me.

"That's the problem with really cheesy pizza," she said. "It turns into rubber and you have to wash it down or else you'll choke. Talk about embarrassing."

I slid the Blue Lagoon back to her and sipped my wine. "I'm not avoiding your question," I said, conscious of the possibility that I had a red wine moustache, but too weary to do anything about it. "I prefer not to talk about my family."

"Well then, can I ask you yes or no questions until you tell me to stop?"

"You may."

"Do you have kids?"

"Shouldn't you ask first if I'm with someone?"

"You can be single and have kids, Margot. Are you with someone?"

"I thought you wanted to know if I have children. Or perhaps you've decided I'm barren."

"This isn't how it works, Margot. Please, just tell me something about you."

"I'm a dual citizen. I was born in Michigan, but I was raised in Québec. Mostly." I summoned the waitress and asked for my derby hat and the bill. Katy tore another slice from the pizza and scarfed it in four bites.

"You could have asked for a take-home box," I said, standing up and dusting flour from my trousers. The waitress returned with the bill, and Katy excused herself to the ladies' room. I said I would meet her at the corner of the street.

I had been successful for the greater part of the day in forgetting that tonight was supposed to be my night with Estelle. Instead, I had treated almost eighteen-year-old Katharine de Wilde of rural New York State to dinner, and I was about to walk back to Le Cabinet Particulier and likely fumble my way through a request to the bellhop to maintain my room indefinitely. The fact that Estelle hadn't phoned or texted all day made me feel insecure about our plans for the weekend ahead. According to Olivier Weinstock's system, we were entitled to a sleepover, but since Estelle always planned everything three days in advance, I wasn't expecting the Weinstock system to work in my favour. I looked at my watch. Right about now, Estelle was probably giving some eloquent speech to the charity dinner guests, standing before them in some spectacular floor-length gown, capturing hearts and inspiring monogrammed chequebooks to flutter open and Mont Blanc pens to scribble like they were in competition with one another. I had to see her. I had to see how everybody else saw her, some unattainable thing of beauty on the other side of the glass, and so when Katy joined me on the street corner, I said, "I feel like a walk after that heavy meal. Come on," and set us off in the direction of my whim.

Thankfully, the benefit dinner was in a ground-floor hotel restaurant on rue Sherbrooke, otherwise I would have encountered some difficulty explaining to Katy what business

we had going into an establishment with a red carpet flanking
its semicircular driveway and two suited, unsmiling men, each
one standing attentive in front of a gold-painted concrete lion.

Two blocks before the hotel, I pretended to search my pockets
for something important.

"Did you leave your credit card at Pizzadeli? Want me to
run back and get it?"

"No, it's not that—but thank you. It completely slipped my
mind that I was supposed to attend a dinner tonight, a charity
event. It's right up there. Mind if we peek in? I want to see if
my boss is there, so I know what story to tell him Monday
morning regarding why I didn't attend."

How fluent I was becoming in the art of lying! I briefly considered blaming this instance on the second glass of red wine
I had indulged in at dinner, but as I sensed Katy's hesitation in
the way she slowed her pace, I knew I had to remain focused
on my goal. Just a few seconds was all it would take for me to
spot Estelle, and it would be easy. The restaurant's wall facing
rue Sherbrooke was essentially one large window, and there
were Gothic-style wrought iron benches in front of the window,
where smokers could enjoy after-dinner conversation along
with their stimulants. Katy and I would sit on a bench, and I
would tell her I was motherless; surely this would launch her
into a self-involved ramble during which I could steal glances
into the restaurant.

But as we waited for the streetlight to turn green and I looked
ahead, there she was, standing in front of the benches, elegant
in an evening gown as I had expected, a strapless cobalt taffeta
one I had never seen in her wardrobe, with pastel grey opera
gloves defining her arms the way white wraps define a Prix St.
Georges dressage horse's legs. She was conversing gaily with a
gathering of tuxedoed men and gowned women seated on the
benches, leather-bound chequebooks balanced on the knees of
the men, gaudy rhinestone-studded European import clutches
tucked under the bare slender arms of the women. Estelle was

the only one smoking. She looked like an orchestra conductor expecting a standing ovation as she raised her hand with the silver cigarette holder to punctuate her soliloquy before she puffed on the cigarette. (I would have to be crafty, later, about how I incited her to confess she had broken her promise of twenty years to me.)

Katy grabbed me by the ribcage and begged me away from the street. "Holy shit!"

Although I regarded her as a girl sorely in need of refinement, I was surprised to hear her swear. Profanity didn't suit the profile of someone who still believed in the childhood stories from her father, about how carousel horses could steal paint and gallop off into sunsets.

"We can't go over there. I'm a slob! Is that Gwyneth Paltrow? It's Gwyneth Paltrow, isn't it?" She pulled me along as she babbled. She was as stunned as I was.

"No, that's not Gwyneth Paltrow."

"So you know who it is. Tell me. Is that your boss?"

I shook Katy from me and turned us back toward rue Sainte-Catherine. The thing to do was find out where she lived, and either propose to put her in a taxicab or walk her to the corresponding metro station. However, she wouldn't stop babbling like a star-struck fool until I told her about the blonde. I had never heard anyone compare Estelle with Gwyneth Paltrow (I could scarcely picture what the actress looked like), and I was a little envious of Katy. When was the last time I had rejoiced over something so utterly inconsequential?

"Katy, you must calm yourself. I assure you, that woman is neither Gwyneth Paltrow nor my boss nor anyone I know. In fact, since I don't have the address with me, it's possible I've confused the location of the charity event."

When we reached rue Sainte-Catherine, I asked Katy how she would get to the Fortins' home.

"I'll go back to La Ronde and start over from there."

"That's nonsense."

"It's the only way I know how. I told you, I never come into the city."

I calculated in my head how much it would cost to send Katy home by taxicab, and then I took out my wallet to make sure I had enough cash to follow through. She put her hands up when I counted out eighty dollars. "You can give me the change next time I see you."

"Nuh-uh. No way. You already paid for dinner."

"*Bonsoir,*" I said to the taxi driver. "My friend is designated for L'Île-des-Sœurs." I was pleased to have waved him over on my first try. Unless I was with Estelle, for whom drivers veered across busy intersections, normally I had to either schedule a pickup by telephone or walk the extra blocks to a taxi stand.

I opened the rear passenger door for Katy. She gave me a look of reproach but ducked inside the car. She didn't roll down the window to protest more after I closed the door, which meant perhaps she was as ready to end our day as I was.

CHARITY EVENTS ESTELLE attended for work always carried well into the night, so I knew I had enough time to go to the loft and collect some items to see me through the next days. I wanted my Sensodyne toothpaste, not Le Cabinet's granulated complimentary brand. I wanted fresh clothes and my straw Panama hat (why hadn't I recognized sooner how preposterous it was to wear my derby hat in August?), and I wanted a moment on my mohair settee to sip loose-leaf peppermint tea. All of this I could accomplish in under one hour. After Estelle arrived home and phoned me to ask why I hadn't waited on her, I would say I was respecting her boundaries. As I climbed the stairwell to our floor, I prepared myself to feel like a visitor in my own home, which would surely be more disconcerting than feeling like a visitor in my home city. We were still moving in, had personalized parts of rooms rather than entire rooms, and who knew now how long it would take for the task to be complete?

My hand shook as I tried to fit the key into the lock. I dropped my keychain twice and cursed out loud. The man in the loft across from ours peeked into the hallway and asked if everything was all right. He looked as new to me as he had the day we moved in, or like I hadn't seen him in a year when I had passed him in the stairwell the day before on my way to Olivier Weinstock's. Time was behaving unsympathetically, denying me even the mundane comforts of my reality.

The loft was dark except for the recessed lights under the kitchen cabinets. The iPad above the kitchen sink was programmed to *Radio-Classique*. Estelle's confusing arty vase from the bathroom was now on the temporary Ikea table, and it boasted an arrangement of flowers whose stems appeared freshly cut on the diagonal, and whose fragrance I found invasive.

Hissss-hissss!

I leaned on the table to collect myself. My guilt over being here was so powerful that it was causing me to hear things.

Hissss-hiss-hissss!

The noise sounded like it was right beside me, though, not inside me, and when I moved away from the table, two inimical Siamese faces glared up from underneath. They curled their lips and bared their vampiric little teeth: Wolfgang and Puzzle, the evilest cats known to mankind. I set off pacing in an attempt to compose myself; no, I would not let my conscience frighten me off with hallucinations. But the cats, as real as the thundering in my chest, followed at my heels, hissing and spitting and swatting at my oxfords. Whenever I reached the endpoint of a room and turned around, the cats scrambled in front of me and arched their seal-point bodies into serpent shapes to prevent me from getting away. They became particularly aggressive the second time I entered the bathroom and tried to close the door so I could relieve myself. Puzzle, or Wolfgang (I couldn't tell the damned things apart), howled when his body got caught between the door and the doorframe, prompting the other cat to leap four feet in the air and through the opening so he could accost me from inside the bathroom and liberate his friend. He wrapped himself around my calf and tried to climb my leg, though mercifully he had been declawed on all fours, so the best he could manage was to hold on tightly and sink his teeth into my flesh. Even there, he failed. His teeth caught on the fabric of my trousers and I was able to shake him off before he could try again. He fell to the floor and slid across the tiles, where he stayed and growled until his companion realized he was no longer caught between the door and the doorframe and was free to rescue his rescuer. I still had to relieve myself, and I decided to do so with the cats where they were, since they had become involved in grooming away each other's trauma, and their ears didn't so much as flicker when I crooned their names.

"Thatta boy, Puzzle. Thatta boy, Wolfgang. I despise you more than all the arty vases in the world. You're terrible, ugly creatures. Why are you here? Did your mother abandon you in a garbage dump? Did she..."

"GoGo?"

Estelle stood in the bathroom doorway, pigeon-toed and limp-armed, her voice small and hopeful like a girl's on Christmas morning when she discovers all the presents under the tree. *Are they really all for me?* Both of our minds were playing tricks on us.

"Hello, Estelle." I pressed the issue of *Cigar Aficionado* I had been thumbing through onto my bare thighs, and wiped the sudden perspiration from my face with the ball of toilet paper I had fashioned in case the cats decided to collude against me while I was compromised.

Estelle dropped her handbag on the floor and leaned woefully against the doorframe. "I must be fucking *grisée* out of my mind."

"I came to collect a few things, then I'll be on my way."

The cats were unfazed by the presence of another person; Puzzle (or Wolfgang) was lying on his back, limbs akimbo while his companion licked and kneaded his belly.

"You couldn't wait until tomorrow?" Estelle kneeled down for her handbag and recovered a tin of mints. She shook the remnants of the tin into her mouth. My impulse to inform her I had seen her smoking seemed entirely ill-timed, and creepy. I would have to wait until my pants were up before saying anything incendiary.

"I didn't know we had plans for tomorrow."

"Of course we do. We just talked about it this morning. *Dieu*. Why do I feel like you're trespassing?"

"Trespassing? You're joking. Elle."

"Don't call me that. Not right now." Estelle swung the bathroom door shut. The cats sprang to all fours and stared at me like they were ready for another round of "cops and robber." I threw the balled toilet paper at them and hiked up my trousers.

I found Estelle on my settee, nursing a syrupy amber liquid from a tumbler. She had an icepack across her forehead.

"Hurry up, get your stuff. I'll call you in the morning," she said, keeping her eyes closed.

I went to the burled walnut futon across from the settee. The cats trotted over and jumped onto the futon to resume their spa.

"Why are they here? You know I hate cats. You know I especially hate Marianne's cats."

Wolfgang (or Puzzle) yawned his body long on the futon cushion, until his head was pushed against my leg. Puzzle (or Wolfgang) sat on top of him and regarded me not with hostility but with adulation, or so I assumed since he kept squinting at me.

Estelle threw her icepack across the room and the cats became two blurs vanishing down the hallway.

"Now look what you've done," I said.

"I told Marianne I would look after them. She's going through a divorce. You know this."

"I thought that already happened?"

"Really? You think a divorce ends as soon as you sign the

papers? *Fantastique*. I'll keep that in mind." Estelle stood
and pointed to the door. "You can get everything you need
tomorrow. You can spend the day and pack a whole box if
you want." Her voice had that familiar *I dare you* edge to it,
and she was certainly drunk enough, but I was too distracted
to test those waters. I didn't like how she kept looking at the
wall clock above the futon.

"Have somewhere to be?"

"Yes. In bed. I really fucking want you to leave, Margot. It's
not your night."

And then it hit me. Between my wife's overreaction to finding me in our loft, and Puzzle (or Wolfgang) stampeding back
into the living room and reminding me how strongly I disliked
Marianne, it hit me: "You're sleeping with her. That's why you
want me out of here, isn't it? Marianne's on her way over so
you two can fuck like you fucked last night after you went
clubbing. Or did you fuck in the bathroom *while* you were
clubbing? Are you letting her experiment with you until she
finds a new man with deep pockets to marry? Are you going
to look for matching men? Twenty-five years with a woman
long enough for you? Or are you trying to convert Marianne?
Tell me, Estelle, tell me all about it. Are you going to rename
the cats and play house together?"

Once I started, I couldn't stop. The recriminations and the
wild assumptions came forth in torrents, while Estelle squeezed
her fists to her temples and backed away from me. I pushed
her against the wall with my demands for answers. I dragged
tears down her cheeks with the threat of never looking back
after I left that night. All of what was mine would be hers to
deal with, and she would never be able to shred the letters
from my parents without reading them first, and so she was
welcome to read them all until her heart renewed for me, when
she realized I had protected her, not lied to her, but I wouldn't
be there anymore. By the time I did leave, Estelle was locked
in the bathroom with her tumbler of amber.

How could Marianne be vulturing in so soon to take my place? Or maybe something had been brewing between the two beforehand? Maybe they had been secret lovers since grad school in Savannah—the timing made perfect sense, since that was when Estelle got bit by the "I need to see more of the world" bug, and I felt convinced I was going to lose her. I was too distressed to catalogue all the occasions when I might have missed cues, but I couldn't return to my hotel room until I had proof of my conviction—which I would deliver to Olivier Weinstock at dawn's break. No. I would wait until Estelle's next individual appointment with him, the following Thursday at two p.m., when I would drop in to share the news. How I delivered the news was immaterial if I didn't have any news to deliver, so I had to begin my quest immediately, in the alleyway between our loft building and the neighbouring one. I was going to wait there until I saw Marianne (had my Blackberry been equipped with a camera, I could have photographed her slipping into the building, but my model was basic and dated). Thankfully, the night was clear and calm, so I could attenuate my nerves by looking at the stars or by listening to the music carrying from side-street bistros and bars.

"Excuse me, ma'am, but would you happen to have some change you could spare?"

I looked to my left and then to my right, but I did not see anybody.

"Back here," the voice beckoned. A finger poked my shoulder.

I would have jumped out of my skin had I been the type to do such a thing, but even faced with a potential fate as compelling as being mugged, I was at best able to issue an audible grunt.

When I turned around, ready to receive my divine punishment for having yelled so cruelly at Estelle, I was met by the kind expression of a young man holding a stick with a neatly bundled cloth sac hanging from its top. Why was it that lately, a motley of strangers seemed drawn to features about my person that had once drawn Estelle to me—features that had begun, one by one, to repel her from me.

"Sir, have you any idea how threatening it is to a woman standing alone in an alleyway at night when an unfamiliar man materializes from the dark and asks her for money?"

The vagabond leaned his stick on the ground. "I'm sorry. It's just here you are. Also, you don't seem very threatened."

"Certainly not," I said, preferring that my legs were shaking rather than my voice. "And if you were to ask me the same question in the morning—though you would have to be on the street, because I don't normally hang out in alleyways—I'd be happy to give you some change."

"Do you have any now?"

I stepped back onto the sidewalk and gestured for the man to follow. He hoisted his stick over his shoulder and stepped into the lamplight.

"Perhaps you'd like the keys to my loft?" I said, feeling in my pockets for change. "I don't seem to live there anymore, and I can't stand the tenant in my wake, so if you're quick, you can snap up the space."

We conversed comfortably for a spell. I learned the man was twenty-one, from a struggling fishing town in the Maritimes, and that he had come to Montréal in hopes of living like *un bohème*, only he didn't speak enough French and it turned out bohemian life was not government-subsidized like he had heard and thus required one to earn a living.

"I've decided to go back home, but I want to pay my own way so no one knows how badly I messed up."

The click of heels on cobblestone echoed toward us (otherwise we were the only ones on the street), so I shoved the young man back into the alleyway. He understood when I placed a finger on my lips and cupped an ear, and he backed farther into the shadows while I watched the sidewalk like a deer hunter. *Click-click, click-click, click-click.* It could have been any woman coming toward us, but I knew it was Marianne. It had to be. Estelle had wanted me out quickly, before Marianne arrived, and not even ten minutes had passed since my departure. The timing was right.

I had degraded into some wretched, single-minded thing. I had turned into a fusty old bat. Hovering in the alleyway alongside the loft I had purchased for my wife, pinning my blind eyes to the liposuctioned, sequined ass that swaggered past. The vagabond slipped farther into the shadows during the lull in our conversation, and I was relieved to discover he hadn't picked my trousers pocket, though he wouldn't have needed skill to thieve a wallet half hanging out.

"Hello?" I called after him. "I was joking about the keys, of course, but I would be happy to help you get back to your old life. A train ticket or bus fare, perhaps? Hello?"

Rodents scurried as rodents do in midnight alleyways. A window on the second floor of a neighbouring loft complex slid open, and a silhouetted man leaned outside and sought to confirm he was not imagining voices. I pressed against the brick and shimmied to the lamp-lit sidewalk and walked north to rue Saint-Jacques, where I whistled for a taxicab.

*B*EGIN WITH TIE AROUND NECK. *The left end (A) must be longer than the right end (B). Cross A over B then tuck* A *into hole between neck and tie. Fold B at widest part and hold sideways....*

My thumbs and forefingers cramped. I stood in front of the bathroom mirror, stuck on the same step I got stuck on every time. It was my umpteenth try, and failure was not an option. With mounting despair, I referred once more to my father's issue of *Esquire Fortnightly*, spread over the sink. Maybe the diagram was missing a step? What if "A" was really "B"? My father frequently complained about typographical errors in the newspaper, so why wouldn't *Esquire* be susceptible to the same problem? According to "How to Make Manliness Look Easy," the magazine's feature article extolling the virtues of approaching every task big and small in a methodical way, a man could achieve the perfect bowtie in just six steps and walk out of the house as put-together and important as Hugh Hefner. I didn't know who Hugh Hefner was, but it was of highest priority that I achieve the perfect bowtie if I was to meet Les Nessman.

"Margot, *dépêche-toi*. We have to leave soon."

I threw myself backward against the door when my mother jiggled the handle. If she found me fumbling to get ready, she would either moan like I had already ruined her evening, or she would fix me up with the skill of an *Esquire* man's wife. I didn't want her to do either. I was going to do it myself. I was eleven years old.

"*Chérie*," she said, tapping her long nails on the door, "we're going to be late for the concert. Aren't you excited for the concert?"

I was not. I didn't know any of The Who's songs, and I thought the band's name was dumb. I couldn't form it into words, but I could sense the band's failed attempt at cleverness. And even if the music turned out to be enjoyable, my enjoyment would be underscored by the dumb band name, the way a good book could be ruined by a bad title.

It was our annual family vacation. The tradition had started three years before, after my mother exiled me from Wellfleet to Saint-Télesphore to live with her parents while she worked things out with her husband. This time we were in Cincinnati, hardly a desirable place to "vacation" in December. We had spent the previous years in Honolulu, Charleston, and San Diego, all places my mother had begged my father for, but this year my father's business overlapped with her pleasure. One of Wright & Ellis's prominent shareholders lived in Cincinnati and had expressed interest in financing a retail outlet in the city. The people of Cincy played billiards, too, though they preferred to call it "pool," and their working-class incomes couldn't support the high-end models. Nonetheless, business was business, and Morgan Wright, albeit still virile and dashing, was fifty-four and didn't want to work forever.

So, he indulged my mother's every whim in Cincinnati to keep her from setting off in public and tarnishing his professional reputation. Her first complaint was about our accommodations: she didn't like the Netherland Plaza's "burnt out" look, and she believed that an establishment with eight hundred guestrooms invited all sorts of criminal potentials.

"This place is like a small city. I could get mugged on my way to the tea room."

After the bellhop delivered our bags to a top-floor suite with an Art Deco-themed living room and a lovely view of the Ohio River, she flopped onto the tan leather elephant arm sofa and bemoaned her lack of privacy.

"You can't get more private than a penthouse," my father said, going to the minibar by the view window to examine his options. "Look, Marguerite, they have three different types of brandy."

My mother lit one of her menthols and let her hand with the cigarette hang over the sofa, dangerously close to the rug. "Oh, Morgan. This is supposed to be my *vacation* time. Why didn't you get a separate room for her? *Elle est une grande fille maintenant.*"

That night, after my mother fell into a brandied stupor, snoring and drooling all over their bed sheets, my father came to my room, which was on the floor below. He flipped his starched shirt collar up to his chin when I opened the door, and then crept in like Inspector Clouseau. These antics had amused me when I was five and even eight, when I was so happy to see him after his travels that I accepted any behaviour from him, but this time I felt testy and uncomfortable. I hadn't seen him since the December before. I hadn't seen my mother since the summer, but at least she phoned me at *grandmère* and *grand-père* Soucy's every Sunday to ask about my week. Whenever I asked about my father, she changed the subject to all the gifts he had brought home for me, which, when she remembered, she would bundle together and mail to Québec.

My father sat on the bed. He was dressed in brown- and gold-checkered slacks, a pale yellow shirt, and a brown smoking jacket with gold lapels. He produced an issue of *Esquire Fortnightly* from his smoking jacket, along with a sleek gift-wrapped box.

I had grown bored with his continuous, predictable gifts, but the magazine piqued my interest. Most often, gifts from my father seemed like gifts for someone else's daughter—porcelain dolls decorated like Indian tribe girls or Geishas, "Farrah and

Cher's Glamour and Makeup Center," and my first recipe card filing system, made with real Bakelite. My mother claimed those were all the gifts he got for me, but I knew differently. She had been hiding and throwing away the ones that didn't meet her approval. I had seen it with my own eyes that summer in Wellfleet, one chilly evening when she asked me to gather wood from the shed behind the house. There, in a box the size of a chesterfield, I discovered unopened miniature models of Wright & Ellis billiard tables, a battery-operated reproduction of Amelia Earhart's Lockheed Model Ten Electra, a pine and steel handcrafted train set of the Susquehanna railroad, and an illustrated history of the musket. All things I would have loved.

Before I opened the box, my father reclaimed it and made me promise not to tell my mother. "Or make sure you put it on first," he said, winking. "Then she won't be able to resist how smart you look."

It was a truly excellent gift: a beige velvet bowtie with little silver sows all over it. The sort of bowtie Les Nessman of *WKRP in Cincinnati* wore.

"I hear you've been watching the show up in Québec."

"Anaïs really likes it. We watch it together. Her favourite is Jennifer. The secretary? I like Les Nessman. He's a very serious person."

"You should really call her *grandmère*."

"She told me not to. She says it makes her feel old. When can I come back home for good? I heard Anaïs talking to mom last week on the phone, and she asked the same thing."

"Do you have any friends where you are? Do you still read a lot?"

Perhaps I should have been devastated by how little my father knew about my life with the Soucys, but I had succumbed to the magic of the bowtie with the silver sows.

My father opened the magazine to the how-to diagram.

"So!" he said, clapping his hands after we stared awkwardly at the diagram for a spell. "Why don't I use your shower, so I don't wake your mother?" He slipped his smoking jacket off and folded it neatly on a corner of the bed, and then opened the bottom drawer of the dresser, where he had ferreted away toiletries and fresh underclothes after arranging for my separate room. "I have to meet a business associate for late-night drinks. You know how it is."

Of course I didn't know how it was with business associates and late-night drinks. I was eleven years old. But I had begun to form an idea of how it was in the world of my parents, and I felt briefly sorry for my mother, numbed and alone, splayed gracelessly across the most expensive king-size bed in all of Cincinnati.

Before my father closed himself in the bathroom, he said, "I hear your mother's taking you to a little show tomorrow? That should be nice."

"A rock concert."

"Don't be silly, Margot. That's for grownups."

"I'm telling you," I yawned, closing the magazine and placing it on the night table so I could fold down the sheets. I wasn't tired in the least, but I felt embarrassed by my father's cluelessness, and I didn't want any more awkward interactions between us. Also, I wanted him to leave so I could practise my bowtie, which I was going to wear to the concert—the perfect occasion. My mother, I was pretty sure, didn't own any rock-style clothes (though I didn't know what rock-style clothes looked like, exactly), so we could stick out like sore thumbs together, and since we were in the homeland of Les Nessman, people would understand and praise my bowtie, because, naturally, everybody in Cincinnati watched the show. I hadn't taken time before the trip to meditate on any of its positive features. It had been such a hassle for the Soucys to drive me to the airport (Benoît was a nervous driver, and Anaïs was a nervous backseat driver), and once we arrived, then came the hassle of finding my mother, who had flown up from the U.S. to get me, and who was flabbergasted that she would have to fly back at the end of our trip to return me to her parents.

"I don't understand why Morgan won't let you go by yourself, the way I sent you here when you were eight. You did fine, and that was on a bus with no stewardesses to bring you juice and peanuts."

The ordeal had seemed to last longer than the trip was going to last, but now that I was here and tempers had quelled, my mind flowered with possibilities. Maybe before we saw The Who, we could visit the WKRP radio station! I knew the show was make-believe, but that didn't mean we couldn't bump into the actors, who obviously lived in the city since the show took place there. While I wouldn't turn my nose up at Johnny Fever or Venus Flytrap if I passed them on the street, I cared only about meeting Les Nessman. I didn't know the actor's name, because it wasn't important. I imagined the man who played the charmingly hapless news reporter was so involved in his role that he dressed and talked like him even when he wasn't in front of the camera. I loved Les Nessman for his matter-of-fact manner and his lovely bowties, and this was the first thing I was going to tell him. Once his other fans finished pestering him to autograph their TV guides and memo pads, I would emerge, solemn and humble, and ask if he wanted to go to the concert with my mother and me. It would be the event of the century.

"If you don't come out of the bathroom *immédiatement*, Margot Anaïs Soucy, I will leave without you."

It was hopeless. I was never going to get it right. Why hadn't my father taught me how? What good was an illustrated diagram without the guiding voice of a father? I opened the door and scowled. "I'm not going."

My mother tugged at the bowtie, which was hanging loose around my neck. "What's this?"

"You wouldn't get it."

"Don't be such a baby. *Tiens*." Her fingers consorted with the beige velvet, and in what seemed fewer than the six illustrated steps in *Esquire*, I was sporting a perfect bowtie to complement the russet blouse my father had purchased for me after breakfast, when he brought us to the boutique in the hotel lobby.

"Now look," my mother said, turning me to face the mirror so I could watch her. She eyed the diagram over the sink and sighed. "You're a bit young to be practising, *chérie*, and I predict these will soon go out of style, but I suppose it's a good skill to have in case you ever date a boy who can't do it for himself. I don't know why your father couldn't get a room for you on the same floor as ours. Now I have to go back upstairs to get my coat."

As usual, my mother was dressed for a glamour photo shoot. Even though she was twenty-three years younger than my father, he never dissuaded her from taking every measure to preserve her beauty, no matter how much it cost him. She went to a hair stylist that afternoon to have her roots filled in so she looked natural, and she let my father purchase a mink shawl for her, which was hideously inappropriate for a rock concert, even I knew that, and it smelled like chemicals.

"Where's Dad?" I asked, when she met me at the elevator.

"*Tu sais*, he has places to be and women to please other than you and me."

There was a musical energy to her words, even though I knew they meant something ugly. As we waited for the elevator to reach the ground floor of the Netherlands Plaza, I pictured my father giving furs and other excesses to pretty blondes like the ones on Hugh Hefner's arms, on the cover of *Esquire Fortnightly*. My mother was perfectly content right then, and my father had made her that way. Now he was on his way to make another woman happy, or maybe two women happy. Maybe that was all he knew how to do, aside from being a successful businessman. And what was so wrong about that, really? Being good at your job and at making women happy? I would have preferred if he were devoted entirely to my mother and me, but maybe men weren't capable of such devotion—unless they stayed single like Les Nessman and focused entirely on their work. I appreciated Les Nessman's dedication, but wouldn't it be nice for him if he found that one person he wanted to be with forever?

The taxicab dropped us off at the Riverfront Coliseum at six p.m. There was a swollen mass of people waiting to get in. Apparently everyone knew about The Who except for my father and me. I had never been near so many people, and I didn't like how they dropped lit cigarettes on the ground and forgot all about them while they drank from brown paper bags and shouted song lyrics like war cries over one another's heads. This all confirmed what I already thought of the band. The agreed-upon dress code seemed to be open trench coats, T-shirts with images of the band on them, and jeans and sneakers, so my mother and I really *did* stick out like sore thumbs. A guy in line in front of us, shirtless (in the cold of winter no less), with the band's name written in black marker all over his torso, said his name was Pete and then asked my mother if she was media, probably because she was dressed so imperiously.

"Yes I am," she said, flashing her red lips and placing a matching manicured hand on his forearm. "Do you know if there's a separate line for media? I just arrived to the city an hour ago. Damn this jet lag."

"Man, I dunno," Pete said, accepting a menthol from my mother, though not lighting it after he realized it was menthol. "If there's a line for media, it's been swallowed by The Beast. I've been here since three-thirty. I heard people started lining up since one-thirty."

My mother moved close to Pete and whispered in his ear. She slid a folded twenty-dollar bill into his hand.

"Hey, Bruce," he yelled up the line. "Bruce!"

A guy with fly-away feathered hair stalked over to us. He was wearing a yellow vest with reflective tape down the front, and he seemed blasé.

"Bruce, man, could you take this nice lady up to the front?

She's media." Pete intonated these last words.

Bruce pretended not to be associated with us when a trio of policemen walked slowly by. The officers paused to glower and make us feel criminal. After they moved on, their hands close to the pieces holstered to their sides, Bruce gave my mother a once-over. She whisked loose strands of hair from her face and posed like a person of influential lineage.

"I'd be very grateful for any help you wish to extend," she said throatily.

Bruce grunted and pointed at me. "No kids allowed."

"Of course. Her father will be back any minute. You'll wait for him here, won't you, *chérie?*"

My mother was going to sacrifice me to The Beast! It had been her plan all along, her way to punish my father for making her fly all over North America. She had willfully suppressed her madness with brandy and spending sprees until this evening. But I was fine with us each going our separate ways. I would have so many opportunities to find Les Nessman. Someone here had to know him or his whereabouts. My mother slipped a twenty to Bruce, and the two vanished toward the front of the line. I turned my attention to Pete.

"I'm not your babysitter, kid," he said, squirming like he had just been touched by a lizard.

"I don't need a babysitter. I want to ask you something."

"Fine, but you have to smoke this first." Pete lit my mother's menthol and shoved it in my face. He laughed when I stumbled backwards and fell. His teeth were uneven and yellow. "Whoa, kid, *chill.* I'm just joking."

"Do you know where I can find WKRP?" I asked, scurrying to my feet before getting trampled by people who didn't know I was on the ground.

"What the fuck is that?"

"I mean the place where WKRP is taped."

"Say what?"

"Don't you watch TV? It's a show made right here in Cincinnati. It has Johnny Fever and Venus Flytrap, and Jennifer, the secretary with the very blonde hair."

Pete snorted cigarette smoke out of his nostrils and punched a guy in the arm who was standing beside him. "Hey, Mikey, this brother with a bowtie here's got a thing for Loni Anderson. He thinks she's foxxxx-ay."

"I'm a girl, actually, and I'm looking for the man with the round glasses who plays Les Nessman. The news reporter?"

The guy who got punched in the arm hovered forward and tousled my head. His hand was sticky and pulled on my hair.

"Ouch!"

"Hey, kid," he said, swatting at me with his brown paper bag. "Why don't you find Roger Daltry and ask him to write a song about freak wankers? Oh wait, I think he has already. It goes like '*I'm a boy, I'm a boy, but my ma won't admit it. I'm a boy, I'm a boy, but if I say I am, I get it.*'"

And then all the guys and girls as far as the eye could see broke into song and jostled one another and had the time of their lives, and I was used-up space. I set off running. Someone opened a can of soda pop that sprayed all over me as I groped for the back of the line, which was much farther away than when I had arrived with my mother. I called out for her, spurned as I felt, because the reflex in a girl to ask her mother for help takes a lifetime to deactivate. Even if my mother had been nearby, she wouldn't have found me amid all the hoopla. And she wouldn't have wanted to. No one noticed me except to push me away when I tried to squeeze past, not even the policemen, who seemed to be everywhere now, rushing toward the coliseum. It occurred to me how easy it would be to pick wallets out of coat pockets and purses along my way. Since I was penniless and feeling increasingly nauseated from being rammed around and spat on, I paused to consider one girl's cloth backpack, its drawstring mouth wide open.

"Hello, there," the girl said, acknowledging my presence.

I wiggled the drawstring. "You're going to lose everything."

"Awwww, you're so sweet."

"Where's the Netherlands Plaza from here?"

"Are you lost?"

"I need to get to the place where *WKRP in Cincinnati* is taped."

"I'm sorry, where's that?"

I didn't have the energy to explain myself again, even though the girl was curious and started walking with me as I continued my exit. She held my hand as we walked, and I felt moored. The space was opening up. People at the crowd's extremity seemed content to chat civilly and wait their turns.

"Are you here on some kind of school fieldtrip?" the girl asked, taking a second to straighten my bowtie. "You poor thing, you must be scared out of your mind."

Les Nessman receded from my thoughts as the girl untied the red bandana from around her neck and patted me dry, licked her thumb to rub something off my cheek, knelt to eye-level and said her name was Robin. I liked being fussed over by Robin. She was the prettiest girl I had ever seen, prettier than my mother and Hugh Hefner's coterie of women, and she wasn't shy or apologetic or angry about it.

The tone of the evening shifted. More police officers darted past, and the air thickened with a unanimous roar that rippled from the Riverfront Coliseum to where we stood. Robin let go of my hand and jumped up and down to see what was happening. People around us who had been standing quietly threw their arms in the air and hooted.

"If you go up Broadway and turn left on East Third Street, you'll find lots of places to ask for help, okay? Good luck!" Robin hugged me and kissed the top of my head. I watched her disappear into The Beast and hoped she wouldn't lose all of her belongings. The mouth of her cloth backpack was still wide open.

I followed Robin's directions and got to East Third Street. Police cars, ambulances, and a fire truck whizzed by, and their competing sirens somehow made me realize how hungry I was. I hadn't eaten since breakfast, because I had spent the afternoon locked in the bathroom trying to achieve the perfect bowtie. When I got to Sycamore Street, I asked an elderly lady walking her Miniature Schnauzer for directions, and I found my way back to the Netherlands Plaza. I took the elevator to the penthouse floor and knocked on my parents' door. My father was casual in a navy-blue velour bathrobe. He was enjoying a cigar.

"Come," he said, inviting me to the living room, where the television was set to a local news station. I sat beside him on the sofa and grabbed a handful of Planters Cheez Balls from the tin between us. The reporter was speaking from inside a helicopter, and below him was the Riverfront Coliseum. The crowd was gone, but there were still a lot of people milling about. There was litter everywhere. The view from the helicopter wasn't the sharpest, but I could make out the police cars, ambulances, and the fire truck that had passed me on East Third Street. It looked like EMTs were unloading stretchers from the ambulances. The screen zoomed in to a puffy-eyed guy who spoke in quavering sprints. "People were climbing the walls ... I mean, the girl that went down next to me? No one heard her screaming for help ... I tried to help her, but there was no room to move ... it started when they opened the doors then closed them ... I mean, people got mad ... then it just got crazy, and now I didn't get in 'cause I tried to help, so I've wasted my ticket." The screen zoomed out when the guy started to sob, and the sound cut off, which made the scene of motionless bodies covered with white blankets all the more inconceivable. The white-sneakered feet of one body twitched after an EMT draped a blanket over it, but the EMT didn't check to see if the person was still alive.

My father pulled my head to his chest as he fumbled for the remote control. "Jesus, you shouldn't be watching this. I'm sorry, kiddo. Are you hungry? You scarfed down all those cheese balls. Where's your mother? Shall we go find her and have a late dinner?"

I threw up all over his bathrobe. I said, "That's where Mom is," and then ran to the bathroom and threw up some more.

I expected my father to be long gone when I returned to the living room, but he was not. He had changed into a business suit, and he was speaking to someone on the phone while he shined a pair of pleated dress shoes.

"You're fine like you are," he said, inspecting my clothes and hair.

"Where are we going? I don't understand. What's happened to Mom?" I had never behaved hysterically around my father, but then nothing momentous ever happened when he was around. His visitor's role in my life had granted him the ease of experiencing me in my best moments. I waited for him to seize my shoulders and shake me like my mother sometimes did, maybe even smack me across the face, but instead he smoothed the frizz from my hair and puffed on his cigar.

"One day, your mother will learn."

"Is she hurt? Is she okay? Do you know for sure she's okay?"

"*Okay* is perhaps not the right word to describe how your mother is, Margot, but let's not get all excited around her at the police station."

My father was speaking the language of adults to me, but I couldn't grasp the subtext. That he seemed in no rush to get to my mother, however, helped me calm down. As we waited in front of the hotel for a taxicab, I began to worry for Robin. Even though I knew it was a part of life to meet people I would never see again, I wished I had never met her, because I had no way of knowing if she was one of the bodies under a white blanket.

We waited at the police station for two hours before my mother was booked and released. Her brilliant idea to pay her way to the front of the line had almost gotten her killed, but she was more concerned with how much money she had wasted.

"And then I get arrested for being in the wrong place at the wrong time? The nerve of that officer. I told him I'm going to report him."

"Report him to whom, Marguerite? And for what? Do you know what happened tonight? Do you have the faintest idea about the catastrophe that occurred?" My father was cross at having been made to wait alongside parents summoned to the station to account for their wild teenage kids, but he was more upset that he couldn't possibly open a Wright & Ellis retail outlet in Cincinnati now.

"Why do you always change the subject when I'm talking about something important, Morgan? Don't you care about how I'm feeling after almost being trampled to death? I saw someone right beside me get *killed*." My mother raved while we walked to the taxicab that my father had commissioned to wait for us. She mourned the damage to her brand-new mink shawl and pointed urgently to a bruise on her wrist.

My father opened the car door and shooed me inside. He closed the door and turned at my mother, and I heard every word.

"I can't open a store here, because my wife just got arrested for reckless behaviour at a rock concert for kids. Are you that stupid, Marguerite? What if your daughter had been trampled to death? You could be charged with murder."

"Don't be ridiculous, Morgan. I wouldn't have trampled my own daughter to death. And she's your daughter, too."

"I give you everything. All I ask for in return is that you not act like a lunatic. Do I have to put you back in that place for longer? Do you want to stay in there for the rest of your life?"

My mother howled and started hitting him with her purse until the strap broke off. I jammed my face between my knees and covered my ears with my elbows, but I heard my father strike her. She pressed a palm to her cheek as she settled warily into the back of the cab with me. My father sat in front with the driver. My mother smelled of perfume soured from excessive perspiration, and of urine. The driver coughed and asked if we wished to return to the Netherlands Plaza, and my father said yes. The driver apologized for the high fare, but two hours was a long time to wait, and my father said of course.

After a long silence, my mother hugged me against her and kissed the top of my head. "I'm so relieved you weren't there, *chérie*. It was a jungle. You were smart to leave." She turned toward me and held me at arm's length, and her tone cooled when her eyes fell on my bowtie. "*Franchement*, Margot, Halloween was a month ago."

JUST TWO WEEKS AFTER Estelle had pursued me from rue Saint-Paul to rue de la Commune to inquire about my trilby hat, I was in love with her. We were in her semi-basement studio apartment on Towers Street, three blocks from where she had studied art at Cégep Dawson. Estelle spread her favourite LPs across the floor: Prince's *Sign 'O' the Times*, Bryan Ferry's *In Your Mind*, The Smiths' *Strangeways, Here We Come*, and Québec folk records my grandparents also owned.

I scooped up an album featuring a sombre Frenchman sitting on a bale of hay. He was playing wooden spoons against his knees, while the blue cow behind him looked onward with languorous ennui. She had white trebles and clefs painted all over her body. "You sure like some gay music," I said.

Estelle huffed. "My family plays this every June twenty-fourth. You should come this year."

I grinned crookedly and slapped my thighs, the way I imagined people did at rural Québec shindigs.

"I'm surprised your grandparents never brought you to a *Saint-Jean* celebration. That's true *québecois* culture." She held up a compilation of The Who's greatest hits.

"Absolutely not."

"Too bad. You only get one exchange."

"I'm serious. I don't like them. Please don't."

The studio apartment grew smaller, and the aroma of Estelle's homemade marinara sauce turned putrid like cigarette smoke and urine. I wondered if I was experiencing a flashback like the sort popularized by the "Purple Haze" and "White Lightning" acid tab crowd. Estelle grew smaller, too, as I floated into a space where lucid recitations of the past were as uncomplicated as the alphabet.

"*Beau dieu*, that's awful," she said, when I told her how I threw up all over my father's bathrobe. "What happened to Robin?"

"I don't know."

"What do you mean?"

"Meaning I flew back to Saint-Télesphore the next day. Life went on. I didn't see my parents for another three years."

"But what does that have to do with the girl? Didn't you want to know? Don't you still want to know?" Estelle looked as sad for Robin with the red bandana as I had felt for her nine years earlier.

I was amazed and touched by how she could mourn such an abstract loss, though I hoped she wouldn't turn out to be susceptible to melancholy the way my mother was susceptible to madness.

"Let's talk about something else," I said, standing to stretch my arms toward the ceiling and surreptitiously check if I needed to deodorize myself (I had sweated profusely during my flash-back). I had high hopes we would make love that night. There had been plenty of kissing and dry petting between us already, but my shameful secret of being a twenty-year-old virgin had driven me to say idiotic things every time Estelle tried to unzip my jeans. What if we were sexually incompatible because she had been with men? What if she got turned off when she saw my sprawling bush? What if I made too much noise? Or not enough. What would we say to each other after we were done?

Estelle fetched a bottle of chardonnay from the refrigerator. She poured two glasses and we toasted to nothing, because everything in the infancy of our relationship merited a toast.

"Tell me what it's like to make love to a woman," she said, lifting her glass to my mouth. "I want you to tell what it's like, so I can do it better."

She sipped from her glass, fed me another sip, and we kissed with chardonnay running down our chins.

"I'm sure it's delightful," I said.

"For real, GoGo. Why won't you tell me? Are you grossed out 'cause I've had boyfriends?"

I loved how after just two weeks, she had given me a nickname. It was entirely too frilly, but I didn't care. No one had ever called me anything endearing without a threat attached to it.

Estelle tugged on my zipper and I backed away. She moved forward as I backed away, until I fell onto the sofa and spilled my wine. She fell on top of me and poured the rest of hers into my mouth, and then she waited expectantly for me to share my secrets of lesbian lovemaking. I wanted to believe that making love to her would be as transformative for me as she believed it would be for her.

"I've never done this before," I said, beginning to feel the elastic effects of the chardonnay. "I don't know what I'm doing."

"Don't worry," Estelle said, rolling up my T-shirt. "I've seen *Desert Hearts*."

"What's that?"

"Some lesbian you are."

I lifted my arms and she removed my T-shirt. She lifted her arms and I removed her camisole. I stared at her breasts until she nudged me.

I knew the next step, but I was mortified by how I hadn't groomed my most critical zone. I had convinced myself this was a safeguard against having sex until I was ready. My safeguard was neurotic and utterly embarrassing. I was ready.

"I have to warn you," I said, pressing Estelle's hand against my zipper. "I didn't come prepared."

"GoGo, silly, we don't need protection." She sat onto her ankles and regarded me like I had just spoken Italian but was convinced I had spoken German. "I mean, if you're that worried, I can show you the results from my last doctor visit."

"No, no, I mean … just one more thing?"

"Mmmm-hmmm?" Estelle peered down her nose at me. There were speckles of marinara sauce under her chin.

"What was it like with men? Did you like it?"

"They were boys, if you think about it. So do you want the Coles Notes, or, like, everything?"

"Just avoid the word 'penis' and all of its cousins."

"*Alors*, first there was Marc-André. He was also a virgin, and we did our best. Then there was Mathieu. I really liked him—he was that jock every girl thinks she wants. But in bed, I didn't like how his biceps were the size of my head. He was a totally sweet guy, but every time we had sex, I became aware of how powerless I could be in the wrong situation. Then there was Sébastien."

"And?"

"He dumped me the year after I moved here."

"That dick!"

"Not really. He saw it before I did. This boho will never be a farmer's wife. Now, stay right where you are."

Estelle went to her bed, but ten feet across from the sofa, and gathered her down comforter. She caped it around herself and swooped back to me, and for the rest of the night, shrouded in goose feathers and each other, we made love.

"I RECOGNIZE HOW I'm grossly encroaching on your privacy, and if you're unwilling to help me—which I wouldn't fault you for in the slightest—then I'll turn myself over to St. Mary's hospital. But would you let Estelle know? If she comes in next week and says, 'I haven't heard from or seen Margot since last Friday,' would you tell her I've admitted myself to psychiatric? If I say anything to her it might cause a fight, and I'm tired of fighting."

The static of presence on the other side of the intercom system ceased, and I hoped this meant I was going to be buzzed inside. Standing on a doorstep at three in the morning and drivelling into a stone wall was not how I had pictured myself after I watched Marianne swagger up to my loft. I couldn't remember the last time I had seen a building, aside from something large and commercial, with an exterior intercom, but I thought this peculiarity of 19 Redpath Street suited its top-floor occupant. Also, it made me feel less like I was scaling the ivied Victorian triplex to peer into a window and more like I was accepting the intercom's invitation to employ its services, which had to be as-needed, otherwise the device would have been installed inside the front door, which was locked, as most city doors were at this hour.

Two figures in platform shoes clopped north toward Mount Royal. They leaned against each other for balance and talked breathlessly about the latest spree shooting in America.

"That's what they get for letting people bring guns into Disney World. Florida used to be such a safe place. I used to love going there with my family."

"Wasn't the shooter Mexican?"

"Racist."

"No. It's what I heard. Didn't your brother date a Mexican girl once?"

"Not really. He banged a local when he went to Cancún. He said her cum tasted worse than a mouthful of hot sauce."

"Guess that means he didn't swallow."

The girls flung their arms around each other and laughed uproariously. What did it matter that they were on a sleeping street? One of them spotted me standing on the doorstep. She lifted her hands to the heavens, as though I had been placed there solely for her convenience, and then pulled her friend over. The pair reeked of the signature club-scene combination of fruit-scented body mist and saccharin cocktails. They looked to be somewhere in their twenties, but it was possible that under the heavy eye makeup and rouge-scorched cheeks, which made their faces look tight and dehydrated, they were younger. One of the girls lit a cigarette and exhaled smoke down the plunging neckline of her friend's tank top.

"*Excusez moi*, madam," the smoking girl said. She gave her friend a thumbs-up, like she had just acted on a dare. "*Je veux aller au* purple cross? On Mount Royal?" Her friend whacked her on the behind and told her to speak English because I didn't look very French. The smoking girl continued, "We were told it's the coolest thing ever to see, and we're, like, going back to Toronto tomorrow morning. Hey, that's a really awesome hat you've got on. Do you like *Mad Men*?"'

After I stared at her dumbly, with no body language to suggest I was going to answer her question or say anything at all, she and her friend laughed nervously and continued on their pilgrimage. A few feet away, the smoking girl looked back. I was still staring dumbly, and I felt satisfied when the girls hastened their clopping.

The day had lasted too long. I had no wisdom left to impart to fathers who snuck off to hot dog competitions, or to young men who hid in alleyways of affluent neighbourhoods and dreamed of bohemia, and I certainly had nothing to say to frivolous girls who couldn't distinguish Black from Hispanic from Latino. Everyone seemed so young to me, suddenly, even Estelle. We were forty-five, but that evening I had seen her look youthful and radiant on rue Sherbrooke—like Gwyneth Paltrow, according to Katy. Katy was scandalously young. I hadn't cared at the time about how treating her to dinner could be regarded as inappropriate, depending on the audience, but now I understood I had committed a colossal *faux-pas*, only I hadn't gotten caught. But what if? I wouldn't have known how to explain the lispy, bow-legged teenager grabbing onto me and pointing at Estelle, for I didn't know who she was to me. *Some girl I met at the carousel. Someone to keep me company.* From Estelle's perspective, it would have looked like I was spying on her from behind the throng of Friday-evening foot traffic, and Katy's dramatic reaction would have impelled questions of the sort Marianne's cats had impelled. *Who's that girl, Margot? Are you trying to flaunt her? Are you trying to get me back for going out with Marianne last night? Do you like this young girl? Are you planning to fuck her?*

The more I replayed events of the last forty-eight hours, beginning with my overdue first visit to Le Galopant, the more deranged I felt. Really and truly, my marriage was in a perilous state—a state other people might call "over." This state preceded Estelle's discovery of the letters, my inertia since resigning from Le Canon Noir in the spring, and our move to the loft, only I couldn't say when it had started, or why. It couldn't all be me. Surely our twenty-five years together had to be testament we could make it through another twenty-five. Our joys and troubles were the standard domain of married life, and it was normal, after so many years, for partners to miscue and mistreat each other, to be forced to recalibrate; however, when I tried to focus on the unique qualities of our union, the good and the bad and everything that made us Margot and Estelle Soucy-Coté, my introspection yielded a titanic mystery.

A third-storey window opened, and Olivier Weinstock peered down at me. He was backlit by a prism of soothing hues that gave his small, round stature a beatific impression.

"It's such a lovely night," I called out, desperate to distract myself from more conjecture. "Perhaps you'd like to join me for some air?"

Olivier rubbed his face with both hands and scratched behind his ears. He produced a kerchief and blew his nose. "Please, sit on the doorstep and wait for me. For goodness sake, it's not safe for a person to be alone on the streets at this hour."

"I'm as safe as a doily, though I could talk at length about the strange encounters I've had tonight."

Olivier stared at me a moment longer, perhaps in case I

wasn't really there, and then closed the window. I sat on the doorstep and waited.

Ten minutes later, when I was about to leave (my energies had waned significantly, so I figured sleep would be a reasonable next step), Olivier cracked the front door open and asked me to open it the rest of the way. He emerged with a silver tea tray and sat with me on the steps, placing the tray at our feet. He poured us each a cup of loose-leaf Lady Grey. The ceramic teapot reminded me of the kind local Wellfleet artists made, the kind my mother used to make fun of because she couldn't take ceramic art seriously.

"What do you mean, she couldn't take it seriously?"

"Who knows? She was a fickle woman. One day it was ceramic art, the next day it was anything made with clam shells. I'm sorry, have I offended you? It's a lovely teapot, and the tea is delicious." The tea was, in fact, delicious, and I thought I should dwell on it to keep the tone between us causal. Olivier, however, seemed alert and prepared for involved discussion. He had even arranged a generous serving of Le Petit Écolier cookies for the tray.

"I don't have a better snack food," he said, when I eyed the cookies. "Unless you prefer soda crackers? I think the ones I have are stale."

I selected a round-shaped cookie with dark chocolate covering. "Thank you, Olivier, this is fine. No, this is delightful. I've never thought of mixing Lady Grey with dark chocolate. I need to try things like this more often."

We sat on the doorstep, sipping tea, nipping at cookies, appreciating the slumbering Victorian buildings across the street. Olivier Weinstock had earned my respect. Instead of sending me away or phoning the police ("Yes, officer? The wife of one of my clients is lurking outside my home. She's a firearms dealer."), he had remained calm and resourceful. I knew he wasn't acting out of genuine concern for me, but I nonetheless felt comforted by his attention, and so I sipped my tea as slowly as I could. I still wasn't ready to go back to Le Cabinet Particulier and puzzle out how to get through the next incomprehensible day.

"So what were you hoping to gain by waking me up at this hour?"

"I didn't come here expecting a session, though I'm happy to compensate you for the disturbance."

"This isn't a session, Margot. And I'm afraid I won't see you again after you leave. I don't continue with clients who violate my protocols, unless a medical doctor has referred them to me."

Olivier surely wanted me to wince when he used the word "violate," and I did. He was perfectly within his rights. Why had I come to him at three in the morning? The short answer was I had allowed my jealousy to drive me where it would, and how lucky for me my single-session therapist lived in the same building as his practice. Now, of course, I was rightly chagrined by my folly. The long answer was frothing around inside me in all sorts of permutations. I expected that Olivier had already drawn a mock-up of who I was, based on his sessions with Estelle (wasn't I one of the reasons she had sought him out?), but he couldn't possibly understand how the things frothing around inside me had begun to resemble my mother's paranoia and delusions, for Estelle hadn't known of their extent until she found the letters.

"You'll have to speak with her about finding another couples counsellor, too—if you both agree to travel that path. I'll continue with her separately."

"Frankly, Mr. Weinstock, your first homework assignment made things worse."

"Oh? How so?" Olivier poured us some more tea and offered the plate of cookies to me. "I like the little rectangle ones myself, even though they're the exact same ingredients as the round ones."

"I'm living in an Edwardian-themed hotel that doesn't serve breakfast waffles. There are two detestable Siamese cats and an even more detestable redhead squatting in my loft—I'm sure you know all about the redhead. And my box of letters? The whole reason I came here yesterday? Nowhere to be found. I mean, I get why Estelle wouldn't want it in plain view, but where in hell did she put it? And earlier today, when I visited my former business partner, I learned he's afflicted with some horrible illness. And finally, I spent the afternoon with a seven-teen-year-old-girl I met at the carousel. We rode some hideous roller coaster called the Vampire, and then I took her out for gourmet pizza. To a teenager, that's called a date, except she's engaged to some guy in New York. So what's missing from my tale? Oh, yes, the part where I'm supposed to be with Estelle right now, tucked into our divinely comfortable bed and dreaming about my still unused Belgian waffle-maker."

Olivier said, "I see," and looked at me levelly, like a thera-pist would. I assumed he was translating my grievance into a textbook explanation he could send me off with along with a new homework assignment. The tea had cooled, the cookies were gone, my courtesy session had expired.

"Margot," he said, when I stood and smoothed the creases from my trousers.

I considered ignoring him, hurrying away from this stranger to whom I had revealed too much outside the protective bounds of therapist-client confidentiality. But when I looked at him, I wondered if he was perhaps a little sorry to see his impromptu company leave so soon.

"I apologize. I'm all twisted out of form. I'm sorry for accusing you of making things worse. I really should be on my way."

He rose and shook my hand. He kept hold of it after we stopped shaking, which incited me to reach for my wallet. By itself, "Thank you for your time" seemed inadequate.

"May I be forthright with you, as an objective listener?" he said, dismissing my money.

"So not as a therapist?"

"I already said I won't take you as a client."

"Will you tell Estelle I came to see you?"

"Margot, your lack of curiosity about things that don't overtly affect you is the equivalent of ignorance. Simply put, you're an ostrich."

And with that, an incredibly unpolished—rude, really—statement of the obvious, Olivier bid me a good early morning and collected his tea tray.

I already knew I was a self-absorbed recreant, so his statement didn't bother me. What bothered me was knowing my wife consulted this man for advice—relied on him, even. She was wasting money on his facile analyses and prescriptions for self-betterment, and I had been willing, however briefly and reluctantly, to waste money on him, too. Maybe this man was part of the problem. After he had helped Estelle through her issues at the gallery, what if he had begun to probe at her marriage by asking nebulous but damaging questions like, "How do you really feel?" and "Are you really happy?" Such questions were impossible to answer and quite capable of spurring people back to therapy until they invented answers that corresponded with their delicate realities.

I would have buzzed the intercom to tell Olivier he hadn't duped me, but a police cruiser turned onto Redpath and decelerated as it approached number 19. I nodded civilly at the officer when he rolled down his windows, and then I set off for Le Cabinet.

PART II

9. LE MALHEUR

I FELT AS HYPED UP as a Kentucky Derby racehorse. After two cups of Lady Grey and Olivier's cavalier pronouncements, I was ready to take on the day. I checked out of my room at Le Cabinet Particulier and sat in the lobby, beside an older, very svelte man outfitted in black cycling spandex and cleated shoes. We traded issues of *Elle Québec* and commented on the baffling fashion predictions for the coming year until the hotel café opened for breakfast. In the café, I tucked into a corner and read every page of *The Globe and Mail* and *National Post*, even the classifieds; I read like a fiend so I wouldn't have even a moment's opportunity to reflect on anything Olivier Weinstock had said. I hadn't slept in twenty-four hours, and I was afraid my lightheadedness would make me suggestible to his dross.

"*Quelque chose à manger, madame?*"

"Some more tea would be wonderful."

Every time the waiter came to my table, I asked for more tea (the café promised unlimited refills). I ignored him every time he lingered in case I decided to order an overpriced meal. During the first hour, he checked on me every ten minutes, until finally I requested the muffin *du jour*. And still he lingered, tallying bills for his other tables, feigning unawareness that the menu tucked under his biceps was open to the *prix fixe* page. Two hours later, he turned aloof, even if I stared him down as he walked in my direction. At a quarter to ten, feeling bothered by my inability to make sense of my horoscope in the newspaper (*Dear Capricorn: Your glass is neither half full nor half empty. It's brimming with soy milk*), I realized I would have to force myself to get on with the day. Restiveness on its own was not enough. The waiter zipped over as soon as I stood up, and he acted surprised when I tipped him a crisp ten-dollar bill. Of course I shouldn't have, my tea and ubiquitous blueberry muffin cost a mere five bucks, but I wondered if an act of benevolence could put me in a better mood. The waiter probably lived in a dank closet-sized apartment in the east end of the city, among the gainfully unemployed, drug runners for biker gangs, and prostitutes, the way Estelle and I had lived on top of the gentlemen's club in our early twenties. He probably had fantastic, unattainable dreams like most people did, but none of the patrons at Le Cabinet café cared. I didn't care either, but I could at least make some small, positive contribution to his illusion. Olivier, so it turned out, was right about one thing: I needed to be a little nicer to people.

From the café, I ventured into Montréal's underground city and wandered the channels until I found Estelle's store of choice when she wanted to throw something stylish together on a budget. I had been in with her a handful of times, and every time I had ended up waiting on the offensive breast cancer pink bench outside the store. The bench was designed to make you feel utterly miserable for not paying more awareness to all the women courageously battling for their lives, and what better way to atone for your unearned health than to be proactive and purchase items whose proceeds (but only a small percent) were donated to research? As I sidestepped preying Saturday morning shoppers, I wondered if Marianne and her terrible cats were still at the loft. I found a rack of T-shirts and yanked a half-dozen off their hangers. *That bitch.* I fought my way to a rack of casual pants and grabbed two pairs of khakis with handprints ironed onto the back pockets (it was either those or stonewashed jeans with silver studs along the outer leg seams). *How dare she steal in on my space like that?* I went to the footwear aisle and confiscated a pair of Converse sneakers from a teenage girl who spotted them a second too late. *I should have told Estelle years ago how I really, truly feel about Marianne: Marianne is the worst of all her pretentious arty friends.* After I paid for the items, I went to the dressing cabins and changed out of the button-down and trousers I had donned since my exodus to the hotel. As I tore the price tag off my new sneakers, I realized they weren't Converse but knock-offs planted to ensnare the rushed shopper. I pressed my forehead to the cabin wall and imagined Puzzle and Wolfgang clawing Marianne's face to shreds.

"*Mon esprit!* Every time you come back to me, some poor farmer *dans le nord* wins the lottery. Thanks to you, he will never have to till the soil again."

Le Canon Noir was closed on weekends, but I had never known a Saturday when Bertrand wasn't there, applying paste wax to wood gun stocks, padding display fixtures with foam, sorting through queries and invoices. He lumbered outside and wrapped me in a sweaty hug, squeezed me until I said I couldn't breathe, and then stepped back and beheld me with amazing fondness, given we had seen each other the day before. His eyebrows wiggled up and down, and he seemed curiously wired, but I let myself indulge in his affection for a bit. I felt humble and needy in my handprint khakis and knock-off Converses.

"Ask me anything you want," I said, bending to my duty to address the "my life has turned to shit" issue before any other.

Bertrand closed the shop door and sat on the stoop. He tried to mask his wheeze by stretching his arms far above his head and yawning loudly, but he couldn't hide his pallor even under the blush of high-summer heat.

"I'll tell you everything if you tell me everything," I said, nudging him in an effete attempt at playfulness.

"What do you mean, *esprit?* What are your plans for today?"

He wiped perspiration from his brow and mined the empty breast pocket of his shirt.

"I thought I'd stay here for a while."

"Of course, *esprit*. Of course. This is your place, too. Does this mean you are ready to travel to America?"

"All I need is the itinerary."

We shook hands to indicate we were back to business as usual. We smiled to convey our pleasure. Bertrand started humming a tune he had invented years ago. I joined in until he trailed off. I knew that, really, he was short of breath.

"So, Bert?"

"Yes, *esprit*?"

"May I go inside?"

He looked away guiltily.

"Have you seen a doctor?" I said, crouching in front of him. "Who's taking care of you? No one, I'm sure."

Bertrand waved when the owner of the deli next door came outside to sit on his own stoop and smoke a cigarette. The deli owner grunted, and Bertrand said, "*Shalom*." In all my years at the shop, I had only heard the deli owner grunt to Bertrand, and I had never heard Bertrand say anything to him except *shalom*. Every Christmas, the deli owner left a pound of smoked meat on Le Canon Noir's doorstep, and every Passover, Bertrand left a carton of *Gauloises* cigarettes on the deli's doorstep. I respected their relationship.

Bertrand clambered to his feet when I stepped around him to let myself into the shop. "*Attends!*"

"Why? Are you closing down? Are you retiring? As your business partner, I have the right to know! Even if I bailed like a jerk."

Bertrand muttered "*bon dieu*" and bowed his head. Right as he bowed his head, the door opened and there stood Estelle with a steaming turquoise teapot.

"Hi," she said, breathlessly, like she had just run up a flight of stairs.

"Hi," I said, looking from her to Bertrand.

"*Allô,*" Bertrand said, as though we had all just met up after a morning jog.

"Would you like some green tea?" Estelle asked. The ceramic lid clinked against the pot from the slight tremble in her hands.

"Don't mind if I do," I said.

"It's gun powder green tea," Bertrand said, emphasizing "gun powder" and slapping his great belly for comic effect.

"Would you like to come in?" Estelle asked, looking behind her like a housemaid checking to see if the master was ready for guests.

"That would be nice," I said, feeling like I had suddenly entered into a game of Charades with Gérard Départdieu and Gwyneth Paltrow.

I was relieved to discover that nothing inside the shop was bubble-wrapped or under throw sheets. Everything looked the same, including the dimmed annex, until I got to the office in the back, where there was evidence Estelle and Bertrand had been plotting against me.

"I tried calling you," Estelle said, placing the teapot on the Formica table. "The hotel said you checked out at six a.m. I was worried."

I pointed to the Xerox box on the orange sleeper sofa. "Read anything good lately?"

Estelle avoided me in the same guilty way Bertrand had. There were puffy half-moons under her eyes, and her hair was pulled back with a red bandana. She looked like someone who had been scrubbing toilets since dawn.

"Last time I was here," she started. "Nothing's changed. It's a little weird."

"Tell me, is your plan to move all of my stuff over here one box at a time?"

"I phoned Olivier this morning."

"I hope you told him to consider using Rogaine."

Estelle bit back a smile. There was the faintest stain of lipstick on her lips, and I had the wildly ill-timed urge to kiss her until the stain disappeared.

"We're going on a trip," she said.

"A trip?"

"Yes."

"As in you, me, and Bertrand go to Disney? Please tell me what's going on. You know what surprises do to me."

"I'll tell you in the car."

I turned to the pushpin board and glared at my gun postcards. It was better than glaring at Estelle. *Nicer*. I had to be nicer. "Will Puzzle and Wolfgang be joining us?"

Estelle picked up my box of letters and hugged it against herself with the vigilance of a girl hugging textbooks to her new, incomprehensible breasts. She spoke slowly, and I experienced the discomfort a crowd experiences when someone delivers a rote speech. "Hyannis, Massachusetts. We're going to visit your mother. I'd like to meet her. Say a few things to the old bitch. Then we're going to Wellfleet to see your old home—I'm sure there's no harm in knocking on the door. Then we'll fly to Grand Rapids and deal with your father's estate. I thought we'd spend the last few days in Lanaudière. The Coté clan misses you, Margot. Plus I asked Jean-Jacques for two weeks leave and he actually agreed without a fuss."

I pulled the pins from my postcards and attempted a new arrangement. The postcards had been in place for so long, they had made imprints in the cork. It appeared Estelle's journey through the enchanted land of therapy was complete. Now she wanted to lead me by hand through the dark forests of my childhood, and then cure my bad feelings with bonfires and musical wooden spoons. I pictured Olivier Weinstock fairies buzzing around our heads like mosquitos. It made me laugh.

"It's just as much my fault," Estelle said, coming up behind me and perching her chin on my shoulder. Her breath was balmy and cinnamon-scented. "It's not like I didn't know something was up, but you always get so disturbed talking about your family, even the good times. Why make you feel worse? Remember the first time you told me about the hermit crabs? I never knew a person could literally cry for days on end. So I let it go, and go and go and go. I also wanted your parents to be dead. Better than having in-laws who don't even know you exist. It's fucking crazy. What were we thinking? Why didn't you just leave the fucking letters here?"

Estelle needed to express her feelings, and I let her—I was impressed by how she had revised them since Thursday morning. I didn't interrupt with excuses or, god forbid, new lies to explain the old lies. She was giving me a chance as gracefully as anyone could dare hope for. If I refused to go on this trip, I was essentially admitting to the end of our marriage, even if our marriage took another five years to end, so I knew I was supposed to feel more inspired than I did about having a second chance. But I felt the same lassitude I had felt on Wednesday, before I finally got myself out the door to take pictures of Le Galopant.

Outside the shop, Bertrand gave us each a vigorous hug. He behaved like this was any other Saturday, and he chastised Estelle for allowing such long gaps between her visits. "You are family, *beauté.*"

Estelle went ahead to get the car—Marianne's car, which we were borrowing in exchange for letting Marianne and her cats stay in the loft while she worked through the final phase of her divorce from Antoine. So it turned out she wasn't after my wife (though I wasn't ready to let go of my doubts). I complained about her to Bertrand, hoping to catch him off guard; before I left, I wanted some evidence that he would be okay. With the exception of one uncomely, cynical girl twenty years ago working the cash at Le Real Deal, Bertrand had absconded all varieties of romantic and family life in order to sacrifice himself to the business of antique firearms; the idea that he might be on his way out of my life was insupportable.

"*Vas-y, mon esprit,*" he said. "Visit the places you've stored in your head for so long, and when you come back, we will show *monsieur Vieux Montréal* that guns are more spectacular than blondes in Budweiser bikinis."

"HEADS OR TAILS?"

"Merry-go-rounds."

"Margot, be serious."

"I'll take the one with the dapples, please."

Estelle tossed the quarter. She caught it on her wrist and cupped her other hand over it, and then deepened her voice like a television game show host. "Sir, think long and hard before you make your choice. I'm willing to let you have heads this one time."

"In public? I don't think I could."

Estelle shook her fists in mock frustration. The quarter pinged against the pavement. Heads or tails, it didn't matter: No way in hell would I ever sit at the wheel of Marianne's spoiled-milk beige Fiat 500 Cult convertible. You become conscious of two things when travelling in such a car, and neither thing is agreeable. First, you discover that you can apply Darwin's theory of natural selection to cars, as even a Volkswagen Beetle becomes enormous and predatory next to the Fiat 500C. Second, you automatically become a member of the Soft-Top Leisure Car Club. Said motorists, mostly middle-aged (hardtop convertible sports cars are the domain of younger, intrepid types, or wolfish businessmen) honk as they pass you, waving and grinning stupidly like they couldn't be more pleased to see you. Something else had become clear to me during the first two hours of the drive. I could not stand the feeling of wind in my hair. On Estelle, the windswept style worked beautifully. She had removed the bandana before we set out, and her mane whipping cinematically behind her, and occasionally in my face, had earned every last thumbs-ups it received. I returned my Panama hat to my head, prepared to hold it in place all the way to Hyannis.

"What happens if it rains?" I said, looking over Estelle's shoulder as she programmed a new playlist for our trip. We were parked at Boutique Hors Taxes de Philipsburg, because I had found the first playlist grating and demanded she fix it. Two hours of Welsh singer-songwriters and their tales of mariners, hearts made of gemstones, and women who loved so deeply they drowned was more than I could bear (not to mention we were in the entirely wrong car for such music).

"The forecast says we'll be fine."

"But what if it rains anyway?"

"Then we'll close the top."

"But you said it takes fifteen seconds. We could get drenched in fifteen seconds."

"Margot, *lâche-le*. I've got it. I know this car well."

As we merged onto QC-133 south, toward the Québec-Vermont border, I tried to connect with the reality that in about six hours, we would be in Hyannis. We were scheduled to have dinner with my mother at Folsom Retreat Center, the white-collar seaside asylum where she had lived since the new millennium, when my father committed her. Estelle said we would be meeting my mother in the Bluefish wing of the manor, and I pictured old men in tailcoats carrying trays of baked yams. After a few songs from Morrissey's *Maladjusted*, I muted the car stereo and initiated the next in our series of difficult conversations to be had.

"Are you disappointed you'll never get to meet Morgan?"

"What does it matter?"

"So when did he croak?"

"A few years ago. Heart attack."

"Well I'll say. One of my lies was prophetic."

Estelle squeezed the steering wheel until her knuckles turned white. "He must have loved you some, Margot. He left you a nice big trust—I'm surprised you dropped the ball on that one. You'll have to get in touch with the lawyer who probated the will. I have his letters in the bag behind my seat. Hopefully you didn't screw us by waiting so long."

"Screw *us*?"

"*You*. God! Hopefully you didn't screw *yourself*. Maybe there was a provision to give the trust to someone else if you weren't around."

"Of course. Because all my life, I've just wanted his money. That's a pretty rotten thing to say, Estelle."

"I feel pretty rotten right now."

So. Morgan Wright had kept me in his thoughts even after I expelled him from mine. He had certainly gone above and beyond standard husbandly obligations, leaving in his wake an inexhaustible fund to board his wife in a "manor" for the mad. For the first time, it occurred to me he might have fathered other children. Perhaps my trust wasn't as hefty as Estelle assumed. I reached behind her seat for the bag, which looked suspiciously like a beach bag. Estelle had never been to Cape Cod, so it was natural for her to expect we would take advantage of its amenities, especially since she had spearheaded the whole affair. But I knew—and she did, too—ours was not to be a beach-going sort of trip.

There were a bunch of envelopes in the bag. They were from Marguerite Soucy (according to the postage marks, she had sent one every week during the month leading up my to father's heart attack), and a Hunter Levin of Levin & Patterson Law PLLC. There was an unopened envelope at the bottom of the bag, addressed to me and ready-to-go with a "Janis Joplin forever" stamp. It bore no sender or postage mark.

"For me?" I held it to the sun to see if I could guess what was inside. I had always enjoyed guessing the contents of the envelopes Estelle mailed to me at Le Canon Noir or left on the kitchen table or in our bedroom. Even when she left them for me at home, they were stamped. She loved the aesthetic of physical mail. At work, I usually received handwritten confessions from her. The confessions were always unprompted by me and about trivial things, which made them at once vexing and endearing. *I keep hiding your slippers because you're so ferociously sexy when you storm about looking for them. I plan to put flowers in the "confusing arty" vase forever so you'll keep noticing that I bring home flowers.* At home, particularly on the kitchen counter, I might find an apology if we had argued the night before. The apologies were standard, and I always replied with the owl feather quill pen she left for me. On mornings after Estelle had succeeded in dragging me to events at L'Espace Vif, I could anticipate an envelope beside me on her pillowcase when I woke up after she'd left for work: *Meet me at the corner of Ste. Catherine and St. Denis @ 7 p.m. Wear your zoot hat!* I hadn't received an envelope of any kind for five months. Maybe longer. There was a photograph in this one.

"Actually," Estelle said, touching my hand, "that's for later."

I dropped the envelope inside the bag, not feeling a scrap of disappointment over having to wait until later or curiosity about why. The truth was (since I was now in the business of truths), I was beginning to feel angry about being forced to go on this trip. Just as I hadn't appreciated Estelle's Olivier Weinstock ultimatum, I didn't appreciate this one—and that she assumed she could make it not only bearable but also agreeable. While she had evidently found time between Thursday morning and this morning to research my secret history and plan an itinerary suited to the way she was open to feeling about the whole situation seemed to me as dangerous as my revived unwillingness to repair our relationship. How could we do either before we knew what in hell we were doing? Obviously we didn't. The titanic mystery of our twenty-five years together reared against logic, and the events of the last four days, the only events that seemed tangible to me, were swiftly losing definition. We might as well hope for epiphanies to shoot like meteorites from the sky and blast us out of Marianne's beloved convertible back to a time when we knew what we were doing and didn't have to think about why or possible future corollaries. I had grown bored, I knew it, and Estelle had grown so insecure she was willing to visit a fortuneteller if it could buy us some time. I wanted to yell at her. This exquisite, sanguine woman among whose passions for beautiful things once included me. I had ruined her with my rigidity, the little cruelties I imposed whenever something new excited her: *Can we go to the carousel? No. Please can we go now? Not yet. When can we go, Margot? When I'm ready.* I hated the smell of her despair, and I knew I would resent her before the trip's end.

A half-mile from the border crossing, I began considering viable escape routes. It was unlikely Estelle had neglected to bring my passport, so I would have to be creative. Perhaps when we got to the booth, I could start sneezing and coughing when the officer asked if I was bringing anything into the United States. Or when we stopped for gas, I could refuse to get back inside the car after strolling about to stretch my legs. Threaten to humiliate us both and hitchhike home if Estelle wasn't willing to forfeit this ludicrous journey. What we needed, I would tell her, walking backward along the edge of the road with my thumb out to show I was serious, was a weekend home together, alone. Marianne and her cats could fill someone else's space, or she could get over her spoiled-girl, new-age claim that Antoine's "aura" still clung to everything in their condo, even though he had left months before. I needed to sleep in my own bed and wake up to the sound of Estelle laughing softly while she listened to CBC Radio's "Cultural Hall of Shame" and sipped espresso. Estelle needed to sample the delights of my Belgian waffle-maker, and we needed to talk, just the two of us, until either we remembered how to be in a relationship with each other or we had nothing left to say.

"And who's this with you?"

"My wife."

"Purpose of your visit?"

"Family."

The officer returned the passports to Estelle. Estelle unmuted the car stereo and smacked my thigh. "Let's find a way to have a good time, okay?"

"Sure thing. Let's start by ditching Marguerite and going to Provincetown for a night of dance clubs and drag queens."

And off we went, the gas tank three-quarters full.

My crossness notwithstanding, I respected Estelle's will to tackle the indomitable monsters in my closet. A part of me hoped she would succeed. To her, they weren't indomitable, or even monsters, and she was handling the situation with the same sunny pragmatism she handled me with on my barbarous menstrual days, the same dogged patience she showed to artist "A" when he threatened to withdraw his work if artist "B" was to be featured on L'Espace Vif's prime wall space. After so many years, I no longer had a clear vision of who Marguerite Soucy was, and who Morgan Wright had been—a woman with acute schizoaffective disorder, according to Folsom Retreat Center's resident psychiatrist, and a retired billiards salesman, I imagined, whose passion for rib-eye steak had knocked him dead in his Japanese kimono one evening as he watched the sun dissolve into the celadon waters of the Pacific Northwest. I had retained only a few childhood memories, which I had distilled to their ugliest so I could feel justified if ever I questioned whether or not emancipating myself from my family, with no chance for absolution, had been soulless and extreme. Extreme behaviour tinted the Soucy-Wright blood, after all, and it had broken us completely apart—and yet my father had honoured his word to Benoît and Anaïs Soucy until his end and cared for Marguerite, was even caring for her posthumously, and my mother (at least according to her letters before I had stopped reading them) seemed as consistently enraged by everything my father did and enthralled with his greatness as I had known her to be. Whereas I had even ceased all communication with *grandmère* and *granpère* Soucy after I left Saint-Télesphore on my eighteenth birthday.

I had been determined to move as far away from silos and corncob pipes as my savings would bring me. From my first day there, the Soucys had paid me a paltry weekly allowance for sweeping the aisles of the dairy barn and carrying buckets of milk to the cooling tank, while the bulk of my savings had come from my father during our annual family vacations. There was no future for me in Saint-Télesphore, unless I chose to surrender myself to livestock husbandry or waiting tables at diners, and my grandparents, even after I had lived with them for ten years, excluding summers and one or two weeks each December, still didn't know what in hell to make of me. They treated me like a pensioner in their home, a presence that startled them every morning at the breakfast table and reminded them that the fifty-thousand dollars Morgan Wright had given in exchange for Marguerite's hand was money spent—money I would continue to outlive (but of course my father subsidized my upkeep).

On the minus forty degrees Celsius January morning of my eighteenth birthday, Anaïs sat on the army cot in the attic and watched me pack a week's worth of clothes into the same brown leather duffle bag I had arrived with as an eight-year-old. I was leaving with the musket postcard and "M" *Encyclopædia Britannica* I had come with, some history books I never intended to return to the French immersion high school I had attended in Alexandria, Ontario, and a vague plan to go to college until I figured out what to do with my life.

"*Bon!*" Anaïs said, smiling with strained enthusiasm after I hitched the duffle bag over my shoulder and turned around to get the unceremonious farewell over with. "Eighteen. It will be good years for you, *oui?*"

"I don't need Benoît to drive me. I'm going to hitchhike."

I knew already that Benoît wasn't driving me to Montréal (I had seen him leave with the truck while I ate breakfast), but I wanted to spare Anaïs the discomfiture of explaining why he had gone off without me. Also, I knew that on such a dangerously cold day, I wouldn't have time to flip my thumb before someone pulled onto the soft shoulder and offered me a lift. I had been hitchhiking to Montréal since autumn, studying the city and figuring how I might fit in, visiting historic sites like Bonsecours Market, Chateau Ramezay, and Sulpician Towers, praying for a tempest of motivation to set me in some direction.

Anaïs folded her hands piously on her lap. They were cracked and split, and the contour of her mouth was swollen and red from her nervous habit of licking her lips whenever it was just the two of us in the same room. A life of unremitting Québec winters and manual labour had left their mark, but still she carried her small shoulders at a proud ninety-degree angle to her neck, the same lovely neck as my mother's. I could never look directly at her when I was upset with my mother, which I was that morning for having not yet phoned to wish me happy birthday. In such instances, Anaïs became the placeholder for memories I wanted to expunge. The time my mother squatted with me in the mud and helped me dig trenches in the marsh behind the gallery to protect the hermit crabs from careless tourists. The time my mother helped me with my first bowtie. I would confuse my grandmother's quiescence for kindness, which would make me long to be hugged, though I had never been hugged the entire time I lived with the Soucys.

"*Un chocolat chaud avant de partir?*"

"Okay."

We climbed down the trapdoor ladder and I followed her into to the kitchen, where she poured fresh milk into a tin and set it on the potbelly stove. Benoît's half-finished plate of brown beans and lard had begun to congeal from the cold. I offered to gather more firewood from the shed, but Anaïs shooed me to a chair as she cleared her husband's dishes.

A car severely corroded from travelling too many salted roads fishtailed up the driveway and issued a honk.

"Keep you eye on the milk to boil," Anäis said in fumbling English, before patting her hair behind her ears and stepping into Benoît's sealskin workboots. She hurried outside and spoke to the driver, their exchange creating dense puffs of white between them, and from under her apron she produced a roll of bills, which the driver accepted.

I heard the phone ring, once, twice, three times, but I was too upset to answer. Anaïs heard it too, as she scuffled back to the farmhouse as quickly as she could on the icy driveway. She ran to the phone without removing Benoît's boots, and then extended the receiver to me after saying a timorous, "Yes, thank you," to the caller, whom I knew was my father. The milk began to boil, but I didn't bother to take the tin off the stove; I was too busy glaring at Anaïs for making the circle of Soucy-Wright family transactions complete.

"Margot, happy birthday," my father said, when finally I huffed into the receiver.

"Isn't it."

"You should receive a taxi soon, to bring you into the city."

"It just got here."

"You'll phone your mother when you're settled in? Do you have a number where you'll be staying?"

"I don't know where I'll be staying."

"Well, don't tell your mother that. She's been all over the place the last couple of days with her nerves. She's convinced you'll be kidnapped."

"Better than being homeless."

"I don't understand why you don't stay with the Marions. They would be happy to have you while you get yourself set up."

"No thank you." I heard a muffled female voice. "Is that Mom?"

"I have to go take care of something important. Don't forget to phone your mother."

"Dad?"

"Yes, Margot, what is it? Can it wait?"

"Goodbye."

When I turned around, Anaïs was inches away with a mug

of hot chocolate and a second roll of bills. I almost told her to just get on with her day like I wasn't there, like I had never been there, but she seemed genuinely sorry. I'd wanted every reason to hate her for paying some guy in a clunker to take me away, but it was my father who had arranged my transportation into the city, and it was he who had commissioned Benoît to be absent when the taxi arrived.

"WAKE UP, GOGO. Wake up, we're here."

Estelle poked my thigh until I relented and opened my eyes. I checked the time as I gracelessly protracted my stiff limbs, and I was surprised to learn, given how miserable and unrested I still felt, that I had slept for almost four hours. Estelle's face was swollen from sunrays and windburn, and she was fretting about the Fiat's soft-top. We were parked in front of a silver train car diner.

"It's a bit finicky," she said, rummaging through the glove box, which was stocked with the essentials for a woman in crisis—shades of Kat Von D lipstick for every season, a three-pack of tampons, a pocket paperback of *Don't Sweat the Small Stuff*—and nothing essential like an instruction manual. "There's something you have to do before closing it, but I can't remember what. Shoot. I guess I could call Marianne."

"But I thought you knew this car well. Your words exactly: 'I know this car well.'"

"Let it go, Margot. Okay? Can you check under the seats for the manual?"

"Please call Marianne."

"She's on a date. I don't want to bother her."

"I hope this date is not in our loft?"

"So what if it is."

I pointed to a digital keypad above the rear-view mirror. "I believe this is what you're looking for."

Estelle smacked my hand. "Did you hear me? I said there's something you're supposed to do first." She got out of the car and ducked into the back. I got out as well, feeling unmoved by her distress, and completely displaced by dreams about my grandparents—they couldn't possibly still be alive, could they? No, of course not. Estelle would have said something.

"Where are we?"

Estelle emerged empty-handed from her forage. "Watertown."

"Why are we in Watertown?"

"Why not?"

"I see your point."

"Do you?"

"Not really, dear. Are we here to eat? I'm famished all of a sudden."

Estelle got back into the Fiat and examined the two-option keypad like it was some complex system. She was so unlike herself, hyper and bent out of shape by something trivial. "See the problem is, if you don't do it the right way, the roof gets stuck halfway up, and then you have to go to a mechanic."

"Baby girl?"

"What?"

"Remember the first time you had people over for dinner, after you started working at that weekend gallery?"

"You mean after we got back from Savannah?"

"Right. And Marianne was supposed to help you?"

"Margot, I would really, I mean *really*, like it if you dropped your Marianne bone."

I promised Estelle this wasn't about Marianne—except for the tangential detail that after two weeks of planning the event together, Marianne phoned on the morning of and claimed she had woken up with a sore throat and wouldn't be able to help Estelle with the final arrangements, which amounted to a full day of finger-food preparation, a labour-intensive rearrangement of our quarters, a rove through the city for decorations and other kitsch, and pleading with neighbours to whom we hadn't yet introduced ourselves to lend us things Marianne was supposed to supply.

We were barely settled into our new apartment after our year in Savannah, and Estelle, normally level-headed and systematic about last-minute changes, shook me awake after Marianne's phone call and declared the dinner a pending catastrophe.

"I can't believe she's doing this to me! And I know exactly why," she said, tossing yesterday's jeans and ringer-T on top of me. "She's jealous. She wants to be the host."

"Why can't you both host the dinner? Heck, I'm sure I'll get roped into hosting tonight, too. I sure hope one of your arty friends likes guns. Or tea. I can talk for hours about guns and tea. Otherwise, I'm afraid I'm of no use."

Estelle pulled on the window blind and snapped morning sunlight into the bedroom. "I don't know how you got it in your head that all artists can talk about is art. And you can talk about more than guns. You never even said a peep about them until Bertrand dragged you out of your pawnshop funk."

"That's not true at all."

"Okay, fine, you liked muskets and rifles."

"And longarms."

After I was dressed and caffeinated, Estelle gave me a list of items to purchase—the evening was going to be modelled after the game *Clue*, which I thought was delightful and inventive, even after Estelle admitted she had gotten the idea from Marianne, who had gotten the idea from a mutual acquaintance, who had gotten the idea from a television show. Estelle was going to play Mrs. Blanche White, the game's nosey but kindly maid, who was rife with secrets. Marianne would have played Mrs. Elizabeth Peacock, a high-society type with a penchant for bad behaviour. Estelle and Marianne had spent the previous day running from one consignment store to another in pursuit of the perfect outfits. Estelle succeeded in cobbling hers together for ten dollars, while Marianne went home dissatisfied and whiny.

"Maybe she's pissed because she wants to be Mrs. Vivienne Scarlet," I said, hugging Estelle while she moaned about everything that had to be accomplished before six p.m.

"We agreed Isabelle should be Scarlet, and Alain should be Professor Plum. Everyone else will draw from a hat. One of yours, as a matter of fact."

"Oh? Well then use the Bourbon Pork Pie."

I couldn't envision how we were going to accommodate six people in our teeny-tiny apartment, as boast-worthy as it was with revived hardwood floors and nine-foot ceilings with Colonial-style crown moulding, so I was amazed, when I returned with the party favours (a coil of rope, a toy candlestick gun and butcher knife, a wrench, and two magnums of the cheapest champagne on the planet) to see how Estelle had repurposed the space. Our living room futon, the coffee table, and the television had been relegated to our bedroom, as had all the books and other knick-knacks on the six-storey bookshelf. Estelle had adjusted the heights of the shelves to fit tumblers and champagne flutes, bowls for cucumber wedges and fruit salad, and plates for crackers and cheeses, and she had taped the profile card of one *Clue* character to every shelf. There was an oval rug in the centre of the living room, which Estelle had borrowed from a neighbour, along with an oval table only a foot high. Everyone would sit around this table, their derrieres cushioned by the rug, while they ate and chatted. The final touch, borrowed from a different neighbour, was a crimson Japanese paper lantern suspended above the table.

"Pretend it's a Swedish drop chandelier," Estelle said, as she hid the game props throughout our apartment. Even though it was only late afternoon, she had already changed into her floor-length black and white ruffled dress and pulled her hair into a tight bun under a white bonnet.

I sidled up behind her while she plastic-wrapped a plate of sandwich triangles to refrigerate. "And whom shall I be, Mrs. Blanche?"

"Looks like you'll have to play Mrs. Peacock."

"I beg your pardon?"

By the time guests arrived, Estelle had convinced me of Mrs.

Peacock's appeal (and perhaps she had done so during an hour or so of lovemaking and playacting), although I wasn't entirely comfortable engaging in conversation with the troupe, so I assumed the role of myself while everyone else clinked glasses and chatted gaily in farcical English accents.

"Margot! You must join us," Isabelle exclaimed, feigning shock when I filled her empty flute with more champagne.

"*Oui*," cried Alain as I replenished his flute, "come play with us. We want to hear all about you. Estelle is so *silencieuse* at work. She never wants to take a break and gab about her affairs, like Miss Marianne and her tales of late nights with Antoine."

But I was convinced they didn't really want to play with me, and they didn't care about who I was beyond their caterer; and Estelle, though she made eye contact with me regularly, and trickled her fingers along my back whenever we passed each other, looked so pleased with how the evening was going, was so engrossed in conversation that to me sounded like a foreign language, that I chose to inhabit the only role I believed wouldn't dilute the merry vibe she had worked all day to create.

Once everyone graduated from champagne to food, Estelle turned to Éric, a thirty-something painter whose toupée kept slipping sideways.

"I just love your work," she said, visibly trying to keep her voice from quavering as though she were before an idol of her teenage years. "Your landscapes are so brooding, and yet your colours are so enthusiastic. Can you tell me more? I studied the surrealists a bit as an undergrad, the obvious ones like Dali and Tanguy, but I put most of my energy into photography."

Yvon, the artist designated to play Colonel Mustard when finally the game began, picked lint off the sleeves of his purple brocade frock coat. "The only thing surreal about Éric's work is what people are willing to pay for it."

Isabelle and Alain toasted to this statement, and Estelle hurried in with her next, mediating question. She was the newbie to this group, and she would never be a true part of it because she wasn't an artist. They needed her to sell their work, but I could easily imagine them snipping to one another behind her back about how she was the reason they would never become supremely successful. "Can you *believe* she sold my painting to such a gauche collector?" Even though she was doing it for the sake of professional development, I had to wonder where she found the resilience to cultivate relationships with people who loved her only until someone else could open wider doors for them. Her current job at the Thursday through Saturday gallery was merely a layover until she gained enough experience to move on to something better herself (though I knew she would try to keep in touch with everyone), while these self-important, toupée- and frock-wearing posers, regardless of my condemnatory opinion of them, were only as successful as they were because they happened to be friends with the owner of a small gallery.

Estelle rose and poured herself more champagne. "Funny you should mention it, Yvon. I agree, it's wonderful to see Éric's paintings get picked up so quickly, especially since the public seems so fixated on lifeless themes right now. A sign of the times, maybe?" (It was 1995, and Québec was experiencing cultural tensions between Francophone and Anglophone natives that caused both extremely conservative and knee-jerk anti-conservative attitudes to affect even those who weren't paying attention to the political climate.)

Yvon fingered his ascot. "Oh?"

"Well, I just mean people are, how would you say it, afraid of anything they don't understand right away. They want art on their walls for the sake of having art on their walls, and they want work by some exotic-sounding artist, but they're not interested in subject, composition, movement, or even a particular artist's oeuvre, if it can't all be explained in a thumbnail. As far as I know, no one's commissioned additional work from you after purchasing a piece from the gallery. *Non?*"

Yvon's face flushed, and I wanted nothing more than to sweep my girl in her Victorian maid's outfit into the bedroom and forget about the dinner guests until they finished the champagne and left, which was essentially what happened, only not quite as immediately and dramatically.

I LOOKED OVER at Estelle, remembering.

"God, we fucked a lot that night," she said.

"You ruled that day, just like you're going to rule this car."

"But I know there's something you're supposed to do first."

"Just press the button and see what happens."

Estelle mumbled something to herself in French, pressed her thumb to the keypad, and we both looked up as the Fiat's black roof spread over us and clicked in place. When we got out of the car, Estelle praised the sky and linked an arm through mine. "Just so you know," she said, leading us to the Watertown Deluxe with purpose, "we're leaving the top up for the rest of this trip, no matter how hot it gets, and if Marianne asks, we never had it down."

Inside the diner, we were greeted by a pretty girl dressed in old-style uniform, except for her functional white shoes, which, though they made sense for someone on her feet for long shifts, ruined the otherwise charming effect of the light pink fitted short-sleeve dress and crocheted waist apron.

"I don't understand why she doesn't wear white ballerina shoes," I said, after the waitress ushered us to a booth and implored us to take advantage of the miniature jukebox on our table. "Or even those silly plastic things with all the holes in them—what are they called?"

"Crocs?"

"I wouldn't know. But do you see my point? Why go through all the trouble of looking nice if you're going to wear granny shoes?"

"And how are we doing this evening?" The waitress returned to our table with a pitcher of ice water, apron pockets filled with fresh utensils and napkins, and a wheelie blackboard listing the day's specials in neon chalks. Estelle kicked me under the table to move my attention away from the waitress's shoes. Up close, they were even more unsightly with food and coffee stains.

"We're so happy to be here," Estelle said, indeed seeming very happy all of a sudden. She loved diners, this was true, but she frequented them regularly with Marianne, so I wondered if the events of the last four days were finally beginning to affect her in ways she couldn't suppress. It really needed to be my turn to drive after we ate. I had given up on my immediate escape plan. I would get through the next hours and then try to negotiate.

"As you can see," said the waitress, sweeping her hand in front of the blackboard, "we have tons of specials, but let me say the stuffed turkey breast and mashed potatoes is what everyone comes here for. I'll just leave this here for you to browse, okay? And please, take your time, ladies." She swept her hand around the diner to indicate that there were other blackboards available to patrons, in case we were concerned about delaying anyone. As she spoke, her full lilac lips curled back and revealed unevenly whitened, slightly buck teeth. When she asked us if we were ready to order drinks (a pre-mixed strawberry daiquiri for Estelle, and a root beer for me), she lisped when she said "drinks," and I wondered what Katy was doing. During our dinner at Pizzadéli, she had told me she would be taking a Greyhound bus home for the weekend, to see Ryan. One of his friends was in a band and would be playing for the first time before an audience, and Ryan really wanted Katy to be there. Katy had told me this with as much enthusiasm as she might have told me she was having her wisdom teeth extracted, and she didn't say anything in her fiancé's defence when I said he was a bit of a jerk for not coming to pick her up in the brand new Ford truck he had purchased for himself. (I almost commented on the flimsy engagement ring he had given her, but she played with the ring too often and looked at it too fondly.) Perhaps Katy was also sitting in some diner right now, telling herself over and over she was happy to be there, but really feeling impatient for something out of the ordinary to happen.

"So what do you think?" Estelle asked after the waitress left us to peruse the regular menu.

"I think I'll try the Deluxe Hero. Says here it's been around since the sixties. You?"

Estelle removed the paper tip from her straw and sipped some water. She gathered our menus and tucked them back behind the jukebox. "I mean what do you think of the diner?"

"It's okay. Isn't it? You're the expert."

"Margot, look around you." Estelle seemed at once frustrated and giddy. She followed my gaze as it toured the diner. Every time I paused to consider a detail, she looked ready to jump out of her seat.

Naturally, I saw exactly what I expected to see: A wall of ketchup-red booths, a parallel wall-length ketchup-red counter showcasing homemade fruit pies and take-home treats like chocolate mice and plate-sized cookies, and some tables for four between the counter and the booths. The only interesting feature about the diner (and most diners) was its democratizing powers. Only here could you expect to see, on any day, a peaceful mélange of old townies, young families, long-haul truckers, businessmen, adventurers, derelicts, and people like Estelle and me.

"You don't see it? I mean, you *really* don't see it?"

While I knew I was in trouble, I had no idea how I had gotten myself there. Estelle gulped from her daiquiri after the waitress delivered our drinks. She slammed her glass on the metal tabletop and slouched on her bench.

"Never mind," she said, stretching her legs under the table and pushing my feet out her way. "Sorry I said anything."

"You haven't said anything at all, Estelle. God, what's wrong with you all of a sudden? Are you pissed I fell asleep? Sorry.

I haven't slept in twenty-four hours and there's only so many things we can talk about without getting into a fight..."

Estelle grabbed my hands. Hers were sticky with daiquiri and sweat. "Margot!"

"What do you want from me? You always do this. You say you shouldn't have said this, shouldn't have done that, but you did, you do, and I'm pretty goddamn confused right now."

"What about me?"

"What about you?"

Estelle's face turned from pink to red as she stared at me. I still had no idea what I had done, exactly, to bring us to this point. I couldn't begin to guess why Estelle had brought us to this particular diner, but I knew I had just said something incredibly thoughtless and hurtful.

"Elle, I'm sorry. I'm sorry, darling. I didn't mean it like that." I reached across to touch her face, but the waitress appeared before us with her lilac lisp and a notepad.

"I'll just have another one of these," Estelle said, holding up her empty cocktail glass.

"No, she won't," I said, turning to the waitress so she would understand the seriousness of my interdiction. "And we'd like our food to go, please. I'll have the Deluxe Hero, and my wife will have the club, mustard instead of mayo."

An elderly couple rose from the booth behind Estelle and thanked our waitress for the lovely dinner and service. The wife, austere and matronly in her starched blouse and high-waist linen skirt, leaned past Estelle and pointed to the cocktail glass. "This is the reason people get hysterical," she said, looking at me as though expecting me to discipline Estelle like a mother would her crabby child. I ignored her, assuming her husband with tufts of hair sticking out of his ears was quite ready to leave when he slid his thumbs under the suspenders holding up his brown slacks, so I was caught off-guard when he said to his wife, "Faggots are always hysterical," and then to our waitress, the poor thing, "Tell Bill we're sorry we missed him."

The ogre and his matron took their sweet old time making a punctuated exit, pausing at one table for a stare-down with a pockmarked teenage boy wearing a Metallica T-shirt, who gave them the finger. Next they stopped at the counter to solicit solidarity from a pair of men in leather slouch hats, the sort of wizened Italian grandfathers who played chess in Bryant Park. The pair drew their heads closer together in polite ignorance of the offending couple.

"I'm afraid Bill won't be sorry he missed them," our waitress said, once the flush of frustration left her pretty face. "I'm so awfully sorry for that. Gosh, please, let us pay for your dinners. It's the least we could do. And, please, order anything you wish. I'm so sorry." And while she continued to apologize, and lift our glasses to wipe our table clean even though there wasn't a crumb in sight, she also seemed relieved, like, finally, the seditious event of her shift had taken place, and now she could continue on without worry.

"That's very kind of you," I said, offering my Visa to her, "but why don't I pay for our drinks and you cancel our dinner order? We've got another two hours of driving ahead of us, and it's this one's turn to sleep." I reached across the table and squeezed Estelle's hands. She squeezed back, but only lightly.

When we got to the Fiat, I leaned her against the hood and kissed her. Normally, just witnessing other people's public displays of affection made me feel claustrophobic. But the incident with the bigots, while it hadn't ruffled us the way it had everyone else in the diner, had done nothing to make us feel better about this trip, so I decided it was time to press the "let's start over" button. Just four days earlier, I couldn't remember when Estelle and I had last done something special together, and for that reason alone, I would be remiss to flout this opportunity.

"You said we should try to have a good time," I said, sliding off Estelle's red bandana and massaging above her temples, "so I'm going to try. I can't promise anything groundbreaking, you realize, but I promise to make the best of this ... whatever it turns out to be. So," I said, butting her to make room for me to sit with her on the hood (I was thrilled to be treating Marianne's property with disrespect), "why don't you start by telling me about the Watertown Deluxe? You were so excited about it before. I thought you were adorable."

Estelle kicked off her sandals and slid farther up the hood. She splayed her toes along the fender and played with the silver artisan ring on her big toe. "No you didn't. You were annoyed as hell, but it's okay, I get it. I could have done without those assholes, though."

"Remember that time I told Bertrand I would never again in a million millennia go back to Argusville? Nearly got killed by one of my own pistols down there, I did."

"Sure, in, what was it, '89? In North Dakota? And still, it's not like you went up to the guy and said, 'Hello, I'm here to purchase your Remington pocket revolver and, oh, watch out, I'm a dyke.'"

"Darling, come on. I know you won't admit it because then you'd never want to be naughty with me ever again, but I really am the spitting image of a flaming homo ventriloquist doll."

Estelle laughed and bit my cheek. "No one says 'flaming homo' anymore."

"I could say anything I wanted if I looked like Gwyneth Paltrow."

"Why would you want to look like her?"

"She's pretty, isn't she?"

"If you like that sort of thing. Wait, is she your new Hollywood crush? *Seriously*, Margot?"

"So this diner, tell me about it."

Estelle sighed and opened her purse. She showed me a pack of Peter Jackson menthols. "Sorry."

"Go right ahead. Don't mind me." I couldn't bring myself to act like I was completely stunned that after twenty years she was at it again, and I wasn't ready to say I had seen her smoking on rue Sherbrooke two days earlier, for such a declaration required the backup of a sound explanation.

Estelle closed her eyes and talked about the diner as smoke wafted out of her mouth. "It's not the same place anymore—it used to be called The Watertown—but, *voilà*, this is where it all started."

"I don't understand."

"Yes, you do. There aren't exactly a hundred diners off Route 3 in Watertown. But like I said, it's different now. When I phoned to ask about the poster outside the restroom? The one your mother loved?"

"I wouldn't say she loved it."

"Well, no one here knew what I was talking about anyway." Estelle stubbed her cigarette on the Fiat's front tire, and then took a folded piece of paper from her purse. "I had this brilliant plan to use the bathroom while you ordered our food."

Because at restaurants, I always excused myself to the bathroom when our food arrived (I preferred to wash my hands right before I ate and not a moment sooner), and so I would have seen the Bonheur print taped to the wall the way my mother had seen the poster on the doomful February afternoon of 1965. And then Estelle would have come up to me and told me all about the painting, just like my father had told my mother all about it, and we could have started our relationship all over again.

I spread *The Horse Fair* over my lap and stared at it until I quelled the spasms in my throat. I hadn't seen it in decades. It troubled me that my mother had never experienced the painting's original, unplumbed enormity. Morgan Wright, though he had poured luxuries onto his young wife's lap and toured her across America as Wright & Ellis Billiards expanded, had never brought her to sit on a museum bench so she could study the Percherons trying to break free from their eternal handlers. This absence of completeness seemed to me a continuum of tragedy in the life of Marguerite Soucy.

And it had ruined her for being my mother. "You need to lower your expectations," I said. "This road trip isn't going to change my past."

Estelle looked dispiritedly at the diner. "It was a stupid idea. I don't know. It made sense yesterday."

My anger toward Estelle, which, I was now convinced, had been tricked into submission all day by distractions Estelle had plotted for that very purpose, revived and secured footing as we sped along Route 3 toward Hyannis. Estelle had dozed off, otherwise she would have yelled at me for pushing Marianne's little post-divorce indulgence until it hummed, so I took advantage of running a stop sign and then blasting through a red light at a deserted intersection. Since Marianne was treating our loft like a brothel, I was entitled to treat her Fiat any way I pleased. As the sandy roadsides of my childhood blurred by, I considered new escape options, like swerving into a ditch to avoid hitting an imaginary box turtle, or pulling over and throwing a fit about the enduring stench of perfume inside the car. I was incapable of defying "François," though, the startling Parisian voice built in to the dashboard, as if François were the only one who truly knew where we were going. *Turn right at the next stop sign.* Finally, just after seven p.m., Folsom Retreat Center loomed mockingly before me. I parked across the street, in front of a bait and tackle shop with an inflatable laughing tuna on its roof. Estelle yawned and stretched her arms, looking as disoriented and unrested as I had felt in Watertown.

From the time I had learned about my mother's institutionalization, I had envisioned her living in a red brick, turret-roofed building, with stone gargoyles holding vigil over gardens of Jack-in-the-pulpits, touch-me-nots, and sheep's bits. When eventually this lost its opiate effect on my conscience, I added a topiary maze that led to a courtyard where patients who completed the maze were rewarded with rosewater lemonade and scones. And because my burdened conscience behaved much like an addiction, I was forced to populate the Folsom diorama with Marguerite Soucy of 1976, entertaining courtyard guests and moving her hand like a wand through the air, the corona of her insanity casting on her the same extravagant aura that had captivated me as a little girl. Now before us, the Center looked every bit as generic as I had feared.

When I shared my disappointment with Estelle—Morgan Wright couldn't have afforded his wife statelier accommodations?—she laughed until she clutched her stomach. "It's not like we're going to run into Jack Nicholson or anything."

"You mean R. P. McMurphy, and I'm going to pretend I didn't hear that."

"You're right, Sorry, sorry." She dabbed her eyes with a napkin from the glove box. "Okay, let's do this. The woman I spoke with said social hour ends at eight."

"Delightful. Maybe we can all paint by number together."

"Maybe we can have Marguerite's leftover *bœuf bourguignon*. I wish you'd gotten me that club. I have a hunger headache now."

"Gee, I'm sorry I was too busy defending your honour."

Estelle tilted the rear-view mirror to check her hair. "How am I doing?"

"As in, on a scale of one to ten?"

"Why not?"

"Well, today you've been all over the scale, but on average, I'd say five."

"How generous of you."

"What's up, Elle?"

Estelle raked her fingers through her hair, ripping the knotted tips. "All day I've been wondering, when will Margot ask how I'm doing? When will she pull her head out of her ass and realize I'm here, I'm part of this, and I'm fucking miserable? Do you know my back's still hurting from two weeks ago? And this morning when I used the stepladder, I almost fell again because you still haven't fixed it, because you've been too busy lying."

"Are we doing this or not?"

"Do you care?"

"So that's it? You dragged me all the way out here for nothing."

"Do you want to go in?"

"Nope. You?"

"Give me a quarter."

"We're not flipping a quarter over my mother."

Estelle plucked a coin from the change compartment inside the Fiat's armrest. "We're flipping to see whether we find a motel afterward or…"

"What?"

"I don't know. I didn't think we'd actually make it here."

AFTER WE SIGNED our names and left our drivers' licenses in a small, crudely handmade lobster trap, Estelle asked which way to the Bluefish wing. The tremendous, spit-polished bald man at the check-in desk pointed to an elevator and grumbled the code to gain access to the third floor. The Centre had three floors, he recited, and each floor was named after a local fish.

"You probably get the best view of the port from the top," Estelle tried during a delay on the second floor, where we were crowded to the back of the elevator by a steel food trolley. I breathed against the heavy odours of cold meatloaf and cubed vegetables, divots of chewed-but-not-swallowed food. I nearly gagged when I spotted a pair of dentures peeking out of a slab of yellow cake. Perhaps we were all one meal away from losing our minds.

I had no wish to interact with the young woman who greeted us on the other side of the elevator. Her Tinkerbell-themed scrubs were one more indication of how infuriatingly depressing this visit was going to be.

"You must be Margot," she said, shaking Estelle's hand, peering behind Estelle but not imposing herself further when I didn't return her smile. "I'm Lacey. I'm so happy you made it."

"I'm Estelle. We spoke on the phone."

"Oh. Yes, we did, didn't we? Ha! I was going to say you look just like Marguerite, it's the thing you say to sons and daughters the first time they visit. I'm glad I stopped myself. And so *you* must be Margot," Lacey said, peering anew behind Estelle, patting my arm like I was a rescue dog being introduced to her new forever home. "No need to be nervous, everyone here's nice and friendly—and full from a hearty dinner. Marguerite is going to be so pleased to see you."

"I'm afraid the pleasure, unlike the river, won't flow both ways."

"This really is a wonderful thing you're doing for her. Just follow me so we can sign you in one more time—it's all about signing in and signing out here, and I do apologize for that— and then I'll take you to Miss Marguerite."

The nurse's too-cheery cheeriness gave her the air of a kinder-garten teacher who, though she smiled at parents and gushed about the little joys that were their children, hated her job, which she had thought would be easy-peasy-lemon-squeezy, and she hoped to be recruited some day soon by an older, once-divorced man looking for an uncomplicated wife with an ability to smile through everything. We followed her to the nursing station, in front of which a few slumbering "residents" (as we were encouraged to call the patients) were buckled into reclining armchairs. Lacey mistook my repulsion for concern and pointed to a set of doublewide industrial doors behind the station. "Your mother's in there with the others. We bring some of the residents out here after dinner so they can follow the sunset. The extra natural light makes them feel good, and it's good for them. I'm so happy you're here. Marguerite talks about you every day. This is going to be so special for her."

Lacey's aggressive friendliness toward me was no doubt forced. She knew I hadn't been any part of Marguerite's life in years, and in Lacey's mind that must have relegated me to the same category of soulless people who bilked helpless elderly relatives of their savings and then dumped them at nursing home curbsides on Christmas Eve.

In my mother's first letters after my father committed her, she had seemed the same frivolous, erratic woman from my childhood, interested in the goings-on of my life for one paragraph and then declaiming for pages how deprived her new friends were for having never tasted roe fresh from the sea.

Chérie, you can't imagine the sorts of grotesque things they request for "Feast Friday." Kraft dinner with oyster crackers? Swiss rolls for dessert? One of the ladies from the kitchen laughed when I asked for some loose-leaf chamomile tea at bedtime. Your father will hear about this.

Gradually, her letters opened to the prospect of a two-way conversation, or perhaps my mother had calculated how much time remained before the inevitable drooling stupor of her future.

Do you have a husband yet? I hope he's not as dashing as your father. You know by now that such men are unreliable. Do you have kids? I think the perfect number is two. I wish I had known this, because you would have turned out more sociable with a younger brother or sister to look after. Will you ever forgive my shortcomings and consider visiting me? It's never too late.

Her plea to make amends drove me to stop reading her letters. I had wasted too much of my life pretending I hadn't been injured by this woman who had blamed me for tying her down, who had believed she could sever blood ties simply by sending me away. I wasn't interested in giving her a chance to be someone different. It occurred to me that Estelle knew this, and so her own façade—let's go on a road trip to patch things up—might be her way of proving things between *us* couldn't be patched. My final walk along the plank

The Bluefish wing was unremarkable. I knew from my mother's letters that residents were encouraged to participate in arts and crafts, though I didn't care which pipe cleaner and tissue paper oceanic creature hanging from the ceiling was hers. We stopped outside the social room so Lacey could explain protocol. She pointed to a laminated list taped to the wall and read each item out loud, placing emphasis on the already evident ("*do* ask *how* someone is doing," "*don't* laugh *unless* someone tells a joke"). Estelle slid me a "dear god" look when someone inside the room started playing a terrifically out-of-tune toy piano.

"Usually there's an entrance fee," Lacey winked, "but tonight it's by donation. You've come on a truly special night." She presented me with a netted bag of cat's-eye marbles. "Use these. They're as good as gold to the residents. Just make sure to take them back after you put Marguerite to bed. We don't think she'd try to eat them, but you never know."

"Maybe it would be good for her to swallow a marble or two."

"I know it seems cruel," Lacey continued, impervious, "like taking away a birthday present from a child, but the residents are used to it. If Marguerite gets upset, just promise her she can have her marbles back after breakfast tomorrow."

Inside the social room, folding chairs were arranged in a circle. A handful of audience members were residents. One was a slender teenage boy with a "Volunteer" badge pinned to his T-shirt (he reminded me of elegant Étienne from La Ronde, and I was surprised by the spontaneity of this association), while the other chair occupants were stuffed animals, empty flowerpots, a tiara, and some clam shells. A man wearing a plaid newsboy cap and an oversized Red Sox jersey sat cross-legged on the floor inside the circle, a toy piano on his lap. Beside him, slender as always, savagely elegant in a knee-length summer dress the pattern of a monarch butterfly, her hair no longer dune but the shade of a sable fur coat left for decades to collect dust in some closet, was Marguerite Soucy, *raconteuse extraordinaire*, commanding her assorted audience with the same grandiose satisfaction she had her imaginary one in our Wellfleet living room thirty-seven years before.

Estelle and I stayed by the doorway, unblinking, whispering to each other from the corners of our mouths as though we had suffered a conjugal stroke and our faces were paralyzed.

"GoGo, you have the same teeth. You have the same little pointy incisors."

"I'd rather you didn't highlight our similarities. If you don't mind."

"Sure, sure. Sorry. But you see it, right?"

"I didn't realize my incisors were so interesting to you."

"They're unusually small and pointy. You know I love them."

"Well, now you can love my mother's, too."

Marguerite belted out some lyrics to a Frank Sinatra song, some lyrics to a Céline Dion song, and then she started humming the theme song to *Jeopardy!* The man on the floor gave up trying to anticipate her next whim and started hitting random keys on his toy piano.

Lacey tried to gently herd us inside the social room. She spoke at normal volume into my ear. "After she sings 'I've been to paradise, but I've never been to me,' go up and give her the marbles."

I wiped spittle from my cheekbone. "And say, *Hello, Mother, remember me? Have some marbles.* I doubt very much this will lead to the pleasant visit you're hoping for."

"Don't be nervous. She knows who you are. See how she's looking at you? Funny she's not finishing her act. She must be too excited. Quick, the marbles."

As Marguerite twirled her way over to us, showing off her dress and exclaiming how pleased she was to see me—"And you've brought someone with you!"—I receded into the hallway. Estelle, whose ulterior reason for wanting to meet Marguerite would shortly announce itself, seized her and air-kissed each side of her face in true Québec fashion. "*Madame Soucy, ça me fait gros plaisir de faire ta connaissance.*"

Marguerite couldn't have been more delighted. "*Tu vois, chérie?*" she said, like no time had passed and she was still entitled to scold me publicly for theatre. "This is how I've always told you to behave with people. Always let them know how happy you are to see them even if you're not happy at all."

"But naturally you're happy to see your daughter," Estelle said. "We drove a long way to see you, *Madame Soucy*. It's been quite a hassle."

"*Alors?* Where did you drive from?"

"Montréal."

"Are you Margot's chauffeur? I didn't realize women do that now, though I imagine it was bound to happen."

"I am not Margot's chauffeur, *Madame Soucy*, I'm Margot's wife."

To say I felt numbingly thrilled to watch Estelle take on my mother would be a gross understatement.

Lacey, too, detected the potential for melodrama. "Marguerite, sweetheart, why don't you show your daughter and her friend your bedroom?" She fit the tiara on Marguerite's head, arranged her hair neatly around it, and turned to Estelle and me. "Someone will be by in fifteen minutes to put her to bed. The next time you visit, come earlier so you can stay longer."

"We would love to see your bedroom, *Madame Soucy*. I bet you have all sorts of Margot mementos. As her partner of twenty-five years, I'm eager to learn about her childhood as only a mother could know it." Estelle grinned wickedly, and I imagined her smothering my mother with a pillow, this road trip through my past concluding as a cautionary tale about angry and mendacious women.

After Lacey left us alone, my mother pinched the tiara off like she was holding a pair of soiled underwear and tossed it in the wastebasket by her bed. "I've never met such a stupid girl in all my life."

I laughed, surprising us all. For so long, I had sat on the cruel hope that Marguerite was completely broken. What energy I had wasted, even if passively. Of course she was completely broken. Her hopeful little teenage heart had cracked cleanly in two when *grandmère* and *grandpère* Soucy sold her to Morgan. She had been terminally devastated by the message that even though she was beautiful and well-mannered, she was a commodity, not a beloved daughter. I could see Estelle was ready to confront Marguerite at every turn, pin her to the weakest evidence to explain the present state of our marriage, and in spite of my sudden flash of insight and compassion, I couldn't bring myself to say, "Save your efforts, Elle." It felt good to watch her fight for me.

Marguerite's bedroom was clinical and unadorned, which was the only reason I went in. I didn't want to interact with any "mementos" from my past. Estelle expressed her disapproval of the only artwork in the room, a framed photograph of a sunflower—"I find these flowers so beastly and imposing"— and then commented on Lacey's earlier claim that my mother talked about me every day—"Surely that was an exaggeration. There's no trace at all of your daughter in here, *Madame Soucy*. I'm disappointed." The only personal object was a dark wood handcrafted jewellery box on the night table. When I pointed at it, my mother smacked my wrist.

"What have I told you about sneaking through my stuff? Do you think because I'm right here that makes it okay?"

Estelle took my wrist and kissed it the way a mother kisses a child's scraped elbow. Marguerite didn't blink, whereas I flushed violently.

"Your father got that for me on his last trip. Or should I say some man came here and gave it to me after Morgan died. I almost threw the hideous thing away, but then I thought it might be a good place to keep these." My mother removed the lid and tipped the box until two beige conical shells fell into her palm. "Remember these?" And then, to Estelle, "You're quite pretty for a chauffeur, I'll say. You must have a very confident husband to permit his wife to drive strangers around all day."

"I'm not a chauffeur, *Madame Soucy*. I'm Margot's wife."

My mother spoke to the sunset outside her window. "When Margot was, *bon*, I don't know, five or six, she decided she wanted a pet even though she didn't know the first thing about animals. She thought having a cat or a dog, a dog in particular, was easy, because every summer when the tourists arrived in Wellfleet, they came with their kids and their springer spaniels, and the spaniels were always well-behaved. I said no, but of course her father came home from one of his business trips and said yes, because little Margot always got what she wanted from *Papa*. But I held my ground—Morgan didn't care for dogs anyway—and the issue was put to sleep. Margot sulked about it for a few days. She even refused to come out with us the night before Morgan left for a month. *Tant pis pour toi!* I said. The next morning, she still wouldn't come out of her bedroom, she was on some silly hunger strike or something, and after having breakfast and lunch all by myself, I decided this had to stop. I was so bored eating alone. So I went into your room, remember, *chérie*? And I grabbed your jiggly little hand and we went to Duck Harbor and *voilá*, you discovered hermit crabs."

"What a lovely story, *Madame Soucy*. And did you hear me before? I said I'm Margot's wife. My name is Estelle." Estelle's hands were on Marguerite's shoulders, and she was talking into her face the way one might talk to a slightly deaf senior citizen.

Marguerite's expression soured as she shrugged free. She dropped the shells back into the jewellery box. "Yes, I heard, but I can't be tricked anymore."

"Tricked?"

"Deceived. Believed for *une imbécile*. Whatever you choose to call it."

"I think what she means, Elle, is she's a raging homophobe."

"I'm not raging at all. I'm very content right now."

"Then why do you keep ignoring Estelle?"

My mother cast her eyes toward the ceiling, Ann-Margret style. "*Franchement*, Margot, I don't care if you're a homosexual as long as I don't have to deal with it. And I've already told everyone here that you're married to a man named Christophe, so don't go around all *bisou-bisou*, okay? I have to be careful about my reputation here—you never know what someone might drop into your soup. What bothers me is how you can lie right to my face after everything else you've done to me. Why couldn't you just say, 'Maman, I am married to my chauffeur'? Let me demonstrate: Chérie, these shells are not hermit crab shells. I don't know what they are. I picked them up on my afternoon port walk today so I would have something to give you. That simple nurse told me I should have something to give you. Tu vois? Is it so hard to be honest?"

Estelle produced the Rosa Bonheur print from her purse. "We brought you something, too, Madame Soucy. Maybe you could replace the sunflower with this."

Marguerite accepted the print from Estelle. After a pause, she dabbed her eyes, even though they were dry. "Oh yes, je me souviens. We used to have a full-scale reproduction hanging in the living room, didn't we, chérie? In Wellfleet. Remember?"

"I don't think so," Estelle said, becoming cross and reclaiming the print. "Unless you lived in a mansion, it would be impossible to accommodate a full-scale reproduction of The Horse Fair."

At last, Marguerite appeared willing to take Estelle seriously. "I wouldn't have guessed you for an art connoisseur."

"She manages a photo gallery," I said, figuring if I didn't enter the conversation now, then I would leave without having said any words of consequence.

"Oh?"

"Yes, it's called L'Espace Vif."

"The Empty Space? A pessimistic name for a gallery, don't you think?"

"No, L'Epace V-i-f, the Lively Space, not Vide."

Estelle placed the Bonheur print on the night table. "I'll wait for you by the elevator, okay? It was nice to meet you, Madame Soucy."

I didn't rush after her. If her goal in dragging me to Folsom had been to expose some masterfully concealed sociopathic side of my personality by disproving my claims about a childhood of scorching humiliation, then she had failed, and it wouldn't hurt to give her a few minutes to privately acknowledge her failure. Maybe this wasn't my final plank walk in our marriage.

"Guess that's my cue," I said, splaying my hands and shrugging.

"Oh you look just like your father when you do that. You would have made such a handsome boy." Marguerite's eyes glassed over, but those sorrows and regrets weren't for me. "Will you tell Morgan I miss him? I get so lonely when he takes those long trips, and you're never any help."

"Everything okay in here?" Lacey appeared and handed Marguerite a folded periwinkle blue nightgown. "Fresh from the dryer, sweetheart. Gerald's warming up some milk."

I nodded curtly before I took my leave. There was no need for me to say, "It's been a gas."

ALL I WANTED TO DO was fuck my wife. Inside the elevator, I pushed her to the back and kissed the faint lipstick stain from her mouth that had been antagonizing me since morning. When the elevator opened onto the ground floor, we strode, hands in each other's back pockets, to the front desk, *hemmed* impatiently while the bald man retrieved our IDs. Estelle wanted to go to the beach, so we were going to the beach. We cut behind Folsom to Hyannis Port, feeling as bold and inconspicuous as teenagers; no one came to admire low tide under a waning crescent moon, so we had the place to ourselves. Estelle sat on top of a capsized rowboat and raised her arms for me to undress her. I pulled her onto the sand and rolled her shirt over her head, re-tied the red bandana around her hair so I could kiss every part of her face. After she moaned and kneaded her fists into my waist, she flipped me onto my back and climbed on top of me. We repeated this exercise until our crotches burned and we had sand in our eyes, and then we sat huffing until Estelle said she wanted to immerse her feet in the water. I reached for my shirt but she swiped it away, balling it with hers and tossing both into the darkness. We walked out far enough for the water to lap at our mid-calves before she spoke.

"Everything bad about today is my fault, isn't it?"

"Not everything. It's not your fault my mother's a demented fool."

Estelle held an open palm skyward and revealed two tiny conical shells.

"You stole from *my mother*? That's it, you'll never amount to anything more than a tarty chauffeur—my tarty chauffeur."

Estelle retreated when I tried to kiss her. She hugged her arms over her breasts, and the shells tumbled soundlessly into the water. "It got cold really fast. I think our time here's over, *oui*?"

Under the waning crescent moon I studied the silhouette of my wife's mouth and thought of Katy's. I recalled the way Katy had eaten French fries at La Ronde, how salt crystals had clung to the peach fuzz under her bottom lip. I could not recall wanting, at the time, to wipe the salt crystals away with my thumb, but I wanted to now. K-K-K-Katy: a lisping girl who had the daring to critique my manner of speaking. A girl who believed carousel horses could gallop right off the platform, yet who was engaged to a guy as plain as the ring he had given her. Katherine de Wilde: a girl I had no business thinking about.

"Margot? I said I'm cold. We need to find a motel for the night."

I turned toward the shore. We had walked out farther than I had realized, and I could just barely distinguish the rowboat. "We're going to have a time of it finding our shirts, you know."

"Shit!" Estelle crouched to the water. I crouched alongside her as a flood beam reached for us from the shore.

"Who's out there?" called a male voice.

"Shit—shit! What do we do, Margot? What do we do?"

We stood up. The flood beam blanketed my breasts, which were unfortunately responsive to the cool air, but I chose not to cover myself since the gesture would only emphasize the great flaw of our situation. I placed my hands above my head and smiled amenably at the man wading toward us. "Good evening, Officer."

"And what are we doing all the way out here, ladies?"

The officer adjusted his flashlight to a softer beam. Estelle eyed his trouser legs, which were rolled above the knee, and then covered her face with her hands, her shoulders bobbing up and down from laughter.

"We came to visit my mother at Folsom. She's a long-time resident of the Bluefish wing. Marguerite Wright. Maybe you know her? Now I'm giving my wife a little tour of the area. She's never been to the Cape, and we have to leave early in the morning."

"I wouldn't call Hyannis Port at this hour a prime tourist attraction."

"You are absolutely right, Officer, but it's been years since I lived here—Wellfleet, that is. Off Chequessett Neck Road? I haven't followed the tide schedule since the eighties, I'm afraid."

The officer shone his beam on Estelle. "Ma'am, please uncover your face."

Estelle parted her hands like a grownup playing peekaboo with a toddler. "Hello, sir," she said.

"Ma'am, remove your hands from your face and put them at your sides. How much have you had to drink tonight?"

Estelle dipped her chin to keep her laughter in check. "I apologize, Officer. I'm so nervous right now it's making me hysterical. Please let us be on our way—it's what we were about to do. We'll pay a fine for indecent exposure if we have to, but we're not the sort of people you're looking for." She caught her breath. "Please, Officer, we really did visit Margot's mother, and it's really true I've never been to the Cape. It's also true we came out here to see if we can save our marriage. All in all, you've caught us at a terrible time."

The undesirable after-effect of making love to my wife on the beach was that the aforementioned fact about our marriage could no longer be suspended, and I felt as startled by Estelle's frank statement as the policeman looked. Surely he hadn't expected to find himself at the centre of marital conflict when he spotted two women frolicking in the pungent seaweed.

The officer shone his flood beam toward the shore. "I would like you to walk a straight line all the way back," he said. He stayed close behind as we followed his order. Once we reached land, he helped us find our shirts. He rolled his trouser legs down while we righted ourselves, chaperoned us to the Fiat and verified licenses and registration, and then offered to show us the way to the Hyannis Inn Motel. Estelle smoked a cigarette and favoured her lower back while we waited for the officer to come around with his car, and I picked bits of sea debris off my calves. We weren't bold, inconspicuous teenagers at all; we were middle-aged women caught naked in the dark, our skin stinging from the saltwater and petty scandal.

10. CHEKHOV'S GUN

I AWOKE WITH THE IMPULSE to leave my life the way I had left Anaïs and Benoît Soucy and Saint-Télesphore for good on my eighteenth birthday. Just five days earlier I had answered the call of boredom, and then promptly—as one must with a snake oil salesman—shut the door on it. But instead of appreciating my fortune of twenty-five years with the woman I loved, I proceeded to stomp around the loft and crab about my punishing privilege. Poor bored middle-aged me. If I hadn't been such an ostrich, as Olivier Weinstock believed me to be, I could have destroyed the damning contents of the Xerox box. Of course Estelle would eventually discover them. Oh hell, I could have abandoned Marguerite's fictions in a city alleyway for someone to claim as found art, if I had so badly needed a thrill. Or, as Estelle had snipped after discovering the letters, I could have returned them to Le Canon Noir along with a great big apology to my great big mentor, and then, after sharing with Bertrand a cup of his latest favourite specialty tea, I could have gone home—not before detouring for two blueberry tarts—and prepared a dinner to greet Estelle with after work, and then, over candlelight and white Rueda, apologized for my thick-headed behaviour of late, reached across the temporary Ikea table for my wife's lovely, slender hands, and said, "Baby girl, tonight I am taking you to the carousel," and we would not find ourselves now at a stucco motel in Hyannis, Massachusetts.

Estelle was curled around an extra pillow on the bed. I felt feverish as I returned to order the sofa where I had slept, and by the time I finished showering, I was decided on the things we would not do no matter how much Estelle pressed: We would not drive to my childhood home in Wellfleet to gawk. We would not spend the morning shivering on the beach. We certainly would not fly to Grand Rapids to collect what was supposedly mine from Morgan's estate (and anyway, Estelle couldn't have been serious about that). And we would not conclude our journey in Lanaudière to imbibe St-Ambroise beer and gnaw on sweet corn with the Cotés. Estelle would insist, before the long drive home, that we stop at a local breakfast nook. It would be the least I could do for her, she would say.

I recalled Olivier's edict to be charitable with my wife in situations where my reflex was to be tight-fisted, but I could see no benefit in our spending twenty minutes frowning into free-refill coffee mugs to avoid such paramount questions as, "May I come home now, or should I purchase a timeshare in Le Cabinet Particulier?" In the last five days we had argued every day, made love twice, driven six hundred kilometres to kick up embers from my past, and none of it, though it was the most momentum we had gathered in months, had solved the problem of our sagging, uncertain marriage.

By the time Estelle woke up and stretched her long, naked limbs in the dusty sunlight, her half-smile an invitation for me to join her in bed, I felt the panic of a person being buried alive. When my Blackberry lit up on the coffee table, saving me from the callous act of turning down my wife in her vulnerable state, I nearly cried out from relief.

"Sorry, sorry," I said, grabbing the phone. "Hold that thought." I dipped outside and sat on a plastic deck chair in front of the room, and pressed a palm over my heart.

"*Esprit, qu'as-tu*? You sound like you have taken up the morning jog of the middle-aged."

"I'm afraid it has almost come to that. How are you, Bertrand?"

"How was your visit with *la maniaque* Marguerite?"

I paused to swallow and wipe sweat from my chin. "Delightful. She wore a cocktail dress for the occasion. It was orange and brown—hold on, I'm sorry, there's another line." I didn't recognize the caller ID, but I didn't care. I needed to keep moving. "Yes?"

"Oh, hi, hello. Can I, I mean *may I* speak to Margot? Please?"

"Yes."

"Margot?"

I knew only one person who lisped. "Hello, Katy."

"Thank god! I don't know what I would of done if you didn't answer."

"You *could* have left a voice message, or sent me a text message. Isn't that what your generation's all about?"

"No one leaves voice messages nowadays."

Katy laughed, and I felt a baffling excitement. Perhaps I was still asleep, for I had dreamed about her in the night. In the dream, we were back on the roller coaster she had begged me to ride with her. I kept yelling that I was going to be sick, just as I had yelled on Friday, and Katy kept laughing and unfastening my button-down. When she finished, my button-down flew open as the Vampire lunged around a vertical loop of bright purple track, and then ratchets, pliers, clamps, and drill bits—tools I had no reason to be thinking about, even unconsciously—came pouring out of me. The tools turned to particles and scattered into the air, and Katy said, in the glum, pouty manner of a teenage girl who believes she knows better than her parents, "Good one, Margot. Now we can't fix anything."

My hands trembled as I switched my Blackberry from one ear to the other. "I'm actually on the other line with someone right now."

"I can call you back. Or you can call me. Do you have caller ID? It's when the person's number..."

"This really isn't a good time. Is there some emergency?"

"No, but sort of. I mean I'm not hurt or anything, but I do have some pretty upsetting news to tell you. Can you call me back as soon as possible?"

I looked over my shoulder into the motel room. The bed was empty, so I figured ten minutes before Estelle was showered and ready to leave. I would tell her I had gotten disconnected from Bertrand and needed to phone him back while she returned our room key. "Why don't you tell me now."

"But you're on the other line."

"I can talk with the person later."

"Shouldn't you tell the person? Who is it? You never talk specifically about anyone in your life."

"Maybe I have no one in my life."

"Is it your husband?"

"Katy."

"Oh right, you're barren so you probably don't have a husband. Hey, you never told me who the pictures of you and Napoleon were for."

"I'm going to hang up in five seconds. One."

"I don't understand why you won't tell me. It's ridiculous, Margot. What's the big deal?"

"Two. Three."

"Fine. Are you sitting down? Where are you right now?"

"Four."

"Just tell me where you are and I'll tell you everything. It's not fair that I'm the one who always does all the talking."

"I'm in Hyannis, Massachusetts."

"Where's that?"

"Cape Cod."

"So you *are* with someone. You didn't tell me you were going on vacation. People are usually excited about vacations. And they talk about them. We had dinner together on *Friday*, Margot. That's when you tell people about your upcoming vacation two days away."

"I'm on a business trip, Katy. A last-minute business trip that just so happens to be in a desirable location. Are you satisfied now?"

"Oh. Hey, maybe when you're done there you can come to Canaan and look at my gun. Maybe you'll want to buy it."

"You own a gun?"

"Actually it's Ryan's and I don't think it's worth a whole lot, but he says it's a family artifact, and we do need money for our wedding."

"Heirloom, not artifact. I don't like this Ryan you keep speaking of, but who am I. Now would you please tell me what you phoned to tell me?" I looked over my shoulder again. Estelle was in her underwear, her hair wrapped in a white motel towel, and she was speaking into her phone. I assumed she was speaking to Marianne, the way she smiled, kicked one foot back and curled her toes. Marianne, whose spoiled-milk beige car was our only way home, whose Siamese cats had surely ruined my mohair settee by now, and who, I was certain, had designs on my wife, although at that moment I was more riled by the phone call from Katy.

"Margot? Are you sitting? Make sure you're sitting for this."

"I've been sitting the whole time."

"Okay, see I'm sorry, but there's no other way to say it: They've completely closed Le Galopant. Yesterday morning I got to work and Étienne was waiting for me at the cotton candy wagon, and he said after this summer he's quitting because he hates operating the other carousel and he heard that they're going to put a McDonald's where Le Galopant was. Talk about insulting the injury."

"Insult to injury."

"Exactly!"

"That can't be true, Katy. Le Galopant's an important feature of the park—it's an attraction. Once it's repaired, I'm sure Étienne will be able to resume his role there."

"No, Margot, you don't understand. Yesterday? When Étienne brought me to the carousel? They were taking the horses off the platform and lying them down on top of each other on a flatbed. It was all dirty, but when I told one of the men to clean it off, you know, because the horses are all white, he pretended he didn't understand English. I tried to make Étienne tell the guys, but you've seen how Étienne is when he mopes. He's totally useless. He needs to be on Celexa."

"Laying on top of one another."

"Huh?"

"They were laying the horses on top of one another, not 'lying them down on top of each other'."

"You can't fake it, Margot. I know this is breaking your heart. Look how upset you got when you couldn't find Napoleon on Friday. Because it's so *sad*. Me and Étienne cried together, while they were taking the carousel apart. We held hands and cried openly in front of everyone, because no one else showed any concern. I mean, it all happened before the park opened for the day, so you can't really blame visitors for not caring, but still. By lunchtime Étienne came back to my wagon and said he was leaving—*Foque it*, he said in that adorable French accent—and so I left early with him since that way I could catch an earlier bus home."

"You're back in New York for the weekend?"

"I'm back for good now that the Fortins don't need me anymore."

"When did that happen?"

"I was always supposed to leave the first weekend in August. Julien, the Fortins' little boy, is starting chemotherapy for his leukemia tomorrow."

"Will you be coming back?"

"No, and that's the other thing I wanted to tell you, since I have all this money left from the taxi fare you gave me."

"You don't think *I'm leaving this weekend* would have been a reasonable thing to tell me at dinner?"

"You didn't tell me about your vacation-business trip-whatever. Plus I wasn't expecting you to give me taxi fare. Plus I didn't think you'd care."

"You're right, I don't care. Keep the change. I'm sure you'll come back to Montréal one day."

"But I don't know when that will be. I mean, I'm getting married soon, remember? Ryan swears he'll never go to Canada. One time when he was camping in the Adirondacks with his family, some tourist called them rednecks and that was it, his mind was made up about all Canadians. I know this probably makes me an awful person, but I'm going to miss Napoleon more than the Fortins' kids, even little Julien with his leukemia."

"It doesn't make you an awful person, Katy. You were paid to look after those kids, not to love them."

"I'm also going to miss you, and that definitely makes me a weird person because I barely know you. It's just you went on the Vampire with me, and then you took me out for pizza, and that's the first time I've ever done anything in Montréal with anyone other than the Fortins."

After I hung up with Katy, I remained on the deck chair and watched a family of four pack their silver Honda CR-V. The ordinariness of their routine was mesmerizing, or perhaps my conversation with Katy was the source of my lightheadedness. The father heaved two jumbo-sized suitcases into the trunk, and then his son at his side tucked two netted bags filled with beach toys and other vacation paraphernalia between the suitcases. The younger son, who had been asleep in his mother's arms when she brought him outside, woke up seconds after being buckled into the rear-facing car seat. His face shone with sunburn and tears as he strained with all his might against the buckle. He beat his dimpled fists at the sky, punted his feet so furiously a sandal flew out the window. When his mother crooned, "It's okay, sweetie, we're going home," and he went on to scream every vowel combination in the alphabet, I knew exactly how he felt.

Estelle, still topless, was buttoning her jeans when I went

back inside the room. She had made the bed and placed a twenty-dollar tip on top of the pillows.

"A bit much, don't you think?" I said, looking in my wallet for smaller bills.

Estelle pulled the towel from her head. "How's old Bert doing?" she asked, combing her hair with her fingers.

"Oh, you know, same as yesterday. He wants me to make a little side-trip to Canaan, New York. That all right with you?" I could feel my pulse thrashing in the roof of my mouth.

Estelle took the Fiat key from the coffee table. "There's a Thrifty Car Rental on Ocean Street. You can walk there. I mapped it on Google."

"Everything okay?" Of course I knew everything was not okay, but I couldn't leave before acknowledging my wife's terrifically pained expression.

She spoke in a quiet, deep voice. "Please return Bertrand's call. He phoned me after you ditched him. Why would you do that? Who were you talking to, Margot?"

"I did not ditch him. A friend called and needs my help. I got caught up in the conversation. What? That's never happened to you before?"

"Who can possibly be more important than Bertrand? He's not well, Margot. *Bertrand* needs help."

"Don't be a bitch about this, please. I'll go straight home after I look at my friend's gun. It might be worth something, and she needs money."

Estelle bit down on her knuckles. "*I'll go straight home after I look at my friend's gun.* Just go. Go to this friend in need and come home when it fucking well pleases you." She covered her breasts and looked around the room for her shirt; she turned her back to me when she found it.

"I told you after I came home from La Ronde, remember? A girl helped me photograph the carousel." I wanted to add, "But maybe you don't remember because you were loaded on wine," but I had no right to take the lead in this fight.

Estelle said, "What I don't understand is how this girl has become your friend since Wednesday. Or have you been hiding her in a Xerox box all these years, too?" and then left.

DURING OUR YEAR in Savannah, while Estelle completed her graduate degree in Advertising, I learned about collectible firearms from Bertrand's contacts in the Deep South. I returned to Montréal proud of how my education had shaped me, and confident that with my new credentials I was more deserving of Estelle's devotion than I had been before we left. Before our departure, I had spent full days and nights in anguish as I imagined my girlfriend falling for some fabulous American. The morning of our departure, I begged Estelle to cancel her plans for graduate school, and I would cancel mine to become a dealer. We were in our mid-twenties, still young enough to make up our minds later about what to do with our lives. Maybe I would become assistant manager of Le Real Deal pawnshop, and Estelle's former "Drawing I" teacher would find her steady work posing nude for artists. Also, I wasn't ready to leave our east-end studio apartment above the gentlemen's club. I had moved in the same day I left Saint-Télesphore. After learning I had nowhere to go in January, the first of Québec's two most brutal winter months, the driver my father had paid to remove me from the Soucys stopped at a gas station to use the payphone. When we were on the road again, he said, "Rent is two-seventy-five. First month's free, I'll cover the second." He observed me in his rear-view mirror and then added, "This has nothing to do with your father; it's not him in disguise trying to help you. It's me in a rush to do my one good deed of the New Year." The driver left me on rue Sainte-Catherine and Saint-Alexandre, and instructed me to walk east on Sainte-Catherine until I came to a set of black industrial doors. One door opened to the stairwell leading up to my new home, and the other opened to the stairwell leading down to the gentlemen's club. I accepted enough money for a week of groceries and one month's rent from the driver, and for two years, until the afternoon Estelle pursued me on rue de la Commune, the unsavoury upstairs apartment was my only tether to this world.

The first time I met with Bertrand after Estelle and I returned from Savannah, I showed him my meticulous (though far from skilled) illustrations of every firearm I had handled and learned how to clean with mineral spirits and soft cloths. I had organized the illustrations by type—pistols, rifles, shotguns, muzzleloaders—in a three-ring binder as thick as an encyclopedia.

"*Jeunesse*," he said, shaking his head when I unrolled the map I had marked each time I visited a landmark of the South, "what time you must have spent recording these details."

I was confused by his dismay. Shouldn't he be pleased I had been productive rather than brooding while Estelle was busy with her studies? Wasn't I the investment he had envisioned?

"*Esprit*, you are not *un investissement*. You are someone I see taking over my business eventually. This is a partnership. And I sent you to a new place for a year. A whole year! If I had been in your position—especially at your age—I would have explored every corner of this new place, and then every corner of nearby new places, and then corners of the places beyond."

"Oh. I didn't realize that was part of my job."

"Not your job, Margot: human nature. It is natural to explore, but you are so focused on the surface of things, so worried about disrupting order. I have not known you long and I am positive it is your default way of being. But can you tell me about your *experience* with all those guns you drew? Did you spend as much time handling them as you did drawing them? Caressing them, smelling them, whispering to them until they told you their secret histories? How boring if not."

During my year away, I had become accustomed to Bertrand's frequent affirmations by phone that I was doing marvellous work. So-and-so had enjoyed discussing militaria with me, so-and-so was impressed I had identified on my own a Model 3

Smith & Wesson whose barrel had been cut down. Why was he lacing into me now?

His tone softened in response to my silence. "Let us try again. What did you learn about guns while you were away?"

"It's all in here." I offered him the binder.

"No it is not." Bertrand took it from me and threw it across the shop. The binder landed with its pages open to the floor, and I felt sickened by the possibility that my favourite illustration, an 1810 Belgian flintlock cavalry pistol that had taken me a frustrating week to complete, might be ruined.

"Why did you do that?" I meant to yell at this man who had tricked me into changing my life, but what came out instead was a loud, undignified sob. "I did everything you asked me to!" I glared at him as I sat on the floor and gathered the binder onto my lap. I wanted to run out of the shop and never see this garrulous man again, but the consequence of letting one sob escape was losing control over all the rest. "I hate you, I hate you. You have no right to yell at me. I did everything you asked."

Bertrand flipped the "*Ouvert*" sign to "*Fermé*" and lowered the emerald green chenille blind. He sat beside me on the floor and, for a while, listened to my unhinged confession about being the progeny of a maniac and a deserter. I apologized for having not warned him my DNA might be host to my mother's madness and my father's transactional relationship to everything, so perhaps he didn't want me to work for him after all, and would he please never mention my parents around Estelle? I had told her they didn't want to meet her, and it had broken my heart to see her reaction. But it had been a necessary lie: My parents were self-absorbed bigots, and if Estelle met them and they were cruel enough to her, she might leave me, for how could a person born from such monsters not be at least a little like them?

Eventually Bertrand pried the binder from me. I was so spent I leaned against him while he spoke. "I want to keep you more now than I did before," he said, laying a palm across my forehead as though feeling me for fever. "But you'll need to develop an instinct for keeping your soul happy so that you do not burn out before we even begin this venture—*notre aventure.*"

"In case you haven't noticed, I'm not at all adventurous. It could take me the rest of my life to recover from my year in Savannah."

At this, Bertrand sighed. "Please try to enjoy life now, *esprit.* This way the regrets in your future will not seem so *insurmountable.*"

THE THREE-HOUR COMMUTE from Hyannis to Canaan was exactly enough time for me to experience the appropriate amount of guilt for dropping Bertrand's phone call, followed by the appropriate amount of frustration with Estelle for not saying, "Don't bother coming home after you look at your friend's gun." Our marriage now was not unlike being stuck at the bottom of a very deep and narrow waterless well, where only one person can thrive (though neither will admit it), by stepping on the shoulders of the other to gain traction on the cobbled wall, all the way up to the pinhole of light. Once you've climbed out of the well, there are still miles to go before you figure out where you are (everything looks dull and similar under the full, oppressive light), and remember where you came from (emotional starvation causes amnesia), and when finally you're ready to go back—which you might never be—to rescue she who is still in the well, it's too late: either someone else has come to save her, or she is unrecognizable.

Once I tired of wallowing and conjecturing, I thought about Katy and her fiancé's gun that might or might not be of value. Would I have to meet this Ryan? Would Katy seem less exciting draped over the arm of a guy who had opted for a flimsy engagement ring so that he could give himself a brand-new truck? I could not stand to see her, regardless of the nuisance I found her to be, draped over some dead-end's arm. When I pulled onto the de Wilde property, an expanse of field imprinted with tire tracks leading to the house, I was feeling more anxious than I had when I left Hyannis.

The de Wilde residence was a single-level tumbledown cabin whose corroded steel roof was patched in places with asphalt shingles. Someone had cultivated a lovely garden of phlox and aster along the front of the cabin, and on one side, next to a flourish of Russian sage, a nanny goat with pendulous ears surveyed her land from atop a cluster of logs whittled to resemble a mountain range. The nanny announced my arrival by yelling and shaking her head to clatter the cowbell around her neck, and then two sheep, one freshly shorn and the other mid-shear, emerged bleating and bucking from behind the cabin. Katy rushed after the churlish creatures, pleading with them not to run away. Her hair was pulled back with a red bandana. Estelle had worn a red bandana the day before, and again before I left the motel that morning, but it was Katy's which aroused in me the memory of Robin from The Who concert. I succumbed, momentarily, to the kind of wild thinking that had crippled my mother for most of her life and imagined the loping, lisping teenager before me was the same girl who had held my hand outside the Riverfront Coliseum on December 3, 1979, and anchored me amid the frenzy. When Katy realized I was parked in front of her home, staring at her in surely a dumbfounded way, she tossed her work gloves in the air and ran over.

"You just totally made my day," she shouted, and flung open the car door and hugged me so ferociously I hiccupped.

"This gun better be worth something," I said dumbly, struggling to release my seatbelt.

Katy reached down and released it for me before skipping around to the passenger side. She sat beside me and took an index card from the kangaroo pocket of her denim overalls. Her overalls were coral pink and form-fitting, and underneath, she was wearing the same "Meat is Murder" T-shirt she had worn on Friday, when I had gone back to La Ronde for her. The word "erudite" was pencilled on the index card in spindly cursive, smudged from left to right. The "i," I gathered, was meant to be a spool of cotton candy.

"After we got off the phone I learned a new word just to impress you," she said, laughing the way a person laughs when everything is right in her life. "Now you have to teach me how to say it, and you can't get annoyed if I get it wrong on the first try, because I'm telling you up front that I do not know how to say this word. I found it in this super-old dictionary my dad has. It's basically an antique—my dad says it's from 1980-something. Half the letters are missing. It reminds me of when me and Étienne watched them take down Le Galopant. Soon all the Napoleons will be missing. Margot, you have to promise me you'll go there as soon as you get home—like, if it's too late tonight, then you have to go tomorrow morning, okay? Please? I need you to tell me what's going on with my carousel. Please promise me you'll do it."

She leaned over and kissed me quickly, strongly, on the mouth, and I unravelled into sobs.

AFTER A CONCERTED RANSACKING of her kitchen, Katy located a teabag inside a Frosty the Snowman cookie tin recessed in a cupboard along with other seasonal paraphernalia like baseball-themed beer cozies and a child's smiling pumpkin bucket. "Oh my god, we haven't used any of this stuff in years. Like, I don't even remember most of it ... except the number-9 birthday candle. That's the year my mom died." She examined the teabag against the early afternoon sunlight reclining through the slat window above the stove before dropping it into a mug stamped with *#1 Daughter*. "Tea never expires, right?" In the car, I had blamed my tearful disintegration on too many hours of highway driving, all that repeating scenery gave me tunnel vision, and Katy had insisted a stack of pancakes topped with honey from Mick's Honey Emporium across the field would brighten my day. "Ryan tells everyone my pancakes sealed the deal for him." I told her I would settle for tea, if she had any.

She was an anxious host, deluging me with offers to run a coconut-scented bubble bath or freshen her sheets so I could nap before returning to Montréal. Aside from an impromptu spa day at the de Wilde residence, what I wanted least was to see Katy's bedroom, surely youthful and incomprehensible, and confirmation I had no business, middle-aged and married, being alone with this girl. The more she tried to accommodate me like I was some weary traveller and not someone she had just kissed with vigour, the more foolish I felt. While she went on and on about Elizabeth and Diana, her father's merino sheep who despised Victor, the miniature donkey stallion, but loved Celeste, the nanny goat, I sat, still hiccupping, at the kitchen table, suppressing the competing urges to either heave or sob anew. I indulged in the possibility that our kiss hadn't counted, for why else would Katy have recovered so quickly? To count, surely a kiss had to last longer than three seconds. I couldn't know, because I had never kissed anyone other than Estelle.

"There's some leftover back bacon from this morning. I can warm it in a pan for you. Or eggs? Do you like eggs?"

"Frankly, Katy, I am here to make sure you're okay—you were more than a little upset when you phoned me this morning. I drove out of my way to get here. As for your fiancé's gun, since I haven't renewed my errors and omissions coverage, I can't make any official comment, I'm sorry. I'd be delighted to stay for a cup of tea, but then I have to go."

Katy fiddled with the straps of her overalls. She leaned against the refrigerator, a boxy matte gold GE from the mid-seventies. She crossed her arms like she had a bellyache. Her toes turned inward. "I didn't really think you'd come when I asked you to. I just wanted to keep you on the phone for as long as I could so I said whatever popped into my head. Do you hate me now? Except it's true what I said about Le Galopant. I would never make that up."

Katy had been affected by our kiss, after all. My response to her effusive greeting had stunned her as much as her greeting had stunned me, and she was waiting, flustered and awkward, for me to say what happened next.

I went to the fridge and leaned beside her. She grabbed my hand when the fridge wobbled. "Three questions," I said. "Three. Got it?"

"This time you have to actually answer."

"You just wasted a question."

"That wasn't a question."

"A question was implied. It was: Margot, are you going to answer my questions this time?"

Katy huffed. "Stop talking like a robot. And I need to practise first. Like, your hat?"

"What about my hat?"

"You told me before we got on the Vampire that you always wear a hat. So where is it?"

"This counts as your first question."

"Did you forget it somewhere? Did you travel without it? I can't see you going anywhere without exactly what you need."

"It's in the other car."

"Whose car?"

"Never mind. You're down to one question."

"Margot?"

"Make it count."

Katy released my hand and repositioned herself in front of me, the tips of her Converse sneakers touching my knock-offs, her pulse visible along her throat. "What is your full and complete name?"

If I answered this question like I should have on Wednesday while Katy photographed me riding Le Galopant, then would my fascination with her end as instantly as it had begun? Would it be as though someone poured ice water over me and woke me from the nightmare of being terminally dissatisfied with my marriage? Overlooking an incomplete kiss, it was not too late for me to redeem myself from this situation I had cultivated by not disregarding it, and which had only one outcome if I lingered. As someone who typically did not believe in risking anything greater than a found dollar on a lottery ticket, I surely did not have it in me to squander everything on a teenage girl no matter how unanticipated my appetite for her was or how much it gnawed at me. And so I said: "Margot Anaïs Soucy-Coté."

"I didn't know you're *French*. You don't sound it at all."

"My mother is Marguerite Emmanuelle-Françoise Soucy, as Québécoise as it gets."

"Is Coté your dad?"

"No."

"Then who?"

"My father was Morgan Wright. He was from Michigan."

"No, Coté. Who is Coté?"

"Estelle."

When Katy pressed, "Estelle who? Who is Estelle? Tell me, Margot, please," her lisp the most cumbersome I had known it to be, I redeemed myself with the cruelty of a single statement: "My wife."

"Your wife?" Katy took a step back and cleared her throat. "Your—oh. Your *family*."

"Yes. My family."

Celeste's cowbell clanged for attention, and through a window to the front yard I witnessed the surreal spectacle of a tiny light grey donkey galloping across the property, braying heatedly as Elizabeth and Diana bullied him toward the road. Katy ran outside to corral the bickering beasts, and I was still leaning against the fridge when she returned, clinging to the notion that I was projecting composure even though the rattling of the fridge betrayed my trembling legs. On my way to the kitchen table, I nearly buckled when a pickup truck, floodlight on the hood and chrome guard on the grille, announced its arrival with three arrogant honks. Katy wiped her face clean with her bandana, tucked the bandana into the kangaroo pocket of her overalls, and I blurted that she looked adorable and had no reason to fret. The tips of her ears reddened as she smoothed her bangs behind them.

"You're the first person to think that." She continued waveringly after a pause. "Ryan's gun is a twelve-gage, um, Ithaca Featherlight. His father used it once to shoot a black bear and the bear's head is mounted over their TV. At Christmastime they put a tinsel wig on it."

I remained seated while she went outside to her fiancé. I was tempted to watch them, preview how they behaved as a couple before I met them as one, but I checked my Blackberry instead, since I had turned it off after leaving Hyannis. There was a missed call and voice message from Bertrand, and a conciliatory text from Estelle. *Getting on 1-89 N. Let me know you're safe. Sorry I yelled. Just come home.*

About to look at gun, I replied. *A Featherlight. Wouldn't have bothered if I'd known.*

The only other text was Estelle's from late Thursday night: *Gaufrier.* Waffle-maker. It seemed like years ago when my most significant goal *du jour* had been to finally enjoy my cast iron gift from Bertrand.

I stood when Katy and Ryan entered the cabin. Ryan tucked the Ithaca behind his back and bowed.

"Nice to meet you, ma'am. Katherine swore up and down you wanted to see the Cox family shotgun even though it's not for sale except for the right price. It wouldn't surprise me if she's also complained to you about the bear my father took down with it. Well, she's a big softie, a gatherer not a hunter, and I ask her all the time: Babe, how're you going to live your dash? That little line on a gravestone between when a person's born and when they die? That's all you've got so don't waste it worrying about some merry-go-round in ooh-la-la-frenchland. We'll have real horses when I'm living here—I'm sure she's told you we're getting married."

I pictured my wife rolling her eyes the way I rolled mine at her ridiculous arty associates like Pierrot. In his trendy jeans and plaid polo that reeked of fabric softener, Ryan was just as ridiculous. The stylish rural edition. There was also the issue of his hands as smooth as nubuck, and his face, neck, and forearms, which were remarkably untouched by the elements for someone who regarded himself as rugged, though perhaps the love of a good woman with property would change all that. I understood why a girl like Katy would say yes to a guy like Ryan: He was a few years older than she was, an irresistible fact in the mind of many an adolescent; confidence wafted from him like pheromones; and how many options did she have? Ryan was of the sort a girl married to assure her daddy he'd done a good job raising her by himself, her way of thanking him. I had no idea what aspirations, if any, Mr. de Wilde held for his daughter, or whether Katy had fallen for Ryan because of some unconscious will to please her father, and I preferred to believe she had chosen Cox Jr. out of pragmatism rather than out of passion.

We all sat at the table so Ryan could show off his shotgun. He described the simplest features with the most technical terms, flaunting his belief that I didn't know the first thing about firearms. Katy interrupted skittishly to ask if she could make some fruit punch for us. I told her not to trouble herself, though I was interested in that tea if it was still an option, while Ryan decided he was in the mood for pink lemonade, actually.

"Personally, as something of an expert," he said, concluding his ode to the Ithaca Featherlight Deerslayer that had saved his father from a tempestuous black bear, "I'd say it's worth a coupla thousand, if I actually wanted to sell. But you must know how it is with family hairlooms, being in the antique business."

"I certainly do. May I?"

Ryan laid the shotgun between us. I had noted already its walnut stock was cracked and the barrel was pitted with rust, but I inspected it with the same care I inspected all firearms. "*Esprit*, never make someone feel *criminelle* even when it is obvious they plan to rip you off."

After a respectable pause, I said as congenially as I could, "I'm afraid I don't deal in mid-century American shotguns. Or *heir*looms. It's never easy to tell a mother her child isn't the prettiest on the block, you know? Try a gunsmith if you ever become serious about selling. You could probably get about two-hundred fifty for parts."

We held gazes until Katy placed my tea, Ryan's pink lemonade, and a plate of Golden Oreos between us. We all stared at the spread until Ryan jumped up and said, "Why don't I leave it here," tapping his index finger on the Ithaca's chamber, which was engraved with a scene of wild geese being chased out of a pond by a barking spaniel, and immaculate compared with the rest of the gun. "Maybe you'll change your tune once you see what it can do." He fingered the side pockets of his jeans and retrieved four red Federal shotshells. He stood each one on its steel head in a deliberate row on the table. One. Two. Three. *Four.*

Katy bit down on an Oreo. "Off to see Brittany now?"

"Off to see the game with the guys, babe. Stop worrying about Brittany. We're just friends. And it's Taylor behind the bar on Sundays."

After her fiancé left, Katy slumped onto his chair. "Brittany, Taylor, Lila, Jasmine. All his girl friends are super-pretty or super-sporty, like fashion model pretty and lacrosse sporty. That's a problem when you're not super-either, you know?"

The smallness of her eyes, her neon air of profound unhappiness, made me want to kiss her the way she had kissed me in the car. Now was the time to reciprocate if ever there was a time. Not to challenge inhibitions, but to console her. I could redeem myself again later, in another three a.m. doorstep session with Olivier Weinstock. I grabbed the Ithaca and fed a slug into the loading flap, the distinct click so familiar it felt narcotic. No, I would not kiss this lisping girl.

"What I want to know, Katherine de Wilde, is how are you going to live your dash?"

"I hate Ryan's dash theory—it's not even his. He got it from some movie about two guys on death row. And also, I like to be called 'Katy,' and I hate my last name."

"Well, I like it. I hope you'll keep it once you're married."

"Why?"

"Because of the nobiliary particle."

"I thought you were going to say because 'Katherine Cox' is an even worse name."

I loaded another slug. "The *de* in your surname is called a nobiliary particle. It suggests nobility in your family history. Maybe you have a Danish prince in your blood."

"Sometimes Ryan calls me 'Katherine of the Wild,' like when he says I'm not being reasonable. And one time he called me Buck—you know, the wolf from that movie?—but I told him to never ever call me that again because it's not my fault my dad couldn't afford braces. Anyway, I'm going to get them when I'm twenty-five and I have a fulltime job. Plenty of grownups wear braces now."

I took my time loading the remaining two slugs while Katy opened up about her lonely childhood after her mother passed away from brain cancer, the way her father closed off completely after her grandparents—"The ones that met when Le Galopant was at the World's Fair in New York City"—passed away, one from pneumonia and the other from a broken heart, and the de Wilde family became just two. But what compelled me more than her history was her bottom lip, the fine hairs silhouetting it, the way she anxiously skimmed her teeth across it, causing it to swell and redden. I aimed the shotgun at the slat window above the stove and tracked a fly floating along a sunbeam. "Shall we go out back and fire this thing?"

"I'm no good. Ryan always gets annoyed when he tries to show me."

"Forget about Ryan for five minutes. I'll show you, and I won't get annoyed."

I followed Katy outside past the small log barn behind the cabin to a clearing of chamomile and other wild grasses, and a bucolic view of Mick's Honey Emporium. Celeste rang her bell to warn the others of new activity on the property, and Victor appeared with a clump of Russian sage sprouting from between his teeth. He flared his charcoal nostrils and kicked up his heels as he trotted toward us, unconcerned about being stalked once again by a pair of mean-spirited sheep. Perhaps the de Wilde flock sensed my designs on their lovely young mistress.

"First and foremost," I said, rearing the Ithaca to the sky and sliding the safety from right to left, "if you see red, you're not safe. Safe is from left to right, no red. Here."

Katy backed away. "No, no, I really shouldn't. I'm really no good at it. I might accidentally hurt someone. It's fine, it's okay. I'd rather watch." She stooped to hug Victor, who had deposited his bounty at her feet. "I've only ever seen Ryan do it."

"Then watch me closely. Maybe one day you can surprise your fiancé." I leaned the Ithaca's butt against my shoulder, welded my cheek to the stock. It had been a while since I had fired a gun just because. Years before, I had ceased treating myself to the occasional hour at a shooting range when I travelled for work. Even though Estelle had not requested any such sacrifice, I had come to expect a quick end to our phone calls whenever she detected my enduring satisfaction; and so it became easier, with time and wisdom, to deny myself an infrequent pleasure in order to avert meaningless tension in my marriage.

Katy got into position to toss the clay target discs she had collected from the barn. She stomped at the earth and wiggled her hips.

"The point is accuracy, not a home run," I said, keeping my eyes on the front sight. "And if you could toss from the other side. I'm stiff from a bad night's sleep."

Katy inquired her fingers across my spine as she passed behind me. "Maybe you need a back rub."

However slight her touch, it filled me with uncontrollable joy. The sun became so luminous, the tendrils of summer breeze so crushing, I had barely the agency to secure the gun before setting it down. I meant to scold Katy when I turned to her—"Do you realize what you're doing?"—but I lost all vestiges of self-preservation and pulled her down with me onto the chamomile and other wild grasses, and restrained her by the wrists with the unhinged grief of a lover about to leave for war. I kissed her more forcefully than she had kissed me in the car, yet she felt as vague as air when what you need is the sea. Her shoulders were too uncertain, her eyes were too round, and her scent and sounds were not Estelle's, which were the only I had ever known. She did not protest when I rolled away muttering curses at myself, and we lay panting in the grass for some time before I could say, "That was not supposed to happen. Are you, is everything all right?"

"I landed on a rock or something, but the real question is are you all right? Like, do you have asthma?"

"No, dear girl, I do not have asthma."

Katy patted the ground until she found my hand. "Margot? Can I come back to Montréal with you?"

"Absolutely not."

"I still have a month on my visa."

"Then you should have stayed."

"That's the whole problem, I didn't have anywhere to stay anymore. Can I stay with you and Estelle? I'll leave as soon as I see Le Galopant one more time and say a real goodbye to Étienne. He doesn't know I'm not coming back. He's expecting my cotton candy tomorrow like usual. I'm afraid if I'm not there, he'll quit and I won't be able to find him after. I don't know his last name."

Victor appeared above me and began licking my forehead like a salt block. I sighed but made no effort to recover myself.

Katy sat up and whacked her bandana on the little jack's rump. "Shoo!"

ON OUR WAY OUT of Canaan, we stopped at Town Tavern & Lore so Katy could apprise Ryan of her new plan. He seemed amenable in spite of his earlier statement about her silly preoccupation with Le Galopant, and he offered us a pint of Hoppiest Blonde in the World, the Lore's new homebrew. "Stay for a while," he said. "Watch the Yanks kill the Sox." Neither of us was in the mood for beer and baseball, but we sipped water from plastic cups and gazed in the general direction of the game until Katy kicked me under the table. "Brittany," she whispered. "I knew it." She kicked me again when I looked over my shoulder at a row of stout backsides and high ponytails at the bar. "Don't be so obvious!" When I excused myself to the washroom, she followed and asked what I really truly thought of Brittany, and did I happen to have extra toilet paper? "Brittany," I said, passing a fistful under the partition between our stalls, "is about as comely as a wet towel."

An hour later we stopped in Saratoga Springs, since it was along our route and Katy had never been there. She tried to convince me that she had heard somewhere it was customary to sneak inside the stable behind the racetrack to pat the horses. I told her I had expended my daily quota of adventure and misbehaviour, alas, and proposed dinner at a restaurant where she could build her own crêpe while our server educated us about the photographs of Travers Stakes winners past on the walls. I welcomed the silence when she fell asleep in the car after dinner, though I nudged her awake as we crossed the Champlain Bridge to Montréal, so she could see the night lights of La Ronde reflecting off the Saint Lawrence Seaway.

"Oh, Margot, it's so amazing. You're so lucky you can see this whenever you want. If I lived here I'd drive across the water exactly like this every single night, even in the winter when everything's closed. I bet you it's still amazing then."

Slow bridge traffic due to summer construction allowed me time to take in the sight as well. I was astounded by my failure to recall any other time in my years of regular travel across the Champlain when I had appreciated the amusement park, or even cared to acknowledge it.

Katy rolled down her window and waved. "Hello, Madame Ferris wheel! Good evening, Monsieur Monstre—hey, Margot, look, you can see it going up the first hill! Before I go home we have to try every ride at night. Do you think we can see Le Galopant from here?" She unfastened her seatbelt and leaned out the window. "Napoleon! Where are you, my love?"

The car behind ours honked. Katy turned and waved to the passengers, who, judging by the tenor of their cheers and wolf whistles, were young men on their way to beseech the city for a good time. The attention inspired Katy to lean farther out the window. I yanked the waist of her jeans when I saw police lights flashing up ahead.

"Not my problem if they pull us over and ship you back to America."

Katy scowled at her knees and re-fastened her seatbelt. Minutes later, she was asleep. We arrived at the loft just after ten p.m., and except for Wolfgang and Puzzle, who hissed at me while they wove lovingly around Katy's legs, no one was home.

11. LA RONDE

"IMAGINE MY SURPRISE when I came home after a very terrible night to find a girl brewing coffee in the kitchen—a girl who knows who I am and says I look exactly like Gwyneth Paltrow. I suppose I should be flattered, except there's something just a little bit off-putting about being greeted by a teenager wearing one of your wife's nightshirts that barely covers her ass."

Estelle bustled around the room gathering items for the wash, including the top sheet from our bed upon which I lay. The air conditioning was broken, she said, opening the windows to establish a cross-breeze. A repairman would be over before noon. Please be here. She was dressed for work, and no doubt eager to blame me for costing her the rest of the vacation time she had wrangled from Jean-Jacques. In her version of things, we were supposed to be sipping lattés on some sidewalk terrace in Provincetown, laughing as we licked away each other's foam moustache. We were not supposed to be back in our semi-unpacked loft, which I would resume unpacking today, she recommended, unless I preferred the accommodations over at Le Cabinet. In the daylight, I noticed the Pierrot print of a woman transforming into a serpent had been framed and hung above the Queen Anne highboy, though from my supine perspective it appeared the serpent was turning into a woman. I pondered aloud over how we had never discussed the placement of this particular *objet d'art* in our bedroom. In fact I hadn't realized we were considering it as part of our home décor at all, yet how easily it had become so in my absence.

"Not now, Margot. There was a fire in Marianne's building. All six condos gutted by flames. I'm taking over her accounts at L'Espace for as long as she needs. And she'll be staying with us for as long as she needs."

"That's where you were last night. I tried calling you."

"No you didn't."

I turned stiffly onto my side and tucked my knees toward my chin. "I meant to."

Estelle felt my cheek. "You're all clammy and flushed. Speaking of clammy, maybe we caught something in the seaweed. I've been feeling a little off, myself. Maybe Marguerite put a curse on us. There'll be no chauffeur fucking *my* estranged daughter."

"Well, hell." I resigned to my shivering demi-fetal position. Estelle layered fresh sheets over me until I proclaimed my body couldn't bear any more weight.

"I let her use your waffle-maker. To be young again and eat with abandon." Estelle kissed my hand, and when I awoke next, Katy was in her place, offering me a vaguely menacing waffle with tangerine wedge eyes, a strawberry nose, and a banana slice smile. "Back home I'm famous for my breakfast art," she said. It was as though a thick blue rubber band was squeezing my head, forcing everything shut, but I managed to instruct her to take my keys and wallet from the temporary Ikea table and go to the newsstand one block east to purchase a copy of *The Globe and Mail*. She should call herself family if anyone in the building asked who she was. She should call herself a Coté, since they were all blond.

Some time later, I became aware of Estelle sitting on the edge of our bed, reading my favourite news column to me. "I sent Katy to La Ronde by taxi," she said. "She told me everything."

"Everything?"

All day, beautiful women tended to my needs. Marianne took over for Estelle, and her munificence in spite of her colossal loss consumed me with remorse. My skin hurt as I apologized for my two-decade habit of goading her and not taking her seriously. I declared her ex-husband an imbecile for burdening her with a pair of wretched Siamese cats, and Marianne confided, without rancour, that while she had lost a lifetime of memories, she believed the fire had cleansed her of all lingering negativity from the marriage. "I could never hate Antoine for being true to himself. Plus our sex life was quite steamy all things considered. I'm in fine shape for the dating scene, if you know what I mean." She had excellent homeowner's insurance and expected to receive a lump-sum settlement from the condominium syndicate, so it was best to look at the fire as a sign from the stars to start over. "In the meantime I get to stay here. How cool is that? It'll be like our Savannah days all over again—a reunion. Twenty years later: Where are they now? If you ask me, I think we've done okay for ourselves. When you're feeling better, we should throw a little party, an official housewarming. We were talking about it earlier, a housewarming-slash-unpacking party. Katy's idea, and we think it's great. Don't you?"

"What time is it?"

"Almost eleven."

"Is Estelle home for lunch?"

"Honey, like, hours ago. It's eleven p.m. She's gone to show Katy how to take the metro home from La Ronde."

The next morning Estelle moved like a mirage about the room, dressing for work, twisting her damp hair into a bun, adjusting the sheets around me and touching my face; however, when I asked how she was feeling—had we both caught something in the seaweed?—it was Katy who said, "I really hope I don't catch whatever you've got. Being sick in summer is the worst." I wanted to say she most certainly would catch whatever I had, "Start counting the hours, dear girl," but in my addled state I couldn't be sure whose face I would find peering down at me next.

Katy presented me with a new waffle shape: a horse head, in profile, with one blueberry eye, a kiwi teardrop nostril, and a maple butter forelock. "You've been mumbling 'Napoleon, Napoleon' all morning, and I'd say this is definitely my greatest masterpiece." She set the plate on the night table and felt my forehead—so many hands on my forehead—and then announced it was time for me to go to the bathroom.

"I beg your pardon?"

"Estelle told me to make sure you go. She said, um, that usually in the mornings you have to, and since you didn't yesterday, so." Katy tipped a glass of orange juice to my mouth, but even at room temperature the juice was too cold on my teeth. I curled up under the sheets like a pill bug when she poked at me.

Eventually Marianne returned and maneuvered me out of bed as deftly as if she'd been moonlighting for years as a caregiver to the infirm. My comment, intended as an insult, inspired her to blather on while I peed. "It's true I'd rather run the risk of damaging a million-dollar photo installation than handle a sick person, but you're not some random sick person. I'm really pretty excited it's the four of us living together now. It's been hard, since Antoine left, to come home all the time to nothing but two pissy cats. Christ, even *they're* happier here. There's good juju in this place, Margot. I can feel it."

I flushed the toilet and waited limply for Marianne to lead me back to bed. She started the bath water instead. "I know you'd rather Estelle, but with the air conditioning still broken, you'll just feel so much more human after."

Katy had changed the sheets and plumped the pillows while I was away, replenished the glass of water on my night table, and laid out a cocktail of flu medication. Marianne hugged her and wished her good luck on her first day.

Even in my hazy state, I envied how quickly they appeared to have bonded. My envy flourished when, after helping me into bed, Marianne said, "We're totally falling in love with her,

Estelle and me. We're becoming like a little family."

I was famished for company the next time I awoke. The rubber band around my head had relaxed, and I felt giddy with things to say. I called out for my wife, for Katy, and for Marianne, but not even the inimical Siamese twins bothered to come snarl at me. Other than a mosquito drawing her nightcap from my cheek, and a tuba bellowing inharmoniously from the cobblestone street below, I was utterly alone. When I called out again for Estelle, my mother took shape in the darkness and hurled a smiling pumpkin bucket filled with detritus at me, calling me a *"déserteur"* like my father. I tried to protect myself with the "M" volume of the encyclopedia, but my father took it from me and placed it with the pile of everything else I wasn't allowed to have. "M" is not a letter for girls, he said. I wrote poem after poem for Estelle and mailed each one to her, only to discover them all unopened and stuffed inside empty white Rueda bottles under the bathroom sink. Estelle said it was the only way to save the hermit crabs when I confronted her, and then she ordered me to take Bertrand's phone call. I said, "Bert, no more horsing around: You need to see a doctor," and my mother laughed into the line, sounding fresh and vibrant as she applied a shade of lipstick called 'Mourning Apricot.' Her patchouli fragrance made me sneeze as usual, but I knew better than to refuse when she asked me to dab some along her clavicle. "Oh no," Estelle said, covering her nose, "Look what you've done." Katy knelt on the linoleum floor to round up the shards of broken fragrance bottle with her bare hands, softly singing, "K-K-K-Katy, beautiful Katy, You're the only g-g-g-girl that I adore."

When finally my fever broke, I emerged with the scraping breathlessness familiar to anyone who has ever been pulled under the ocean by a deafening wave and believed her life was over. The first thing I saw was Bertrand and Katy sitting on top of Estelle's chest of novelty cameras at the foot of my bed, each with a ball of yarn and a set of knitting needles in hand.

"*Comme ça, pouliche.* It must be secure." Bertrand tightened a loop of orange yarn around one of his needles, and Katy copied him with her purple yarn. Marianne, who was in lotus position on the floor, with Puzzle (or was it Wolfgang?) perched smugly on one of her knees, pumped a fist in the air. "You got it, girl!"

Estelle came into the bedroom with a sweating carafe of sangria (the air conditioning was broken still). She poured some for everyone, including a splash for Katy, before noticing my situation had changed. "You're awake."

"Don't mind me," I said, too spent from whatever illness had assailed me to show appreciation for my visitors. "I'll just fester away in the background while you all get smashed. Bertrand, I didn't know you knit."

Bertrand hoisted a basket of flashy wools and other knitting paraphernalia from the floor to the bed. "Everyone has secrets, *esprit,*" he said, laughing mightily in an effort to mask his wheeze. He was teaching Katy the stocking stitch technique so she could knit winter paw warmers for Wolfgang and Puzzle, who would be leaving with her at the end of the month.

Estelle stuck a thermometer in my mouth. "She's helping out at the gallery while Marianne deals with, you know, the effects of the fire."

Everyone fell silent until I asked how long I had been out of it. What day was it?

"It's Wednesday," Katy answered, tapping a knitting needle against her front teeth before parting with her next words. "Exactly one week since you met Napoleon, and you might never get to see him again. Get well fast, Margot."

"*Soon.* Get well soon." Everything around me started to dim, and I couldn't be sure if I had spoken out loud or not.

THE NEXT MORNING I pretended to be asleep until Estelle left for work. I willed my breath and eyelids still as she felt my forehead and whispered, "Margot, are you awake?" Now that my timely delirium had passed, she could demand an explanation for Katy at any moment, which was the least of all things I owed her now. But even if I made it seem as though Katy had begged to come home with me (and hadn't she?), I had no explanation for possible follow-up questions like, "What were you doing with her in the first place?" that wouldn't cast me as lunatic like my mother, or creepy like my father circa 1965. I had submitted, of my own agency and stupidity, to the taunts of a midlife crisis, and confessing this to Estelle just to clear my conscience would hurt her needlessly as well as potentially sentence me to eternity in the dark Edwardian world of unsmiling bellhops and furniture bolted to the floor. As one does in desperate times, I was hoping the answer to all that had misfired in me lately—my inquest of life before Estelle and since Estelle, my failure to understand why my happiness with her, our marriage, had flatlined overnight—would reveal itself with the force of a cinematic epiphany while I scrutinized myself in the bathroom mirror as I flossed, or while I attempted once again to use my waffle-maker. *All this time, my whole problem has been "x." Yes, I get it now.* Now we can resume our usual programming.

I found Katy in the kitchen, helping herself to the coffee and fruit salad Estelle had prepared for everyone. There was a pot of tea cooling on the counter for me, which I assumed also prepared by Estelle and thus a good sign. Katy issued a cheerful hello, and then seconds later, as though she had been waiting in the hallway like her predatory cats for an opportunity to spring on me, Marianne glided in looking all limber and pleased with herself in a pair of Estelle's hot-pink exercise leggings.

"No wonder Belle has limbs like a filly," she said, clasping her hands above her head, bearing her clean-shaven freckled underarms. "That morning Yoga workout is *killer*."

I offered her the bowl of fruit salad. "I didn't realize you two are the same size."

Marianne patted her backside. "Oh, we're not. I'm curvier."

She popped a grape into her mouth and winked. "Katy, I can take you to L'Espace after my shower if you want."

"Actually," I answered, before Katy could, "I'd like her to stay here with me for now. Just in case. I'll accompany her to the gallery after lunch."

"In case what?" Marianne sifted through the fruit salad with her fingers, helping herself to the rest of the grapes. I was at once repulsed by how she handled all the other fruit in the process, and mesmerized by how her fingers treaded around the bowl like tiny disembodied ballerina legs.

"In case I get dizzy," I said, pouring myself a glass of water to offset the slight uprising of my pulse. "In case I faint. I don't know. What does it matter?"

"As long as you're in shape for the housewarming tomorrow."

"I will not be in shape for the housewarming tomorrow. Besides, the A/C is still broken."

"So we'll get more fans. Anyway, it's just going to be us, old Bert, and a good-looking friend of young missy's over here."

"I got him to pose for me," Katy said, showing off an image on her smartphone screen of Étienne frowning at an unlit cigarette, ironic as ever in a *Mary Poppins* hoodie.

"Think of it as a symbolic thing," Marianne went on, "a belated christening."

"You can trust that we've christened the place already."

Marianne shook her fists at the skylight. A thin silver ring gleamed from her bellybutton as the hem of her tank top rose up, invoking my curiosity.

"When did you pierce your navel?"

"*Franchement*, Margot, can you please stop being an official dick?"

Other than her intent to break me of my unwillingness to throw myself a party—and there was no one in the world who wanted to throw herself a party less than I—Marianne appeared to have no agenda, no plans to drill me about my deranged mother in the Bluefish wing or my lust for Katy (an apparently fickle lust, for I was now finding it a challenge to ignore the gleam of the bellybutton ring). This could only mean Estelle hadn't confided anything, and so maybe the problems in my marriage weren't as dire as I perceived them to be. Given how reflexively I had exchanged the secret of my mother's *belles-lettres* for the secret of my kiss with Katy, then maybe, as I had suspected the day I set out to photograph Le Galopant, I was the problem.

Marianne snapped her fingers inches from my face. "*Allô?* Why are you folding napkins? Shit, you're all flushed. Your fever better not be coming back. We are having that party tomorrow."

As I folded the last napkin in a set embroidered with blue flag irises, a gift from Estelle's parents on our wood anniversary, I indulged in my most ridiculous fantasy yet, asking Marianne to help me back to bed, "I'm not as recovered as I thought," to then pull her onto the mattress as I had pulled Katy into the chamomile, and smother her with the vexing impulses seeded into my DNA. But unlike Katy, she would buck against me, grab at me and bite me until we drenched the mattress. The kitchen roiled around me as I sipped my glass of water empty and told myself that whatever was wrong with me, this pulsing drive to do foolish things, like a second coming of age, had to be self-limiting. It had to be coming to an end.

"Well? Am I staying here with you today or not?"

"I'm fine, Marianne, but thank you for your concern. Go about your affairs and I'll go about mine, and tomorrow we'll throw a party."

After Marianne left, I invited Katy to join me on the balcony so we could admire the day taking shape on rue de la Commune. We leaned against the glass parapet and observed the *calèche* horses stationed along the sidewalk, nodding off in the already humid morning; street artists and buskers greeting one another as they set up their lots; a shirtless gentleman in suspenders and baggy slacks looking to swap copies of a religious booklet for handshakes. I could smell Estelle's cinnamon body wash on Katy and tried to revive how it had felt to kiss her, how I had gone mad enough to drive two hundred miles for a teenage girl who made her handwritten "i's" look like spools of cotton candy. What came to mind was how limp and baffling Katy had felt underneath me, how pathetic I must have seemed to her afterward, a middle-aged woman undone, perspiring and gasping in the grass. Retrospective humiliation alone was enough to shame my infatuation back to the dark corner whence it had come, a circus lion retreating from the whip, and in its place swelled a renewed desire for my wife—or, rather, a sincere desire to desire my wife. This abrupt metamorphosis, rollercoaster-like as it mingled with my post-viral vertigo, sent me staggering and laughing to the parapet.

"What? Do I have a pimple? Is my moustache showing? I wax it every three weeks, but sometimes I'm a few days late and Ryan reminds me by calling me his boyfriend." Katy touched her upper lip as she crouched to analyze her reflection in the glass. "It's very important that I look good today, so please tell me if I don't."

"What's the occasion?"

"I'm having lunch with Étienne. I have something to tell you, Margot, but you have to be serious. Please. I haven't told anybody else."

I sighed and patted my eyes. "I think I know what you're going to say."

I considered flinging myself over the parapet. In this fantasy, I had slingshot precision and landed on my feet by the gentleman in suspenders, and perhaps, after shaking hands with him, I could use my complimentary religious booklet to shield my eyes from the ridiculing sun, and spy on Katy and Estelle and Marianne as they conducted themselves like the ultimate female nuclear family, wave enthusiastically to them should they catch me gaping like a tourist. My weeklong affair with Katy had been so one-sided and interior that mourning it would be nothing more than an excuse to feel vastly sorry for myself, and I wasn't ready yet to pitch that white flag. I would put the last nine days behind me and instead, move forward as though nothing had happened, as apparently, in Katy's view, nothing had.

Katy grabbed the end of her ponytail and sucked on it. "I think I'm in love. We held hands yesterday while we watched them take down the last Napoleon. And then when I got home I took Ryan's ring off. I had to, right? It's what you do."

She wiggled her denuded ring finger at me in the same cheeky manner she had wiggled her hips in the field across from Mick's Honey Emporium. But my thoughts turned to the world's first galloping carousel with no horses on its poles, no Napoleons or constellations drawing chariots of laughing children, the Wurlitzer organ songless as the basswood platform spun and wobbled like a coin clumsily flicked across a table. I recalled from my second visit the yellow tape with the word "Danger," how the darkened scotch-coloured teardrop bulbs on the carousel's canopy had caused my throat to burn. Shortly after Estelle became interested in carousel horse restoration, she showed me a photograph of Le Galopant she had found online. The horses were racked abreast in the cargo hold of a ship, covered in burlap sacks to protect their lacquered coats from nicks and dings during their voyage from Belgium to America. She loved the image so much she commissioned an artist on exhibit at L'Espace to reproduce it. Though I hadn't cared for the image, I wondered now if the photographer who had chosen that moment to capture, the meticulous fetlocks and hooves barely reaching below the burlap body bags, had sensed an unsettling end for the horses.

BY THE FOLLOWING AFTERNOON, Friday, I was committed to keeping my marriage a success, which meant letting the memory of that fateful Wednesday I went to photograph Le Galopant recede into the penumbra of some other lifetime. For indeed it felt like a lifetime had passed in the last nine days. I even took pains to amend my relationship with Puzzle and Wolfgang, so strong was my will to start fresh (of course no one knew I was starting fresh, which made the experience lonely for me, and my behaviour mystifying to everyone else). Through every interaction with my wife and temporary co-habitants, I had to prove to myself that I was not in any way prone to the triumphant sadness I very clearly remembered my mother describing in her letters to me before I had stopped reading them. *Oh, chère fille. There are days I look back on my life and laugh like a loon when I realize my problems are all because of my parents. There is nothing I can do!* Whenever Marianne asked how I was feeling, I exclaimed, "Much better, thank you," and omitted facts such as my ongoing interest in her navel ring, and a cresting paranoia that she, Estelle, and Katy were building a life without me, tenderly crowding me out of the loft. Katy, I was intent on avoiding altogether. I was even prepared to re-establish residency on the orange sleeper sofa in the back office of Le Canon Noir until she left at the end of the month. She was the midlife crisis—expedited—I had hoped to outsmart after retiring from my job and purchasing a new home. A plainclothes sorceress in Converse sneakers and a "Meat is Murder" T-shirt, following me around with a camera, reciting information about carousels from a pamphlet, altering this information at will, casting spells on me with her lisp. I was the malfunctioning outside horse, flanked by all the others who rose up and down, forward and backward with grace and majesty. I remained impaled and stiff, my disc eyes wide and mummified, as the rest galloped off the platform without me. I was the broken Napoleon.

In spite of my resolve to be a better person, I couldn't make myself look forward to the housewarming party. After having griped all day Thursday through Friday morning, I convinced Estelle to downgrade it to an uncomplicated affair of gimlets, tamari almonds, and Manchego cheese. I let Estelle think my heightened aversion to social activity was an after-effect of the virus; I couldn't tell her I believed something terrifically shattering was going to happen at the party, what I believed would be my undoing. My *dénouement*. I was on the Vampire, creeping up the steep purple track, *click click click clack*, waiting for the drop, and once I realized the drop would never come on its own, the train car would perch and sway on the precipice, a spoon balanced in perpetuity on the bridge of a laughing child's nose, I would perform my final act of stupidity. *Come one, come all, watch Margot Wright royally fuck things up!* Some greater force would ensure I paid for my misdeeds. Perhaps it would be the same force that once drove my mother to declare she had never wanted me, the one that had enabled her to abandon me in a crowd where I could have been trampled to death. Or if no such force existed, then surely after Marianne had found a new place to live and Katy was back in Canaan, my wife would turn away from me in bed one morning, as she had the morning I finally offered to take her to Le Galopant, and admit she had known all along of my boredom, because it was hers, too.

Estelle positioned a gossamer yellow vase at the centre of the temporary Ikea table. "I asked Mare to bring back some daisies. I hope that's not too extravagant for you." Her tone was playful. It was six p.m., an hour before our guests were scheduled to arrive.

My heart trembled more than my hands as I placed a sixties-era jadeite napkin holder beside the vase. I rested my chin on Estelle's shoulder. "Daisies will be lovely, darling girl."

"*Darling girl.* You haven't used that one in a while."

"Darling girl, darling girl," I said, breathing the words onto her neck.

Estelle skimmed the shoulder straps of her sundress down her arms. The dress fell in white cotton scallops around her ankles; she wore nothing underneath but a mist of sweat. "You owe me," she said, her expression impatient and purposeful as she untied her hair. "Ditching me in that shitty motel. What if some lonely, handsome repairwoman had come by after you left? Or a repair*man*? While you were off chasing the girl with the gun. Our little lives could've turned into a big thriller. *Cest ça que tu veux?*"

I stared inappropriately at my wife, the way I had wanted to stare at the dancers in the gentlemen's club above which we had once lived. It seemed impossible to me now that I had ever felt comfortable with her posing nude for the aspiring artists of Cégep Dawson. Estelle swayed her hips and twirled, pausing with her backside to me, winking at me over her shoulder. "You're not even supposed to be here," she chided. "I never gave you permission to come home." She grabbed my hand and began to lick each finger from knuckle to tip, and the perfume of her cinnamon body wash came at me like a storm, pungent and reeling. On Katy, it had been subtler, simpler, like unripe watermelon. I had enjoyed it on Katy, and though Katy had made it clear her affections were now for Étienne, what had happened in Canaan had been forgotten already, I wondered if she had used Estelle's body wash for my benefit.

"Well, this is awkward." Estelle released my hand and took a napkin from the table to cover herself like Eve—a generous attempt at comedy in response to my inertia, my serial rejection of her. Before either of us could blunder into a conversation neither of us was ready to have, I fell to my knees before her and slid her sundress up her legs, pausing to kiss her thighs, each hand holding the napkin in place, her warm belly, the damp, round under-curves of her breasts, her throat. I adjusted the shoulder straps of her sundress, smoothed her hair behind her ears, and whispered, "I'm afraid I'm still too woozy to get it up, darling girl. I'm sorry."

We held each other as our heartbeats slowed, and I could feel how troubled Estelle was by my dishonesty, how she struggled not to say anything serious or consequential, and we stayed like this, clinging to an understanding there had occurred at some undefined point a tectonic and unutterable shift in our couple, until the *clippity-clop* sound of Marianne's high-heeled footfalls released into the corridor outside our loft. When Marianne rapped on the door and hollered, "Extra special delivery for Mrs. and Mrs. Soucy-Coté!" in the style of a newspaper hawker, we jumped apart like teenagers caught in the janitor's closet at school. Estelle smiled feebly and mouthed, "Sorry," as she opened the door to reveal not only Marianne and Katy bearing the cheerful gift of daisies, plus handsome Étienne profoundly overheating in a *Jesus Christ Superstar* hoodie and Bertrand waving exuberantly as he coughed into an emerald green handkerchief, but also Olivier Weinstock in a bowtie, a box of dark chocolate Le Petit Écolier cookies in tow, and the entire Coté clan—Estelle's younger sisters Gabrielle and Véronique, her older ones Caroline and Nathalie, all four with a homemade dish for the dinner table, and her parents, Arnaud and Brigitte, ready to celebrate with Cheval Blanc beer and musical wooden spoons.

"Surprise!" they all yelled.

What better way to court epic failure than to assemble everyone you know in a small space on a scorching summer evening when your air conditioner hasn't worked in days. Following a procession of awkward greetings (awkward on my part, although I noticed Olivier looking similarly stupefied), I defected to the kitchen with Marianne, who seemed as eager as I to escape the very surprise committee she had ushered from Place d'Armes metro station to the loft. She spoke quickly, averting my glare as she poured chilled sangria into hurricane glasses for the guests. "I swear I didn't invite them," she said of the merry Coté clan, who had hijacked the Ikea table to set out their dishes. Meanwhile, Katy was circulating among the bedlam to record drink orders on a notepad even though the only drink options were Cheval Blanc beer or white sangria, Estelle was chasing after Wolfgang and Puzzle to lock them in our bedroom (Olivier apparently suffered from ailurophobia—fear of cats), and Étienne absconded to the balcony to chain-smoke and brood above the new August cityscape.

Katy ran into the kitchen and waved her notepad at us. On it was an order for two white sangrias, both "i's" her signature spool of cotton candy. "Bert and Oliver are getting along like gangsters," she cried, racing off before Marianne could pass her the drinks.

"Bert and *Olivier* are getting along like *gangbusters*," I called out, abandoning my earlier plan to avoid her altogether.

When Olivier came to fetch his order, Marianne stammered, "Please, take as much as you want," and then threw herself into the mindless task of wedging lemons, leaving Olivier and me to appraise each other dryly.

"Dr. Weinstock, it seems fate has reunited us. I apologize for the unbearable climate in here. My wife and I are thinking of turning the place into a greenhouse. What do you think?"

"It wouldn't be Montréal without this uncomfortable heat, would it?" He dabbed his bald, glossy crown with a paper napkin and waited for me to challenge his remark. When I did not, he continued with, "So, cats."

"Cats indeed." I smiled and offered him two sweating hurricane glasses.

"May I ask where they are right now?"

"Confined to the bedroom—though the door tends to spontaneously drift open every now and then. You know how it is with these old buildings." I couldn't help myself from indulging in the therapist's trepidation; he had, after all, called me an ostrich the last time we saw each other. Behind me, Marianne, too, seemed ill at ease, wedging up a citrus storm on the counter.

Olivier dabbed his brow with a fresh paper napkin. He had yet to accept the drinks from me. "You don't strike me as a cat person."

"That's because I'm not in the slightest." I mouthed *they're hers* and pointed at Marianne, who ineffectively feigned nonchalance.

Olivier produced a third fresh napkin from his corduroy trousers, blotted it across his cheekbones, around his mouth, and edged closer to me. "Have you heard of the poltergeist?" His discreet voice was as loud as his speaking voice. Marianne coughed into her elbow.

"I've heard of *a* poltergeist, or *poltergeists*, but I'm afraid I wasn't aware of *the* Poltergeist. A friend of yours?"

Olivier edged closer still, his humid, over-minted breath condensing on my face. "Cats are the perfect conduits for evil spirits."

"Yes, but poltergeists?"

"I've seen it in practise, when I was in Malaysia observing divorce rituals among villagers. When I retire, I'm going to write a book about it."

"I'm sure it will be a fine read."

"Cats are very different over there, you know. Not nearly as smug and overweight as they are here. It's very difficult to be a cat in Malaysia."

I nodded thoughtfully (what else could I do?). Olivier winked at me like we now shared some exclusive strand of knowledge, and then he took his drinks, finally, and whistled a jazzy tune on his way back to the living room. I waited until he was out of range before jabbing Marianne in the side.

"This is your fault, isn't it?"

Marianne gazed down at the sheer waist of her blouson dress. From my perspective, her tastefully bejewelled navel stole the show. "It's the craziest thing," she began, stammering as before. "I brought him as my date, except he doesn't realize he's my *date*-date. And I didn't tell him it was your party…"

"Miss Marianne Lavoie, are you screwing your therapist?"

"No! What is with you? Just because you got it right the first time." Marianne swigged from a nearly empty carafe, which she returned to the counter with the slow, diagonal precision of one convinced she was still sober. The party wasn't a half-hour old.

"What's that supposed to mean?"

"It doesn't mean anything. Never mind. *Pardonnez-moi.*"

I finished my glass and poured myself another from a fresh carafe (whoever had prepared the sangria had skimped on the rum and Rioja). I didn't want to be in conflict with Marianne. I felt anchored by her company, by how our relationship was not, my flourishing attraction to her midriff aside, tainted by any bad behaviour on my part. I tried again: "I take it he's no longer your therapist."

"I stopped seeing him when I realized I couldn't make it through a session without getting wet—why am I telling you this? And you know the rest: Some asshole in my building fell asleep with a lit cigarette." Marianne clinked her carafe against my glass before swigging some more. "Guess how I got him to come?"

"Please don't ask me that ever again."

"I'm paying him. Technically, right now we're in session. I said I had to make an appearance at this party if it killed me, but with the fire and Antoine and work, I just couldn't bear to be alone. We agreed we wouldn't talk the whole time."

I thought of telling her about my own recent pseudo session with the therapist, but I didn't want to seem like I was bragging about benefiting from his services for free—not to mention I hadn't benefitted. It was hard to imagine anyone benefiting from Dr. Weinstock's questionable methods. I poured myself more drink.

Marianne laid a hand on mine. Behind her, the sky glowed with sheet lightening. "We'd better slow down," she said.

A zephyr surged through the window above the sink, hot, fat raindrops and a groan of thunder on its heels, and it made me want to shove her against the counter and plunge under her blouson dress for the ring. What did it feel like on the fingertips, the tongue? There were experiences so much bigger than Katy, and experiences much smaller, of which I knew absolutely nothing in my middle age. Already, middle age! If I were to die the next morning, Estelle would have only "Flossed teeth daily, sometimes twice. Paid taxes on time" to etch onto my headstone, and it was this make-believe tomorrow that compelled me to embrace my unravelling. Whereas earlier in the day I had felt enslaved to its certainty, I now felt its allure, the promise of a black hole of deliverance if I just let myself go. Fuck it. Who was I to believe my marriage, my life, my anything could return to what it had been after all that had happened in the last ten days?

"What?" Marianne felt for her earrings, the bronzed feathers strung around her neck. "Why are you looking at me like that?"

"In all the years, have you ever?"

"Ever what?"

"Been attracted to Estelle."

"Well, I mean, she's beautiful, and I used to think Antoine had a thing for her. And I guess I used to be jealous of her, like back in grad school. That day we first met in the waiting room for international students? I hated her for being so pretty. Then she started talking to me and she was so nice, and I hated her for that. I liked you more in the beginning, if you can believe it. When she introduced us, I thought to myself, 'That Margot Wright seems like a really solid person.' I also thought the way you talked about guns was sexy."

"But can you honestly tell me you've never once fantasized about her?"

"How do you mean?"

"Come on."

Marianne retrieved two bottles of Cheval Blanc from the fridge. "Okay fine. I did once have this dream about the three of us."

"Did you tell Antoine about it?"

"He wasn't in the dream, silly. To be honest, I can't even remember if Estelle was, you know, part of the action. You were really ... you were really tender. You kept telling me to slow down, we weren't trying out for the Olympics. Or something like that. I had a girl crush on you after."

My desire to shove Marianne against the counter ebbed and was replaced with humming curiosity. "How long did your crush last? I don't mean to pry, except I do."

"Remember when I bailed on Estelle the day of our *Clue* party? We'd all been hanging out so much, and I was totally convinced you knew I had a thing for you. I was afraid you were plotting to mock me in front of everyone. Then you went on that South Dakota trip, and Estelle told me about the guy who chased you with his pistol. That was the first time I really understood life's different for you. I hadn't thought of you as gay before then, just the person my best friend was with. I've loved you like family ever since."

Estelle came into the kitchen flaunting an envelope of St. Hubert powdered gravy mix. "*Papa*'s ready to educate us all about the virtues of French fries and cheese curds." She emptied the envelope into a saucepan with water and turned on the stove.

Marianne pretended to gag and Estelle smacked her on the backside (Arnaud Coté's poutine was famously bad, worse than the abject dish itself), and the moment was almost perfectly normal, a cruel exhibit of how things could be again *if*—until the sound of Katy's laughter, like the sizzling end on a stick of dynamite, found its way to me from the convivial gathering in the living room.

BY SEVEN P.M., an hour into the party, we had all settled on the living room floor around an imposing spread of working-class francophone cuisine. Arnaud's voice was taut with pride as he bestowed praise upon the simplest of the dishes—"*La poutine* she is like the reindeer with *le nez rouge* that saves Christmas!"—and urged us all to douse our French fries and cheese curds in the gravy Estelle had simmered. For as long as I had been with Estelle, her father's pre-meal praise of poutine had functioned as a quirky Coté family grace reserved for special events. Apparently this evening was extra special not because Estelle and I were finally admitting to our new home, but because inside our new home there dwelled a loquacious, exotic *américaine* named Katherine de Wilde, and being the hospitable people my in-laws were, they wished to ensure she experienced Québec as authentically as possible before her departure at the end of the month.

Arnaud beamed as he explained in faltering yet unhindered English how he and Brigitte had decided to use the overdue housewarming as an excuse to pluck their daughters away from tobacco fields, husbands, and children, and splurge for two nights at the Queen Elizabeth hotel, where Estelle and I had stayed on our wedding night so many years earlier. "It taken some *négotiations* with the *téléphone*," he said reverently, since guests typically booked their stays months in advance, but finally his persistence and politesse were rewarded with a suite whose king-size bed Gabrielle, Véronique, and Caroline had agreed to share, while he and his wife would share the foldout sofa, and Nathalie would take the cot because menopause had turned her into an unreasonable bedmate.

"What was your room number again?" asked Brigitte, taking the *tourtière* from her husband before he could purloin a second slice.

Estelle, sitting to my left, rubbed my thigh affectionately. "Seventeen forty-two, one of the famous 'bed-in' rooms. GoGo spent a month's pay on it."

"And I'd do it all again." I raised my Cheval Blanc for the sake of my wife, our guests, though what I really felt like doing was joining Étienne on the balcony and taking up smoking as my next poor life choice.

Estelle's youngest sister, Véronique, offered to serve me some of her onion soup, but my lap was already heavy with a plate of Caroline's asparagus crêpe. I wasn't sure how food had made its way onto my lap in the first place, for I had, if anything, an anti-appetite, and no memory of partaking in the feast thus far. Bertrand, on my right, had skipped the appetizers and main course options altogether and dedicated his plate to equal helpings of sugar pie and Poor Man's Pudding, desserts Gabrielle and Nathalie had baked for the occasion. He paused between fits of chewing and swallowing to catch his breath or grunt into his handkerchief, yet no one, not even Estelle, seemed to find anything troubling about a large, jolly man labouring over his meal. No one seemed concerned about how this Humpty Dumpty of a guy was going to get back onto his feet. Except for the low stoop outside Le Canon Noir, where Bertrand liked to share quiet company with the deli owner next door, I had rarely seen him sit on the ground, and this realization perturbed me. Surely, along with the wheezing, secret knitting, and recent attempt to lure me back into firearms dealing, it foretold of grave news about my long-time mentor's health, which I was in no state to receive.

Across from me, Olivier was eyeballing Brigitte much too openly as she told stories about young Estelle's dream of becoming a veterinarian.

"*Maman*, that's not true," Estelle said, leaning forward to swat at her mother and cast warning at Olivier. "That's what you and *papa* wanted me to become. And anyway, I was never good at *les maths et sciences*."

At this, Arnaud curled his hands around his mouth like a bullhorn and declared a toast to not becoming what our parents once wanted us to become. "*Vive la liberté*," he cried, collecting the musical wooden spoons by his side and clapping them jubilantly against his thigh. Brigitte grabbed her set and matched her husband's rhythm, and the living room became an opus of clinking hurricane glasses and beer bottles, and guests fondly complaining about the shortcomings of their parents. Katy scooted along the perimeter of the circle to Marianne's side and hugged her (poor Marianne did look miserable sitting beside feline-fearing Olivier without being able to interact with him), Bertrand profited from the din by loading the rest of the Poor Man's Pudding onto his plate, and Étienne clipped his cigarette on the balcony to come share an anecdote with us about his parents, who were not affluent professionals as I had so deliberately speculated the previous week, but a mother who worked at a hospital gift shop and a father who repaired used appliances—the combination of which made him a natural fit for the role of carousel operator, I thought.

Two hours into the party, I was practically enjoying myself, until I noticed the Coté sisters slipping off one by one to the kitchen with stacks of plates. I had barely said hello to my in-laws, which meant an awkward procession of goodbyes loomed before me, and to dodge this I excused myself to the balcony, claiming the need for fresh air as I was still feeling weak from my bout with the flu. Outside, I leaned over the parapet and watched rue de la Commune change into its nighttime persona. A young couple wearing black capes and tall boots with silver spikes lugged instruments along the cobblestone and sang Leonard Cohen's "Hallelujah" as they searched for a place to unpack their movable cabaret. A man on stilts pitched white and blue flower petals at the sky as he careened down the street in the direction of setting sun. *Calèche* horses whinnied and stomped their hooves as their owners counted the day's earnings before retiring them to the stables. Just yesterday, I had stood here with Katy and hoped she would tell me things I had no right to expect from her, no right to expect from anyone other than Estelle—and did I have that right anymore? Eventually Bertrand joined me on the balcony, resting his big, familiar hands on me the way a father might before opening up the world for his daughter.

"*Esprit*, we are preparing to leave for the second surprise of the *soirée*."

"You'll have to go on without me," I said, startled by how the words jammed in my throat, the anguish that made me want to hurl myself into the dusk.

Bertrand held onto me until I relented and leaned against him, releasing my tears as we looked over the dark, reflective waters of the Saint Lawrence Seaway.

"*Tu dois lui dire*," he said after a while. "Whatever is troubling you, *esprit*, you have to tell her so you can be troubled together."

"You're one to talk."

"Why do you say this?"

"Because you're dying."

"I am dying?"

"Aren't you?" Finding it difficult to articulate myself, I turned and pointed at Bertrand's chest until the words came to me. "The wheezing, the coughing. You were so pale when I saw you last Friday." By the time I finished listing my arsenal of facts that proved he was keeping a diagnosis of some terrible, life-eating disease from me, he was slapping his great belly and roaring with laughter.

"*Oh là là*, hexcuse my henglish!" he cried, after accidentally passing wind. "*Mais, jeunesse, q'est-ce-que tu dis là?*"

Estelle dashed out to us clutching her smartphone. "My god, what's going on? Should I call an ambulance?"

Bertrand, on his knees and sweating profusely through his Expo 67 T-shirt, waved to signal that everything was just fine. Estelle crouched beside him and spoke loudly, over-stressing each syllable, which only drove him further into hysterics.

"Margot, what on earth?"

"I asked if he was dying."

"Dying?"

"Well is he?"

"No! At least he wasn't ten minutes ago. Marianne says we have to leave soon. She's very adamant. Wait here, I'll get him some water."

Marianne was seeing the Cotés out the door, thanking them for their lovely company and recipes, when finally Bertrand was composed enough to admit he may have consumed too many sugary desserts throughout the evening. Olivier left with the Cotés, and Katy and Étienne went downstairs to hail taxis for us.

"We're having brunch with my family tomorrow," Estelle said, returning with two cups of water.

Bertrand drank from one, splashed water from the other over his face and neck, and then went to help Marianne close all the windows in case it rained while we were out.

"I never know what to say to your sisters," I fumbled, now regretting how I had avoided them all evening—yet again, I had behaved like an ostrich.

"'Hi, nice to see you' is never a bad place to start."

Marianne appeared in the balcony doorframe, curvy and silhouetted by the dimmed light of the living room. She was wearing my merino wool derby hat, which she swept off her head as she bowed. "Ladies, the chariots are waiting. You two'll ride together and follow us, okay? The driver knows where to go—don't ask where. It's a surprise!" She tossed a purse at Estelle and my derby hat at me, and then twirled back inside loft.

THE INSTANT WE MERGED onto Pont de la Concorde, the bridge to La Ronde, I ordered the driver to turn around.

"Ma'am, the lady with the red hair paid me to bring you..."

"I'll pay you twice as much to do what I say instead."

Up ahead, Katy leaned out the back window of her taxicab and vied for everyone's attention by imitating a wolf howling at the moon, until Étienne's slender arm appeared and pulled her from sight. I wished I could resent her for her verve and oblivion, her magic and how it had tricked me into believing I could be anyone other than who I was—a girl whose mother had repeatedly given her away, whose father had told business associates he was childless while his daughter was right beside him. "That's my niece. Isn't she a gag with her little bowtie?" I was the eighteen-year-old who had let some strange man drop her in front of a strip joint to begin her adult life, and the twenty-year-old pawnshop clerk who had allowed a beautiful woman to possess her one afternoon on rue de la Commune and tried to become everything for her thereafter. I was Margot Anaïs Soucy-Wright-Coté, but I felt like nobody. The truth Bertrand had implored me to share with Estelle thrashed around my core, primed by the deleterious effects of alcohol and fear of an unrealized life, and it was about to spew from me the way ugliness had once spewed from the family I tried to kill. It was going to happen in the back of a yellow sedan with a running meter and an air freshener shaped like hockey puck. This was where I was going to invalidate everything I had accomplished across twenty-five years.

Estelle tried to soothe me, "It's okay, GoGo. You're having a panic attack. Breathe. I'm here," but she looked anxious as she appealed to the driver. "Sir, you have to pull over right now."

The driver stopped on the gravelly soft shoulder on the other side of the bridge, glaring at me in particular through the rear-view mirror before I stumbled out of the vehicle. Estelle followed me into the flat, barren field, begging for an explanation, some reason she could understand for why the night had suddenly turned frenetic.

I walked farther into the field until the crackling of pebbles beneath our shoes and my wife's palpable disappointment were the only sounds.

"I kissed her," I said, so weakly I had to start over. "On Sunday when I went to Canaan, I kissed Katy."

"Did you fuck her?" Estelle asked, seeming to recoil at the speed and sharpness of her own question.

"She's seventeen."

After a brittle silence, Estelle gave an odd, humourless laugh. "Good. Because I'd hate to discover your bar for creepy behaviour is lower than your father's was. Thank god you stopped at a kiss."

"That's not fair."

"Neither are you! So do you love her? Were you hoping we could have a threesome? I mean, you brought her home with you and everything. *I knew it*, you know. I knew there was something going on but—and you're going to die when you hear this—I thought you were suddenly all hot for Marianne. It made sense, she is hot and she took care of you the most when you were sick, and I was totally willing to let it slide."

"Estelle, I'm sorry."

"Show me how you did it. I want to know what it's like to be kissed by someone who doesn't love me."

"But I do love you! Please, can we go home and talk?"

"No, Margot, we cannot go home. I want to see the carousel. That's where we're headed, right? I get it now, why you're freaking out, but too fucking bad for you because I want to see this carousel you never took me to the first twenty times I asked you. Are you really going to stand there and say no to me again?"

Anything more I could think of saying was cowardly and trite, and soon Estelle rushed back to the cab and took her seat in front with the driver.

Marianne was waiting for us outside the entrance to La Ronde. Estelle turned to me before we got out of the car and said, "I texted her with the excuse we had to pull over because you drank too much."

The park was closing in half an hour, so the young woman at the admissions kiosk let us in for free. Bertrand had already gone off with Katy to learn how to make cotton candy.

Estelle, having never been to La Ronde, wanted a tour of the grounds, and Marianne volunteered to show her. I hung back, still trying to process my conversation with Estelle in the field. I wasn't worried about her telling Marianne—everyone adored Katy, and even in her most wounded state Estelle was not a vindictive person—but surely Marianne would figure things out. If not tonight, then tomorrow or the next day, while the four of us still shared living space.

The after-dinner park-goers were much more sufferable than the daytime ones. There were no shrieking kids or flustered parents, and even the people swirling and dipping overhead on sparkling fluorescent tracks cheered with more restraint than those I had encountered during my trial on the Vampire. The Ferris wheel came into view as I walked toward the rear of the park, a slow-spinning supernova so low in the sky you could touch it, and the roller coasters I had found harsh and imposing the previous week were now practically spellbinding as they burst into the twilight.

As I neared Le Galopant, I listened for the sound of Wurlitzer music. Like a frivolous child, I told myself if the Wurlitzer was working, then my wife would forgive me for kissing Katy, and for lying to her about my family, and for turning into a killjoy the same day we moved into the loft, and we would stay happily together for the rest of our lives. But if the Wurlitzer wasn't working, then Estelle would tell me not to come home tonight, or ever, and I would spend the rest of my days repenting in a mouldy basement apartment with only my musket postcard for solace.

I was the last of our party to arrive at the carousel, and I was surprised to see a pair of men in hard hats unloading an immaculate horse from a trailer—his coat whiter than I remembered, his silver hooves more silver, his forelock more precise. The men carried him into the gazebo, and I followed until Katy popped out of the dark and urged me to come with her to the control booth, where Étienne was running his elegant pianist's fingers over the buttons and dials, caressing them impatiently.

Somebody had clearly understood how vital Le Galopant was not only to La Ronde but also to history and the practice of preservation. No other amusement park in the world could claim something as extraordinary as the world's first galloping carousel, and even if the vast majority of people who frequented La Ronde came across it only by accident, by wandering to the rear of the park where there were no other attractions, there would always be people who came to the park for the sole purpose of leaning against the metal railing to admire the splendid fleet as it loped around the axis to melodies of carnivals past.

"They still have about ten Napoleons to repaint," Katy said, jumping up and down beside me, "but Étienne knows people here and he got permission to show me the carousel tonight before I leave. I couldn't come here without you."

"You're leaving?"

"Ryan wants me to come home. He says he misses me, and, actually, I miss him, too."

Even though Estelle was engaged in conversation with Marianne and Bertrand—Bertrand was supremely pleased with the spool of rainbow cotton candy he had made himself—I felt her watching me as I talked with Katy. I didn't feel anger coming from her, though, but fragility, and maybe even a need to connect. I excused myself from the control booth and went to my wife, trading places with Bertrand and Marianne.

"*Esprit*, can you believe I have gone my whole life without tasting *la barbe à papa*?" Bertrand exclaimed when we passed each other.

Estelle lit a cigarette as we watched the men in hard hats install the last Napoleon of the night. They turned off the floodlight inside the gazebo once they were done, leaving us all in shadows while Étienne cursed eloquently at his station. About a minute later, the scotch-coloured teardrop bulbs fluttered awake along the carousel's canopy, the basswood platform quivered as the engine's gears shifted and clicked into place, and then the tallest flue pipe on the organ released a puff of steam to announce the restored Galopant's maiden voyage.

"I shouldn't have accused you of being like Morgan," Estelle said, inhaling shakily on her cigarette. "But if you look at it from my perspective." She stubbed her cigarette out on the sole of her shoe, and then pushed an envelope into my hand.

"I found this after I found your mother's letters. I couldn't stop myself from going through all your stuff."

It was a photograph of me riding Napoleon (when I had thought there was only one) my first visit to La Ronde. I thought I looked uptight and abysmal in my derby hat, oxford cuff trousers, and inconvenient spectator shoes—who dressed like that to go to an amusement park?—but Estelle had a different opinion.

"I want to blow it up to wall-size and hang it at L'Espace. It's amazing. It's one hundred percent you. Katy took it, didn't she?"

I gave the photo back to Estelle. "You have my eternal permission to do whatever you wish with it. As you know, I'm really not one for pictures."

"As *you* know," Estelle said, tucking the photograph into her purse and leaning against me, "I really am."

I took her hand and kissed it, and together we watched Katy spring, light as a twig, onto the platform, and then climb onto one of the Napoleons and wave to us as she disappeared around the curve.

Into that world inverted
Where left is always right,
Where the shadows are really the body,
Where we stay awake all night,
Where the heavens are shallow as the sea
Is now deep, and you love me.

     —Elizabeth Bishop

ACKNOWLEDGEMENTS

It is an honour to be an Inanna author. Luciana Ricciutelli, Editor-in-Chief; Renée Knapp, Publicist and Marketing Manager; Val Fullard, Cover Designer; Mel Mikhail, Copy-Editor; and everyone else on the publishing team: You have turned my decade-long dream into a book. A book! Thank you.

Jonathan Sadow, thank you for the years, your expertise, your heart. For making sure I finished this novel.

Colleen Curran, Cora Siré, Kimberly Elkins, Anna Leventhal, Brad Windhauser, Greg Santos, Annita Perez Sawyer, James Grainger, Claudine Guertin, Karen Kovacs, Julie Licata: Thank you for your gift of readership and support.

James Simon, Antonella Fratino, George Hovis, Suzanne Black, Mel Lewis, Lauren Dunlap, Gina L. Keel, Franco Zoccali, Maia Troide, Mom: Y'all have stuck with me through my difficult times, and I love you so much for it.

I would like to also thank SUNY Oneonta's English department and IDAP committee members for funding my creative research while I taught writing at the college (2012–2017); Alison Gadsby for including me in the October 2016 Junction Reads author lineup; Jennifer Wertkin for hosting me at the Wellfleet Public Library in June 2016; the Salt Cay Writers Retreat committee for awarding me a full tuition scholarship in 2016; *Short Story Journal* for featuring "The Who Concert" in NS Vol. 22, No. 1; Ian Ferrier for offering me a public space to read from my novel in-progress for the first time (The Words & Music Show, December 2014); and Ucross Foundation for welcoming me as a Writer in Residence in May/June 2013.

Photo: Bernardo Fernandez

April Ford's first book, *The Poor Children*, was shortlisted for the international Scott Prize for a debut short story collection, and her story "Project Fumarase" is among the winning pieces featured in the 2016 Pushcart Prize anthology. April received her B.A. in Creative Writing and Professional Writing from Concordia University (Montréal, Québec), and her M.F.A. in Fiction from Queens University of Charlotte (Charlotte, North Carolina). She has spent time at Virginia Center for the Creative Arts as a Robert Johnson Fellow, and at Ucross Foundation as a Writer in Residence. From 2010–2017, she taught French and creative writing at State University of New York at Oneonta. She lives in Montréal, where she helps at-risk youth and other vulnerable populations express themselves through writing. www.aprilfordauthor.com.